"What we shared in there was ... magic.

"Why are you trying to convince yourself you didn't feel it, too?"

"All right, maybe I did," she admitted, "but that doesn't mean I have to do anything about it. You'll be gone by Labor Day. I'm not modern enough or liberated enough for a summer fling."

With that, she tried to brush past him. He grabbed her arm before she could, releasing her when she turned on him with a glare.

"What makes you so sure you'd only be a summer fling?" he asked. "How can you know that if you won't give us a chance?"

She sighed and shook her head, then gave him a bittersweet smile. "Think about it, Sinclair," she said softly. "I was born to be a red-necked cowgirl. I couldn't fit into your life if I died tryin'. I haven't had all that much experience with men, but I've had enough to know you're way out of my league."

"Becky, are you still a virgin?"

"That's none of your damn business." Her spine straight and stiff, she let herself out, marched across the porch and down the steps.

Peter watched her disappear into the darkness outside. He felt like a jerk for asking her such a personal question ... but he still wished she'd answered it.

Dear Reader,

Welcome to Silhouette **Special Edition** . . . welcome to romance. Each month, Silhouette **Special Edition** publishes six novels with you in mind—stories of love and life, tales that you can identify with—romance with that little ''something special'' added in.

May has some wonderful stories blossoming for you. Don't miss Debbie Macomber's continuing series, THOSE MANNING MEN. This month, we're pleased to present *Stand-in Wife,* Paul and Leah's story. And starting this month is Myrna Temte's new series, COWBOY COUNTRY. *For Pete's Sake* is set in Wyoming and should delight anyone who enjoys the classic ranch story.

Rounding out this month are more stories by some of your favorite authors: Lisa Jackson, Ruth Wind, Andrea Edwards. And say hello to Kari Sutherland. Her debut book, *Wish on the Moon,* is also coming your way this month.

In each Silhouette **Special Edition** novel, we're dedicated to bringing you the romances that you dream about—stories that will delight as well as bring a tear to the eye. And that's what Silhouette **Special Edition** is all about—special books by special authors for special readers!

I hope you enjoy this book and all of the stories to come!

Sincerely,

Tara Gavin
Senior Editor
Silhouette Books

MYRNA TEMTE
For Pete's Sake

Silhouette Special Edition

Published by Silhouette Books New York

America's Publisher of Contemporary Romance

My thanks to the following people for help with research for this book: Kay Peterson of the Pinedale Clinic, Pinedale, Wyoming; Melody Harding of the Bar Cross Ranch, Cora, Wyoming; Alice Dame, Robin Lozier and Chera Temte of Lozier's Box "R" Ranch, Cora, Wyoming; and Debra White of Laramie, Wyoming.

This book is dedicated to Glenda Steffek and Gordon Gum, the two people who taught me about siblings. I love you guys, even if you did pick on me all the time.

 SILHOUETTE BOOKS
300 East 42nd St., New York, N.Y. 10017

FOR PETE'S SAKE

ISBN: 0-373-09739-5

First Silhouette Books printing May 1992

Printed in the U.S.A.

Books by Myrna Temte

Silhouette Special Edition

Wendy Wyoming #483
Powder River Reunion #572
The Last Good Man Alive #643
For Pete's Sake #739

*Cowboy Country

MYRNA TEMTE

grew up in Montana and attended college in Wyoming, where she met and married her husband. Marriage didn't necessarily mean settling down for the Temtes—they have lived in six different states, including Washington, where they currently reside. Moving so much is difficult, the author says, but it is also wonderful stimulation for a writer.

Though always a "readaholic," Ms. Temte never dreamed of becoming an author. But while spending time at home to care for her first child, she began to seek an outlet from the never-ending duties of housekeeping and child rearing. She started reading romance and soon became hooked, both as a reader and a writer.

Now Myrna Temte appreciates the best of all possible worlds—a loving family and a challenging career that lets her set her own hours and turn her imagination loose.

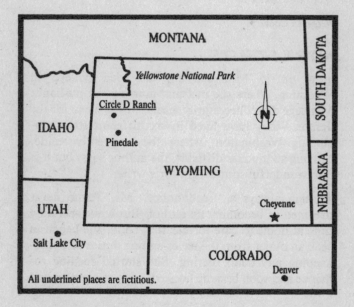

MONTANA

SOUTH DAKOTA

Yellowstone National Park

<u>Circle D Ranch</u>

IDAHO

•

Pinedale

•

WYOMING

NEBRASKA

N

UTAH

Cheyenne

★

•

Salt Lake City

COLORADO

Denver

•

All underlined places are fictitious.

Chapter One

"Whoa. Wouldja get a load of that?"

Becky Dawson glanced up at the note of fervent admiration in her brother Hank's voice, then turned in the direction indicated by his pointing finger. Sexy. The word popped into her mind the instant her gaze fastened on the low-slung, shiny black sports car parked next to the house. Definitely sexy.

"What kind is it?" she asked, rotating one tired, aching shoulder. "A Porsche?"

Hank shot her a disgusted look. "You've been on this ranch too long if ya can't even recognize a Corvette."

"Hey, I was close," she answered with a wry grin. "Who do you suppose it belongs to?"

"Nobody from around here. These gravel roads would tear it up in no time. C'mon. Let's go find out."

Becky grabbed her brother's arm before he could leave. "Aren't you forgetting someone?" she asked, nodding toward the patient, weary horses tied to the corral fence.

"Oh, yeah. Well, let's get to it, then. I want a closer look at that baby."

Turning away to hide a smile at his eagerness, Becky unsaddled Sioux, the blue roan gelding she'd been riding since dawn. After a long winter of being cooped up in the house, her muscles weren't used to the heavy work involved in mending fences. But, Lord, it had been wonderful to be out in the fresh air and sunshine again.

Hank finished with his buckskin gelding, Barney, in record time and took off for the house. Becky chuckled at his long, ground-eating strides and automatically took care of the tack and tools her brother had been in too much of a hurry to remember. After turning both horses loose in the pasture, she paused to watch them roll in the dirt before they trotted down to the creek.

Becky leaned one hip against the gate, heaving a contented sigh as she looked across the valley at the mountains her mother had loved so dearly. The jagged, snow-capped peaks of the Wind River range rose above foothills, still emerald from the spring runoff. The fleecy trail of a jet passing high overhead cut across a cloudless blue sky. Dark clusters of cattle spotted the pastures on either side of the narrow gravel road leading away from the ranch.

A sense of peace and security seeped into her soul at the familiar sight—until her gaze landed squarely back on that sexy little car. Parked next to the rambling old white ranch house the Dawsons had called home for four generations, the sleek Corvette looked as alien as a spaceship out of a *Star Wars* movie.

Who in the world could it belong to? They weren't expecting anyone that she knew of. It was pretty early in the year for it, but once in a while a tourist looking for one of the area's dude ranches got lost and ended up at the Circle D. And sometimes one of Hank's old buddies from the rodeo circuit would drop in for a surprise visit. Yeah, it was probably something like that.

Dusting off her palms on the seat of her jeans, she ambled toward the house. She shot a quick glance at the license plate as she approached the vehicle, doing a double take when she saw it was from the District of Columbia. You didn't see many of those in Pinedale, Wyoming, even at the height of the tourist season.

"Well, there's only one way to find out who it is," she muttered, and trudged up the back steps into the mudroom. Immediately, her grandmother's voice rang out from the kitchen, carrying a note of excitement that intrigued Becky even more.

"Is that you, Rebecca Anne?"

"Yeah, it's me, Grandma D."

"Come on in here. There's somebody I want you to meet."

Becky hung her Stetson on a peg beside Hank's, and noted that her other brother, Sam, hadn't come in yet, because his hat peg was still empty. Then she tugged off her muddy boots and padded toward the kitchen in her stockinged feet. The rich aroma of a beef roast in the oven greeted her at the doorway. She sniffed appreciatively before turning toward the sound of laughter coming from a long oak table on the far side of the room.

Coffee mugs sat in front of Grandma D, Hank and his fiancée, Janice Fairmont, on one side of the table. Hank's six-year-old daughter, Tina, sat on the other side, next to a dark-haired man Becky was immediately certain she'd never seen before. But the lively, congenial atmosphere told her he wasn't selling insurance.

She poured a mug of coffee from the ever-present pot sitting on the counter and approached the table. Grandma D looked up, then jumped to her feet, flapping an excited hand at Becky.

"Here's my granddaughter, Pete. This is Rebecca Anne."

The stranger pushed back his chair and rose to his feet, turning to face Becky. *Good Lord,* she thought, suddenly feeling petite, an uncommon experience for a woman who stood five feet, nine inches in her bare feet, *he's even taller than Sam. At least six foot five or six.*

"Becky, this is Pete Sinclair," Grandma D said in a rushed voice. "His grandpa was my old friend from back east, Jonathan Sinclair. You remember hearin' me talk about him, don't you?"

Becky nodded absently, her gaze riveted to the man's face. It wasn't a picture-perfect sort of face—his features were too bluntly cut to call him handsome, exactly. But there was a power or maybe a strength in that rugged jaw, broad forehead and bold nose that somehow reminded her of the mountains surrounding the ranch.

Her stomach felt as if an elevator had suddenly dropped two floors when she met his dark eyes. They crinkled at the corners and sparkled with a glint of intelligence and humor as his mouth curved into a friendly smile.

"Hello, Becky," he said in a deep, resonant voice, and enveloped her free hand in a warm, solid grip that sent a jolt of sexual awareness right down to the soles of her feet. "It's nice to finally meet you. Grandfather showed me a picture of you once when you were about thirteen."

"He did?" she asked, wondering idiotically if her voice sounded as thready to everyone else as it did to her.

"Yes, he did." His gaze drifted leisurely from the top of her head down to her knees and back up again, lingering for a moment at the third pearl snap on the front of her shirt. His smile took on a devilish twist. "And may I say, you've grown up very nicely."

You can say that anytime you want, buster, Becky thought. Cripes, did this guy have charisma, or what? A snort of laughter that could only have come from Hank made her realize she must be gawking at the man. Feeling her neck and cheeks flood with heat, she removed her hand from Pete's and stepped back.

"Well, uh, th-thank you," she stammered. "It's, uh, nice meeting you, too."

He pulled out a chair for her, and Becky slid onto it, gratefully stretching out her sore leg muscles. Hank rolled his eyes toward heaven, then soulfully batted his thick eyelashes at her. Oh, nuts. He'd seen her blush and now she'd never hear the end of it. Barely resisting the urge to kick him under the table, Becky sipped her coffee and smiled at her future sister-in-law instead.

Unfortunately, Janice looked as immaculate as she always did, her shiny blond hair draped around her slender shoulders in a smooth curve. How did the woman manage to look as if she'd just stepped out of a beauty salon after working in the ranch kitchen all day? Her fingernail polish wasn't even chipped, Becky thought, glancing with distaste at her own work-roughened hands.

She flipped her long, no doubt messy, braid over her shoulder and settled back to finish her coffee. Pete Sinclair might well be the most attractive man to visit the Circle D in a decade, but she was too darn tired to care much about how she looked.

A moment later, she noticed Grandma D's gaze flitting back and forth between herself and the man sitting beside her. There was a speculative, hopeful quality to the old woman's glances that Becky recognized immediately, much to her dismay.

Grandma D inclined her head toward Pete and raised a questioning eyebrow at Becky. Becky frowned and gently shook her head. Pete turned and gave Becky a slow, friendly grin that curled her toes up inside her socks. When Becky finally managed to look away, she caught her grandmother nodding at her with a knowing smile.

Don't start, Grandma, Becky begged silently, but the gleam in the old lady's eyes told her it was already too late.

The sound of a pickup's door slamming filtered into the kitchen through an open window. Hank draped his arm across the back of Janice's chair and chuckled.

"Sam's home, ladies. Whaddaya bet he comes through the door bellerin' for supper?"

Grandma D gasped. "Oh, it can't be suppertime already!"

She squinted at the clock on the opposite wall, then rushed to the stove, her neon pink Nikes and sweat suit creating a blur of color across the room. Becky and Janice scrambled to their feet, hurrying in her wake. Janice grabbed a stack of plates from the cupboard while Becky washed her hands at the sink. Sure enough, a moment later, the back door banged shut and a cheerful bass voice boomed from the mudroom.

"What's for supper, Grandma? I'm so hungry, my backbone's talkin' to my belly button. Whose fancy car is that outside?"

"Come on in and find out, Sam," Grandma D retorted. "And try mindin' your manners for once, will ya? We've got company."

Becky bit back a laugh as her oldest brother walked into the kitchen with a bewildered, mock-wounded expression on his handsome face.

"Now, was that a nice thing to say?" he asked, leaning down to kiss his grandmother's soft cheek and reaching around her back for one of the freshly baked dinner rolls cooling on the counter.

She slapped at his hand in a halfhearted gesture. "Stop that! You'll spoil your supper."

Sam held up the roll, his eyebrows raised in surprise. "This little thing? Shoot, Grandma, it ain't even big enough to be an appetizer. Where's the company?"

Grandma D set down the fork she'd been prodding the beef roast with and led Sam over to the kitchen table. Becky counted out silverware as she watched the little woman perform the introductions with obvious pride. Though Grandma D adored all three of the Dawson siblings, Sam had always been her favorite. Becky didn't remember ever feeling resentful about that; behind his gruff exterior, Sam was such a sweetheart it was impossible not to love him.

Now, Hank was a different breed of critter altogether. Becky loved him dearly, and knew she could always count on him in a pinch. But the varmint liked to tease and torment people in general and her in particular, just to provoke a reaction. She figured she'd really be grown-up when he couldn't make her lose her temper anymore.

Becky's attention returned to the table when she heard Grandma D protest loudly, "Oh, Pete, you can't leave yet!"

"It's been wonderful meeting you and your family, Mrs. Dawson, but I've taken enough of your time," he replied.

"Well, at least stay for supper. There's plenty, and I've got a hundred more questions to ask about your grandpa. And I've got a lovely photo album I know you'd love to see. There's even a few of your baby pictures in it."

Sam and Hank echoed Grandma D's invitation, and a moment later, Pete graciously accepted it. Grandma D packed the men off to the living room, each with an ice-cold beer in hand, then scurried around the kitchen. Becky started peeling carrots for a salad, and nearly jumped out of her jeans when Grandma suddenly clamped a hand on her shoulder and pulled her away from the sink.

"What in the world—"

"We'll take care of dinner, Becky. You get yourself cleaned up," the old woman ordered. "Put on something decent and for God's sake, do something with that hair. You look like you've been pulled through a bush sideways."

"Well, I feel like I've been pulled through a bush sideways," Becky answered. "And why should I get all gussied up to have supper in the kitchen?"

"Because we have company and because I told you to. That's why. Besides, you smell like a damned horse."

"I always smell like a damned horse," Becky retorted with a grin. "Look, Grandma. Pete's your company, not mine. He's only gonna be here for supper, you know."

"He might. But then again, he might not. It never hurts to look your best in front of an eligible bachelor."

"How do you know he's a bachelor?"

"I asked. He's thirty-eight and a doctor," Grandma D added, giving a quick nod to emphasize the word *doctor* as if it were every sane woman's dream to marry a physician.

"Well, so what? A man like that would never be interested in me."

"I'd like to know why not," Grandma D replied tartly. "Don't you think you're good enough for him? Or are you just bound, bent and determined to be the first old maid this family's ever produced?"

Becky shook her head, struggling to hold on to her patience. "It's not that. The man lives in a huge city, about as far from Wyoming as it's possible to get, Grandma. Do you really think we'd have much in common?"

"Your grandpa and I didn't have much in common at first, either, Miss Smarty Pants, and we rubbed along all right together for fifty-five years. Now, get on upstairs and don't argue with me."

Becky studied the determined glint in Grandma D's eyes, the stubborn set to her jaw. Then, realizing that, in order to get her own way, her grandmother would stand right there until everyone starved to death, she smacked the carrot onto the cutting board and marched out of the kitchen, certain that smoke must be rolling out of her ears.

A low rumble of masculine voices reached her as she passed the living room doorway and climbed the stairs. She paused for a moment with one hand on the banister in an effort to calm herself down. After all, Grandma was only trying to be helpful.

Still, it graveled Becky's drawers that the old lady never nagged Sam about getting married and he was forty. Hell, she'd just had her thirty-fourth birthday last month. Did that make her an old maid? In Grandma D's eyes, it sure did. In fact, Grandma had been harping about the subject since Becky was twenty-five.

Shaking her head in disgust, Becky fervently wished she hadn't fallen all over herself and blushed like a stupid schoolgirl when she'd met Pete Sinclair. Granted, there weren't many eligible bachelors her age in the Pinedale area. Definitely none who had ever attracted her so strongly on a physical level. But a sensible person didn't put all that much faith in physical attraction.

Sighing, she continued up the stairs, stripped off her dirty clothes and stepped into the shower. The pounding hot water eased her aching muscles and revived her spirits. After drying off, she studied her meager wardrobe for a moment, then decided it was time to take a stand against Grandma D's matchmaking once and for all.

She combed the tangles out of her wet hair and let it hang down her back in spiky tails. She slathered on some moisturizer to combat her day in the sun and wind, but ignored the rest of her makeup. As a finishing touch, she pulled on her most comfortable pair of jeans—the ancient ones with a rip in the right knee—and a faded, oversize navy T-shirt with Reno, Nevada emblazoned across the front in garish gold letters.

It struck Becky as ironic that she probably would have done more gussying on her own if Grandma had kept her mouth shut. But now that she thought about it, she was glad Grandma *hadn't* kept her mouth shut. If Pete Sinclair or any other man was ever going to like her, he could darn well like the real Becky Dawson. She'd tried to change herself for a man once, and that had been one time too many.

When she went back downstairs, Becky ignored her grandmother's disapproving scowls and pitched in with the final preparations for the meal. After Sam said a quick grace, Becky calmly refilled serving dishes, poured coffee and topped off water glasses, treating Pete Sinclair as if he were simply another big brother.

He was an extremely interesting man and had no trouble holding up his end of the conversation. Everyone else appeared ready to accept him as part of the family. But the more covert glances she sneaked at him, the more Becky realized how vastly different their backgrounds were.

His glossy, black hair fell casually across his forehead and lay smooth as an otter's pelt along the sides, highlighting a distinguished touch of silver at his temples. Becky would bet her best saddle that someone who called himself a stylist cut his hair. He wore a pale pink knit polo shirt, a pair of khaki slacks and shiny black loafers.

He used his hands a lot when he talked, and, though they were as big as Sam's or Hank's, they were smooth and unscarred, the nails clean and neatly trimmed. Shoot, his hands looked better than hers did.

And, it wasn't only his hair and his clothes that set him apart from the Dawsons. His excellent table manners prompted everyone else to shape up, and his grammar and vocabulary revealed evidence of an extensive education. Becky admitted he wasn't snotty about it. Not at all.

In fact, she enjoyed hearing about his trip across the country from his home in Washington. It beat the heck out of listening to another discussion about the stock or the weather. But she wondered what he would say if a heifer splattered one of those shiny loafers with manure or kicked him in the knee.

Still, there was something about him that made her feel as jumpy as a pond full of frogs. She figured he was a nice enough guy, but she'd be glad when he finally left. Sort of.

Peter Sinclair speared another bite of meat with his fork and closed his eyes in pleasure at the luscious flavor assaulting his tongue. His arteries were probably screaming from all the cholesterol he was ingesting in this one meal. Beef, gravy, real butter on the rolls and vegetables, salad dressing that didn't even pretend to be "lite." And, oh, dear God, were those homemade pies sitting on the counter? He wouldn't be surprised if the Dawsons topped them off with fresh whipped cream or ice cream.

It was wonderful. After all the hospital food he'd eaten, all the care he'd taken to keep his diet low in fat and high in fiber, his taste buds thought they'd died and gone to heaven.

The amazing thing was, none of the Dawsons were the least bit obese. He supposed they must burn an amazing number of calories working this ranch. Sam and Hank certainly hadn't developed their impressive physiques in a health club. He found all of them fascinating.

Peter had been curious about Amelia Dawson for as long as he could remember. She'd been Jonathan Sinclair's playmate when they were growing up in Philadelphia. From the stories his grandfather had told about Amelia, Peter suspected the old man had always wished they had shared more than a close friendship. After meeting the woman, Peter could understand why.

Grandmother Sinclair had been gentle, quiet and loving. Peter didn't doubt that his grandfather had cherished her during their fifty years together. But Amelia, well into her eighties, had such spirit, such a joyous passion for life that Peter could imagine what a firecracker she must have been in her twenties. That quality would have been hard for an aggressive, self-made millionaire like Jonathan to resist.

After finding and reading sixty-five years' worth of letters from Amelia among his grandfather's personal papers when the old man had died last year, Pete had made up his mind to meet her. He was glad that he'd followed through on that decision. She was every bit as outrageously outspoken in person as she'd been on paper, but there was a kindness and generosity in her personality that made up for an occasional blunt remark.

"Have some more meat, there, Pete," Sam said.

Pete accepted the enormous platter and helped himself to just one more slice, smiling inwardly at the nickname Grandma D and the rest of the family had automatically given him. The interns and nurses who worked under him at St. Luke's would die of shock to hear him addressed in such a casual manner, but Peter found that he liked it.

"So, where are you headed next?" Hank asked. "Back to Washington?"

Peter shook his head. "I just started a three-month leave of absence. Meeting your grandmother was the only stop I'd planned."

"Well, then," Grandma D said with a delighted smile, "there's no need to rush off. Stay with us a while. The whole summer if you want."

Surprised, but immensely flattered by the invitation, Peter felt his pulse start to race. The welcome he had received from the Dawsons had touched him deeply in a way they would never understand. Despite the tragedies he had read about in Amelia's letters to his grandfather, they were a solid, happy family, the kind he used to dream about in whatever boarding school or camp his parents had shipped him off to.

Being with them was like having his grandfather, the one person who had really accepted and understood him, back again. If Peter had grown up in a family like this, would he have made such a miserable mess of his life? Somehow, he didn't think so.

But was the offer sincere? No. It couldn't be. People didn't open their home to a stranger on the strength of an afternoon's acquaintance. Not in this day and age.

"That's a generous offer, Mrs. Dawson," Peter said, "but I couldn't impose—"

"Oh, we'd make you earn your keep," Sam assured him with a broad grin. "We can always use another hand."

"I don't know anything about ranching. I haven't had much experience with horses, either."

"That don't matter," Hank drawled, shooting a grin at his sister. "Becky's a great ridin' teacher. She'll be *real* happy to show you the ropes."

Peter looked at Becky and chuckled inside at the quick blush that suffused her cheeks and the dirty look she shot right back at Hank. He hadn't missed the family's efforts to get him to notice her—not that he'd needed any encouragement. God, no.

It had only taken one look at her firm, supple curves and those big, beautiful green eyes of hers to send his testosterone level soaring. He doubted Grandma D would be so eager to have him stay if she knew about the intense lust her granddaughter had inspired in him. It was tempting, however, to find out if Becky was as interested in him as he hoped she might be.

"Well?" Grandma D urged, "whaddaya say, Pete?"

"I'd love to stay, Mrs. Dawson."

"In that case, you might as well call me Grandma D like everybody else does."

Within the next thirty seconds, the little woman mapped out his activities for the rest of the evening and the next week. Peter suspected she would map out the rest of his life for him, given half a chance. Since she seemed determined to put him into continual contact with Becky, he honestly didn't mind.

It was going to be a wonderful summer, he thought, digging into the slab of apple pie à la mode that had appeared in front of him as if by magic. The best summer ever. His cholesterol count would just have to suffer.

After dinner, Grandma D dragged Pete off to the living room to look at her photo album. Janice wheedled Hank into taking her into town for the evening. While Janice ran off to primp, Hank and Sam sat at the table, drinking the last of the coffee and keeping Tina company as the little girl finished her pie.

Becky cleared the table, then rinsed the dishes before loading them into the dishwasher. Ambivalent emotions warred inside her mind while her hands worked automatically.

On one hand, she was appalled that Pete Sinclair was going to be staying at the Circle D all summer. Her family would drive her bananas with their matchmaking and teasing, and the man couldn't be more wrong for her if he had two heads and four feet. And since when was it *her* job to break in new hands? Especially a greenhorn who probably didn't know one end of a horse from the other?

But, on the other hand, when Grandma D had issued the invitation, Becky couldn't deny that her breath had caught in her chest and anticipation had hummed through her veins. The thought of showing him the ranch and teaching him what skills she could wasn't really all that unpleasant....

Aw, c'mon, Beck, an inner voice said, *you're dyin' to know what it would be like to kiss him, maybe even do a whole lot more than that.*

Becky shook her head, laughing quietly at herself. Well, she'd just have to wait and see what happened. She wasn't about to mollycoddle Pete Sinclair. After a couple of long, hot days of backbreaking work, he might well bail out and head back east.

She filled the dishwasher's detergent dispenser, shut the door and switched on the machine. Then she turned to find her brothers huddled together, talking in low tones punctuated by deep chuckles. Despite their massive sizes, they looked like a couple of little boys snickering over a dirty joke.

Her lips curving up at the corners, she put her hands on her hips and studied them. "All right. What are you guys up to now?"

"Not a thing," Sam answered, striving and failing to maintain an innocent expression.

"Try again," Becky suggested.

Hank's grin broadened. "Well, sis," he drawled, "we were just talkin' about what a nice guy Pete seems to be."

"Uh-huh." Wishing she'd ignored them, Becky grabbed the dishrag and wiped down an already spotless counter.

"We thought he seemed a mite interested in you, Beck," Sam said.

"Oh, really? I didn't notice."

Hank snorted with laughter. "I guess you were just blushin' every time he looked at you because of the heat, then."

"I did not."

"Sure, ya did, Beck. It was damn cute," Hank assured her. "Reminded me of that time you had a crush on ol' Danny Johnson. Course ya didn't have much more than goose bumps on your chest back then and Danny never knew you were alive, but you've filled out all right. What are you now, hon? B cup or a C?"

After rolling her eyes in disgust, Becky scowled at him. "Knock it off, Hank."

He slouched back in his chair and gave her such a thorough, masculine appraisal, she suddenly felt naked. If any man but her brother had looked at her that way, she would have belted him a good one. And Sam, damn his rotten hide, was joining right in with Hank.

Sam cleared his throat, then turned to Hank. "She looks okay in a pair of jeans, too. For an old-maid sister, she's not really all *that* ugly."

"It's been a long time since I've short-sheeted your beds or starched your underwear," she threatened, rinsing the dishrag with cold water while her face burned.

Hank rubbed his chin thoughtfully. "Now, Sam, if we could just get her to wear some makeup and comb her hair once in a while, maybe brush her teeth and use a little deodorant, why, Pete might get downright interested in her and take her off our hands."

That was it. Becky fired the dishrag at Hank's smug, infuriating grin. It smacked against his nose with a satisfying splat. Then she whirled and stomped out of the kitchen, banging the screen door to the mudroom behind her.

Hank peeled the dripping cloth off his face and turned to Sam. "Ya know, I think poor ol' Pete just might be in for one helluva long, hot summer."

Chapter Two

"Is this the one your grandpa showed you?" Grandma D asked, pointing to a photograph of Becky standing in front of a big bay horse.

Peter nodded. "That's it."

"I like the ones where she's bald and naked, better," Tina said with a giggle.

Looking down at the little girl happily ensconced on the sofa between the two adults, Peter had to smile. Becky had looked a lot like Tina at that age. Their hair was the same rich auburn, their eyes were the same shade of green and their noses had an identical sprinkling of freckles across the bridge. Even their generous lips had a similar shape.

"Grandma, not those old bathtub pictures!" Becky's voice came from the doorway, laced with a dramatic groan. "You'll bore poor Pete to tears."

Chuckling, Peter turned to watch her approach. "I'm not bored at all," he assured her. "You were a beautiful baby."

Becky grinned at him, then stopped behind the sofa and looked over the top of Tina's head to the photo album opened across the little girl's lap. She ruffled her niece's bangs affectionately and bent down, growling with mock-threat in the child's ear. "Are you makin' fun of my nudie pictures, Tina Dawson? Why don't we show Pete some of yours?"

"No!" Tina squealed, twisting around to face her aunt, her eyes shining with mischief. "Don't you dare, Aunt Becky."

"Well, then, you'd better come get ready for your bath, kid," Becky retorted, leaning closer until their noses almost touched.

"Aw, do I hafta?" Tina whined.

"The school bus'll get here at seven-thirty tomorrow. If you want a story tonight, we'd better move along."

Grandma D hauled the album onto her own lap and closed it. "Aunt Becky's right, Tina. We'll look at the pictures again later. Go on and do what she told you, now."

Tina obeyed, somewhat grudgingly until Becky faked a swat at her bottom. Shrieking with laughter, the little girl raced up the stairs. Leaning over the banister in the hallway, she called down, "Ya missed me again, Aunt Becky."

"Yeah, well, I'll get you one of these days, shorty," Becky answered.

Peter observed the exchange with fascination. Though Grandma D had confided to him earlier in the afternoon that Hank's first wife had abandoned him shortly after the little girl had been born, Tina appeared as happy and well adjusted as any child he'd ever seen. He suspected her relationship with her aunt was partially responsible. Compared to his younger patients, she was one lucky kid.

Grandma D interrupted his thoughts by speaking to Becky. "I'll put Tina to bed if you'll help Pete get settled. Since Janice is using the guest room, I think the most comfortable place for him would be the old foreman's house, don't you?"

Becky frowned thoughtfully for a moment before nodding in agreement. "Nobody's been out there since last summer. It'll need a good cleaning."

"Don't go to any trouble," Peter said immediately. "I can take care of it."

Both women stared at him as if the thought of a man doing household chores were truly mind-boggling. "Hey, I've been cleaning my own apartment for years," he said, defending himself. "I can swab toilets and scrub floors as well as the next man."

Becky laughed in delight and patted his shoulder reassuringly, warming him clear through to the bone. "That's great, Pete. We didn't mean to make you uncomfortable. It's just that Sam and Hank are worse than helpless when it comes to housework."

"And with the two of you workin', it won't take long at all to get that place whipped into shape," Grandma D added.

"Come on, then," Becky said, inclining her head toward the kitchen, "let's get to it."

Peter stood, said good-night to Grandma D and followed Becky from the room. He admired her long-legged, no-nonsense stride, finding the gentle sway of her hips and the way the tips of her hair bounced against the small of her back incredibly appealing. She stepped into a narrow room he hadn't noticed before that lay off the kitchen and switched on the light.

Shelves lined three sides of the room, stacked with everything from canned fruit and soups to laundry detergent and first-aid supplies. Peter whistled in surprise. "Wow. You've got your own grocery store."

Becky handed him a box and chuckled. "When you live this far from town, you tend to stock up. But this is nothing compared to what we keep on hand during the winter. We're a little low on snacks, but take anything that looks good until we get your refrigerator filled."

She handed him cleaners, toilet paper, tissues, paper towels, garbage bags and three bars of deodorant soap. Next, she added insect repellent, Band-Aids, a bottle of hydrogen peroxide and some sunscreen. A box of graham crackers and a bag of pretzels followed. Then she grabbed a small cooler, went back to the kitchen for some cans of Coke and bottles of beer, and emptied an ice tray over the top.

"Wait a minute," Peter finally protested. She looked at him, one eyebrow raised in query. "Are you people always this welcoming to strangers? You barely know me, and yet, you've been so generous.... What if I'm really an ax murderer?"

"Are you?"

"Well, no, but—"

"Look, Pete," Becky said quietly, giving him a gentle, sympathetic smile. "This is a different world from what you're used to. We trust Grandma D's judgment. Since she accepted you, so did the rest of us. She grilled you when you first got here, didn't she?"

Peter nodded, smiling as he remembered the little woman's rapid-fire questions. "You could say that. I think she knows everything about me but the color of my underwear."

"Then as long as you don't hurt her or anyone else, you'll be treated like one of the family."

"It's amazing," Peter said, shaking his head. "When I drove in here this afternoon, I wasn't even sure she'd be willing to talk to me."

"Your grandpa was really special to her. Grandma cried for two days after she heard he'd passed away. She'll love having you around, and we love seeing her so happy. But if we come on too strong, you'll just have to say so."

"Are you kidding?" Peter asked. "Your family's great."

Becky smiled wryly at that. "We'll see how you feel about us at the end of the week. Sam wasn't kidding when he said you'd earn your keep. We'll work your tail off."

"I always wanted to be a cowboy when I was a little kid," Peter admitted.

"It's not all it's cracked up to be."

"I'll risk it." Peter hesitated a moment, then decided to ask his next question anyway. He and Becky would both be more comfortable if they cleared this little matter up right at the beginning. "Becky, am I imagining it, or is your family hoping we'll, uh, get together?"

Her cheeks turned a fiery red. She looked away and exhaled a gusty sigh before looking back at him. Then she laughed and shook her head. "Hank and Sam just love to get my goat by teasing me, but Grandma D's been dyin' to marry me off for years. I'm sorry if they embarrassed you."

"I'm not embarrassed at all. But I thought you were a few times, and I don't want you to be. My grandfather used to put that kind of pressure on me, too."

"How did you handle it?" she asked.

"Not very well, I'm afraid." He shrugged. "I got married to please him and it didn't work out. I've been divorced for five years now."

"I'm sorry to hear that."

Strangely enough, he believed she really was sorry, not just mouthing the platitudes people usually did when you confessed something like that. "I'm over it now," he assured her, juggling the box so he could hold out his right hand to her. "But I'd really like for us to be friends."

Smiling, she gave his hand a good, solid shake. "I'd like that, too."

She dropped his hand sooner than he would have liked, and turned back to the shelves. After adding light bulbs, candles, wooden matches and a flashlight to the box, she picked up the cooler and led the way outside to his car.

Becky approached the vehicle as if it might somehow come to life and bite her, then slowly walked around it, studying it from every angle. Her lips pursed thoughtfully for a moment. "That's some toy you've got there, Pete."

"Would you like to drive it?" he asked.

"Man, I don't know." She gave him an impish grin that reminded him of Tina. "Maybe on the highway, sometime. But I'd put it in the garage if you value your suspension system. You really need a four-wheel drive for the gravel roads around here. There's usually one available." She jerked a thumb toward a battered blue pickup parked behind the Corvette. "We can take mine now."

"All right."

He transferred his luggage to the back end of the truck, eyeing with interest the variety of tools piled on one side. Becky pointed out an empty stall in a garage across the yard and waited while he parked his car and jogged back to the pickup. She swung herself into the driver's seat and reached for the keys dangling from the ignition.

"You don't lock your truck?" Peter asked as she steered down a rutted path that wound around the side of the house and past the barn.

"Who'd steal this old thing?" she asked, shooting him an amused glance. "The only time I lock it is when I go shopping in Jackson or Idaho Falls."

"Do you lock your house?"

"Not unless we're going to be gone overnight."

"That's amazing," he repeated, thinking of the security system he'd recently had installed in his apartment.

"You're not in the city anymore, Pete."

He gazed out the side window, then the windshield, then twisted around to look through the back window and banged his head on a gun rack mounted behind the seat. He didn't have the faintest idea what kind of rifle that was, but he studied it for a moment with distaste before looking at Becky.

"You can say that again," he muttered, realizing that though he could see for miles in every direction, there wasn't another house or ranch in sight. "Don't you ever get lonely or bored?"

"Bored? There's too much work around here for that." She shifted down, goosing the gas pedal to get them up a hill. "We get a little sick of each other sometimes in the winter if we get snowed in, but I wouldn't say I'm ever really lonely."

"What do you do for entertainment?"

"What everybody else does. We've got a satellite dish and a VCR, although the boys watch more TV than I do. I stockpile books and do a little whittling. In the summer I go fishing up at the cabin. And we go to the football and basketball games at the high school in Pinedale when we can."

A dilapidated white cottage surrounded by towering evergreens came into view. Becky parked in front of it and smiled at him. "Well, here we are. Home sweet home. It's not much to look at, but at least you'll have some privacy."

Despite its chipped paint and sagging front porch, something about the little house appealed to Peter. He climbed out of the truck and lifted his suitcase out of the bed while Becky collected the box of supplies. She swung the front door open for him, and he stepped inside, his mood instantly brightening. It smelled musty, but it *did* feel like...a home.

The living room was furnished with an old, dark blue sofa and a matching overstuffed chair and ottoman. Western prints decorated two of the walls. A rock fireplace dominated the third wall, and a large window framed with light blue curtains took up the fourth. While he set his suitcase on the oval braided rug that covered the floor from the fireplace to the sofa, Becky moved behind him and turned on a brass floor lamp standing beside the chair.

"Your kitchen's right through here," she said, heading for a door at the back of the room.

Peter followed her, and felt as if he'd just stepped back in time. The appliances and the linoleum on the floor dated from the forties or fifties. A small chrome-and-Formica table stood in a corner next to a dusty window.

Becky set the box on the counter, then pointed out another door at the rear of the kitchen. "Your bathroom's in there. The shower's a little outdated, but it works. You can use one of the bathrooms up at the house...."

"It'll be fine," Peter assured her without bothering to look.

He opened the window before following Becky to another door beside the dome-topped refrigerator. A massive antique bed, chest of drawers and a cedar chest took up most of the bedroom. While Peter admired the mahogany finish, Becky opened the chest and pulled out bedding and a set of towels.

During the next two hours, Peter learned what she had meant when she talked about working one's tail off. The thick layer of dust coating every surface in the little house didn't stand a chance against Becky Dawson. He helped as best he could, but he could barely keep up with her, and her standards for cleanliness were certainly more stringent than his had ever been.

Nothing fazed the woman. When the vacuum cleaner wouldn't start, she calmly took it apart with a screwdriver and fixed it. She wielded a wrench like a pro to turn the water back on for him, didn't turn a hair when a mouse streaked out from the cupboard under the kitchen sink and carried spiders outdoors in her bare hands.

By the time they were finished, Peter sagged against the kitchen counter, feeling as if he'd been on duty at the hospital for eighteen hours straight. He gratefully accepted the bottle of beer she handed him from the cooler and downed half of it in one gulp.

"Can you think of anything else we need to do tonight?" she asked.

Peter shook his head. "Not one thing, Becky. Thanks for all your help."

"Do you know how to light a fire in the fireplace? It still gets pretty cold up here at night."

"I was a Boy Scout. I'll be fine."

"Maybe we should check and make sure the chimney's not blocked. The squirrels and birds build nests sometimes—"

"I'll check it in the morning and I won't light a fire tonight, Mother."

She smiled sheepishly. "Well, all right. If you need us, ring the bell on the front porch and we'll come running."

He set his beer on the counter and put a hand on her shoulder, chuckling when she looked up at him, her green eyes clouded with concern. "I'm a big boy, Becky. Don't you think I can take care of myself?"

"Of course I do," she said hesitantly, easing herself out of his reach. "It's just that you're kinda out of your element here. I didn't mean to offend you."

"I'm not offended. But I don't expect to be waited on. Remember, I'm not a guest. I'm your new hand for the summer."

"Okay. I'll see you in the morning, then. Breakfast is at five-thirty."

He stifled an urge to lower his head and drop a swift, hot kiss on her sweetly smiling mouth. As if she'd read his mind, the tip of her tongue made a nervous swipe across her lower lip. Then she stepped back and walked quickly through the living room and out the front door.

Peter followed, watching through the screen as she hurried down the steps and across the grass to her pickup. She started the engine, gave him a jaunty wave and drove back down the rutted lane to the main house. As the sound of the truck's engine faded away, quiet settled in around him, a quiet so all encompassing he thought he could hear his own heart beating.

God, had he ever been this alone? This isolated from other human beings in his life? The thought was unnerving. Before he could let it get to him, Peter went into the bedroom and unpacked. Deciding a shower was in order, he carried his shaving kit into the bathroom.

Since Becky had cleaned it while he'd vacuumed the living room, he hadn't seen the bathroom yet. A bark of laughter erupted from his throat when he caught sight of the shower. "A little outdated," was putting it mildly.

An ancient, claw-footed tub that was at least six feet long covered half the room. A slender pipe stretched into the air and curved over the top of an oval rod supporting a plain white shower curtain.

Curiosity aroused, he pulled back the plastic cloth, turned on the faucets, and found the knob that should divert the water from the spout to the shower head. The pipes rattled and groaned and, finally, a weak stream of water sputtered out. Well, he thought with a tired sigh, at least he had indoor plumbing.

He shed his clothes and opened the faucets all the way before climbing into the tub. Though the pressure improved, the water ran hot one moment, cold the next. Peter endured it with clenched teeth, scrubbing his body and shampooing his hair in record time.

After toweling himself off and slipping his pants back on, he retrieved his beer from the kitchen counter and wandered out to the front porch. The old pine rocking chair he found there cracked when he settled into it. He rocked it a few times and, when it held his weight, he leaned back and propped his bare feet up on the porch rail.

Twilight had descended on the valley, painting the mountains in the distance a deep charcoal color. A cool breeze rustled in the pine trees near the house. Off to his right and down the hill was a pasture holding a dozen horses of various colors. Some nibbled at the grass, others drank from an oblong water tank. Beyond the pasture, he could see the corral and the stately red barn.

It certainly was peaceful here. Maybe too peaceful for three solid months. Had he made a mistake in agreeing to stay the whole summer?

You wanted a break from medicine, his conscience reminded him. *You'll get a break from it here.*

Peter sipped his beer and admitted that that was true enough. A person couldn't get much farther from his normal life-style than the Circle D. He hoped the hard physical labor he'd be doing here would heal his exhausted emotions.

The feature he loved best about his cottage was that it didn't have a telephone. What luxury to know he could sleep through the night without wondering if he'd be called in to watch one of his patients die.

But living with the Dawsons for that long...worried him. Not that there was anything wrong with them. He couldn't remember ever meeting people so ready to welcome him, so open and generous with their home and possessions and themselves. Though that appealed to him, he wasn't used to it, and he wasn't sure he could be as open and generous in return.

Being an oncologist, battling cancer in all of its deadly forms was the greatest professional challenge he could ask for. Unfortunately it had left his personal life an emotional wasteland. In some ways, he'd been more isolated back at St. Luke's than he was out here in the middle of Wyoming.

If he stayed with the Dawsons and really got close to them, he wasn't sure he could ever go back to his real life. Would he even want to? Should he even want to? Just how much of himself did he owe to his fellow man, anyway?

He had liked both Sam and Hank on sight, and was already in love with Grandma D and Tina. As for Becky, the strength of his physical reaction to her had astonished him, while at the same time, he'd found it reassuring to discover he hadn't lost all of his libido to workaholism. How long had it been since he'd felt so attracted to a woman? Longer than he cared to admit.

It might be wishful thinking on his part, but he thought she'd felt drawn toward him, too. And that was another problem. She fascinated him.

One minute she was ordering him around as a drill sergeant would, the next, she was looking up at him with those big green eyes of hers sparkling with humor, treating him almost like a brother. The next minute she was glancing away with a natural shyness that made him wonder just how much experience she'd had with men.

Yes, he wanted her firm, gorgeous body, but he sensed a vulnerability in her, not unlike his own. He wanted to find out what had caused it. He wanted to know why such a nurturing, vibrant woman wasn't married and raising a family of her own. But, God, he didn't want to hurt her, and he was afraid that he might if he got too close to her emotionally or started a sexual relationship with her.

One of the horses, a black one with a spotted rump, lifted its head, perked up its ears and looked toward the corral. A moment later, Becky came into view, swinging a bucket. All of the horses trotted over to the gate to greet their visitor.

Peter set down his beer and climbed to his feet, hoping to get a better vantage point. He smiled as he watched Becky dip her hand into the bucket and feed the animals what he assumed was some kind of grain. Though he couldn't hear what she said to the eager, jostling horses, the sound of her laughter floated to him on the wind.

His fingers wrapped around the wooden railing. He wanted to be down there with her, asking questions, learning about the horses and sharing in what was obviously a pleasant ritual. Then she shooed the animals away from the gate and let herself inside the enclosure.

She approached the spotted horse he'd noticed earlier, talked to it, stroked its long neck and scratched behind its ears. The animal stood patiently while she checked the area under its tail and proceeded to run her hands over its sides and belly.

Peter inhaled a deep breath at the sight, his body stirring when he caught himself contemplating how it would feel to have Becky's strong, competent hands moving over him that way. Shaking his head in dismay, he dropped back into the chair and drained the rest of his beer.

Should he stay or go? Becky didn't know it, but she'd just taken the decision right out of his hands. He wasn't noble enough to walk away from her.

Chapter Three

Becky crawled out of bed at four o'clock the next morning, her mind already running over the list of things she had to do before breakfast. She pulled on a clean pair of jeans and a blue chambray shirt, washed her face, brushed her teeth and twisted her hair into its usual long braid as she hurried downstairs to the kitchen. After starting the coffee, she mixed up two buckets of mash for her orphaned calves, Sadie and George. Then she yanked on her boots, grabbed a jacket and headed out the back door.

The brisk, early morning air made her shiver, but she paused to breathe in the familiar scent of the pines. She started when Clyde, Grandma D's old rooster, let out a full-fledged crow from his perch on the corral fence. Chuckling, Becky continued walking, greeting Bear Dog, the Australian shepherd pup Sam was training to work cattle, at his post near the barn door.

The calves bawled a welcome, and Gertie, the Circle D's milk cow, stuck her head out of her stall when Becky entered the barn. Tina's cat, Mittens, who was obviously pregnant again, twined herself around Becky's ankles, meowing for a treat.

"All right, you guys, all right," Becky scolded good-naturedly. "One at a time. Be patient."

She fed the calves first, then got down to business with Gertie and finished the milking in short order, giving Mittens a squirt or two to shut her up. By the time she got back to the house and poured the milk into the separator in the mudroom, Grandma D had already taken over the kitchen.

Wearing stylish vivid purple sweats and her beloved Nikes this morning, the old woman stood in front of the stove like a soldier manning his battle station. Bacon sizzled in a cast-iron skillet while she stirred flour into the sourdough starter for hotcakes. Grandma shot Becky a guilty, yet defiant look over one shoulder, then went right back to work.

Sighing, Becky lifted the empty milk pails onto the counter beside the sink. Grandma D was surprisingly spry for her eighty-five years, but while time had not taken a noticeable toll on her intellect, her body wasn't as strong as it had once been. If somebody didn't keep an eye on her, she would work until she dropped, and she mulishly resisted Becky's efforts to force her to slow down.

Becky understood, even empathized with her grandmother's feelings, but she loved the old stinker and intended to keep her around as long as possible. Janice was supposed to be helping with the cooking, so that Becky would be free to help Sam and Hank outdoors. But sometimes Becky wondered just how much work Janice actually did. There certainly wasn't any sign of her yet today.

"Morning, Grandma," she said, forcing a cheerful note into her voice as she rinsed out the pails. "Looks like it's gonna be a pretty nice day."

"Morning."

"You mad at me for something?" Becky asked.

"Not if you forget about givin' me a lecture for startin' breakfast."

"C'mon, Grandma, you know I appreciate your help. In fact, I could use a little extra help today."

Grandma tested the griddle's readiness with a sprinkle of cold water. "I'll do what I can."

"Could you hem Tina's costume for the school program?"

"Be glad to. I'll do it while I'm watchin' my stories."

Hiding a smile at Grandma D's addiction to soap operas, Becky nodded. "That would be great."

The two women continued their breakfast preparations in a comfortable silence. Promptly at five-thirty, Sam and Hank walked into the room. Still bleary-eyed and yawning, they went straight to the coffeepot. Then a brisk rapping sounded at the back door.

Hank answered it. "Mornin', Pete. Don't bother knockin'. Just come on in whenever ya want."

Becky looked up from the pan of scrambled eggs she was stirring and felt her heart sink. She'd told herself over and over last night that Pete Sinclair wasn't really *that* good-looking, and she wasn't really all *that* attracted to him. But he looked damn good this morning—rested, freshly shaven and considerably more alert than her brothers.

In fact, in his crisp tan chinos, a Washington Redskins sweatshirt and a pair of running shoes, and his cheeks reddened from his walk down to the main house, he looked even more appealing than he had the night before. She sorta liked that fancy haircut of his, now that she thought about it.

"Let's eat," Sam said, taking his place at the head of the table. "We've got a lot to do today."

With delight, Pete eyed the pancakes, bacon and eggs on the plate Becky handed him. "That looks wonderful."

Grandma D smiled at him and turned another batch of pancakes with her spatula. "Dig right in. If you don't mind my sayin' so, you look like you could use a few good meals under your belt."

Pete grinned at her and obeyed with such obvious relish, Becky had to smile. It was nice to feed a man who thoroughly enjoyed your efforts. Toward the end of the meal, Sam and Hank discussed which areas of the ranch their crews would cover that morning.

"Where do you want me to work?" Pete asked.

Sam studied the other man's clothes for a moment, then pushed his empty plate out of the way. "Well, now, Pete, it looks like we might have a little problem."

"What's that?"

"Did you bring any jeans and boots with you?" Hank asked hopefully.

"I've got a pair of jeans, but I don't own any boots." He glanced down at his clothes and shrugged. "But I can wear these until I buy some, can't I?"

Sam shot him a doubtful look. "Maybe you can borrow a pair of boots from one of us. What size are your shoes?"

"Thirteen."

"Shoot, that'll never work," Hank said. "Ours would be too small for him."

"What's so important about boots?" Pete asked, obviously mystified. "I've ridden horses at riding stables before without them."

"And you didn't do any hard ridin', either," Hank explained. "See, a boot heel keeps your foot from sliding all the way into the stirrup. So if you fall off your horse, you won't get hung up and the horse can't drag you."

"Oh." Pete exhaled a sigh of disappointment. "I guess I'll have to go into Pinedale today and buy some things."

"Beck, maybe you'd better go into town with Pete and help him out," Sam suggested. "You can pick up some supplies for me while you're there."

"That's not necessary," Pete protested. "I can do my own shopping."

"If you're gonna be a ranch hand, you'll need the right equipment," Hank told him. "Better let Becky give you a hand. Whaddaya say, sis?"

"No problem," she answered, though the thought of spending a good part of the day alone with Pete sent an uneasy tingle up her spine.

He didn't look too thrilled with the idea, either, she decided, sneaking a glance at him as she gathered up a load of dirty plates. God, he'd mentioned her family's matchmaking last night. He'd been awfully understanding about it, and a couple of times she'd thought he really was attracted to her. He'd certainly looked as if he'd been thinking about kissing her at one particular moment out at the foreman's house.

But maybe she'd just wanted him to find her attractive. Maybe after seeing her in the clear light of day, he wasn't attracted to her at all. Maybe he thought this whole trip to town was just an excuse to make him spend time alone with her. Maybe he'd decided he didn't want anything to do with a desperate old maid whose family kept throwing her at him. The food in her stomach curdled at that humiliating thought.

"The stores don't open 'til nine. Be ready to leave at eight-thirty," she told Pete, her voice coming out in a brusque tone she barely recognized.

He shot her a puzzled look, but she pretended she hadn't seen it and went to fill the dishwasher. Sam scribbled out a list while Hank gulped the rest of his coffee. Then they both headed out the back door, inviting Pete to come along and watch them catch and saddle their horses. Grandma D carried more dirty dishes to the sink.

"You had no call to snap at Pete, Rebecca Anne," she scolded. "You were raised to have better manners than that."

"I didn't snap at him," Becky muttered.

"Did, too. I'd like to know why. Don't you like him?"

"He's all right, I guess."

"He didn't get fresh with you last night when you were cleanin', did he?"

"Of course not. Did it ever occur to you that he might not like me?"

"'Of course not,'" Grandma D mimicked her, a wicked twinkle appearing in her eyes. "But that's the problem, isn't it? You wish he *had* gotten fresh!"

Becky rolled her eyes at the ceiling, then started to laugh. "Grandma, you nasty old thing, now cut it out. When I want a man in my life, I'll find him on my own."

"There's no harm practicin' on Pete. He's a fine-lookin' man. Besides, he looks like he could use a friend."

"What do you mean?"

Grandma D gazed thoughtfully into the distance. "I think that boy's hurtin' something fierce."

"He seems all right to me."

"Most of the time, he does," Grandma agreed, "but every now and then he gets a real sad, kinda lost look in his eyes. It's almost like he's grieving, but I don't think it's because his grandpa died. No, I think somethin' else is eatin' on him."

"If that's true, Grandma, why would he come here? Wouldn't it make more sense for him to go to his own family?"

Grandma D snorted in disgust. "What family? From what Jonathan told me, his son and daughter-in-law were pretty worthless as parents, but he had high hopes for Pete. I'd sure like to help him out."

"We'll do what we can, Grandma," Becky said, patting the old lady's bony shoulder, "but I'm not the answer to his problems. It's really hard for me to act normal around him when there's all this matchmaking going on."

"I guess I can understand that," Grandma said, smiling at her. "I'll try to behave myself."

"I'd appreciate that. I'd better get Tina up for school now, and I guess I'll go ahead and change the beds."

"I'll get her breakfast going and fix her lunch."

Becky hurried up the stairs, woke Tina and went into Hank's room to strip the sheets from his bed, her thoughts in a turmoil. Grandma D had a knack for reading people. If she thought Pete was hurting, he probably was.

Having lost her own father when she was fifteen and her mother when she was twenty, Becky empathized with anyone who was grieving. But that still didn't ease her confusion. It was silly, really, this whole man-woman business.

Most of her married friends seemed to be ecstatically happy one minute and miserable as hell the next. And her single friends were in the same boat Becky was. If you liked a man, you didn't want to come off as being too eager. But if you played it cool, the darn jugheads never guessed you liked 'em and went after somebody else.

Most of the men Becky knew thought they liked dainty little gals who wore high heels and makeup and couldn't change a flat tire to save their lives. They wanted a woman who could flirt and fuss over them and flatter their egos, but were essentially helpless outside of the kitchen. Becky didn't have the time or the temperament for playing those games, and she wasn't about to try again.

Maybe Pete wasn't like that. The way he'd pitched in at the foreman's house last night had convinced her that he wasn't a dyed-in-the-wool chauvinist like her brothers. But shoot, he was probably used to fashionable women who spent half their lives in beauty parlors. Why would he ever want a woman like her?

But what if he did?

Becky shook her head and shoved the load of sheets down the laundry chute. That was just hormones talking, she told herself, and it was stupid to let them get all riled up over a man who wouldn't even be around in September. She'd be a lot better off to settle for a nice platonic friendship with Pete. If only her darn hormones would cooperate and behave themselves.

Feeling like the only kid in the neighborhood to be left out of a camping trip, Peter watched Hank, Sam and their four hired hands ride off toward the west. Then he turned and headed for the main house. A movement in one of the second-story windows caught his eye, and when he looked up he saw Becky rush past with her arms full of...something, maybe sheets or laundry. His mood plummeted another notch.

He stopped walking, shoved his hands into his pockets and stood gazing over the ranch yard and to the mountains beyond. Golden fingers of sunshine winked out from behind the jagged peaks, filling the valley with light and the promise of a new day. He breathed in the pristine mountain air and tried to convince himself that coming to the Circle D hadn't been a terrible mistake.

As Becky had said last night, he was out of his element here. When Hank had swung himself aboard his horse, the animal had actually started bucking like a rodeo bronco! Hank hadn't seemed the least bit perturbed, but it had scared Peter plenty. While the other men saddled up, he'd felt both inept and inadequate, an uncomfortable experience for a man who was used to being in charge and making decisions that could mean the difference between life and death.

He glanced back up at the window, saw Becky flit past again and winced. She hadn't seemed at all pleased at the prospect of taking him into town, and why should she? She obviously had better things to do with her time than nursemaid some greenhorn who didn't even know what kind of clothes and boots to buy. God, he hated feeling as if he were an imposition, and he would go on feeling that way until he was finally able to "earn his keep."

Surely that feeling would pass, he told himself. Bud Jones, one of the ranch hands, had told him he was from Detroit. Bud knew what he was doing around horses now. Peter had made it through medical school, and he could learn the same skills Bud had. Couldn't he? Of course, he could.

His relationship with Becky, however, required some additional thought. Given his inexperience with ranching, he was bound to look like an idiot in her eyes over the next few weeks. Compared to her two hulking brothers and the other hands, there was no way he could impress her with his manly strength. That wasn't his style with women, anyway. But he *did* want to impress her. The question was, how?

Somehow, he didn't think flowers, flattery and intimate dinners would do the trick. Becky Dawson was too straightforward, too honest to play those kinds of games. No, for now, he needed to take his time and get to know the woman. So what if he was different from the cowboys she was used to? Perhaps that would eventually work in his favor.

Squaring his shoulders, Peter marched into the house as if he'd lived there for years. He found Grandma D in the kitchen, hovering over Tina, who was eating breakfast. At the elderly woman's invitation, he helped himself to a cup of coffee and joined the little girl at the table.

It felt strange, sitting around, chatting and drinking coffee, when he would normally have been hard at work. He wondered whether Joey Ackerman had been able to tolerate the new course of chemotherapy.... No! He'd promised himself he wouldn't worry about anyone or anything back in Washington.

While Grandma D was seeing Tina off on the school bus, Janice Fairmont wandered into the kitchen, poured a cup of coffee and fixed herself a piece of toast. She wore a rose-colored blouse with a pair of white slacks, which struck Peter as being slightly impractical compared to the clothes Becky and Grandma D wore, not that it was any of his business. He found her quiet manner extremely pleasant, her questions about his life in the nation's capital flattering.

When Janice left the room ten minutes later, Peter couldn't stand to sit still another minute. He cleared Tina's and Janice's dishes from the table. Grandma D returned in time to find him loading the dishwasher.

"Land sakes, Pete," she said, closing in on him like an avenging angel, "you don't need to do dishes around here."

He grinned at her. "Are you a chauvinist, Grandma D?"

"Course, not." She took a mixing bowl from his hands. "What kind of a fool question is that?"

"I just wondered if you were one of those women who thinks a man can't cook or wash dishes."

"Hmmph!" The old lady snorted. "Most of the men around these parts wouldn't be caught dead workin' in a kitchen. I know Sam and Hank are about as useless as tits on a boar whenever they try to help."

"Did anyone ever try to teach them?" Peter asked, smiling at her colorful phrase.

Grandma D shook her head, making her white curls bounce, then narrowed her eyes at him. "Anybody ever teach you?"

"We had a cook who didn't mind having me in the kitchen when I was home from boarding school."

"Well, I'll be," she said, tipping her head to one side in a thoughtful pose. "You any good at it?"

"Not bad."

Becky walked into the kitchen ten minutes later. Pete and Grandma D stood close together at the work counter, hunched over a cookbook and gabbing away like a couple of old pals. They both straightened up when they heard her enter, and she suddenly felt like an intruder in her own home. She hadn't seen so much animation in Grandma D's face in months, Becky thought with a twinge of guilt.

"Ready to go, Pete?" she asked, hiding her troubled emotions behind a gruff tone.

"Whenever you are," he replied.

She rummaged in a drawer, pulled out a checkbook and stuck it into her hip pocket, then said goodbye to her grandmother and led the way outdoors to her pickup. At first, with Pete, she felt as awkward as a newborn foal. But before long, he spotted a small herd of antelope and started asking questions about the area's wildlife, and the fourteen miles of gravel road to the highway zipped by.

"How much did you want to spend?" Becky asked as she turned south on State Highway 352, which would take them past the general store at Cora and on into Pinedale.

"Whatever it takes," he answered with a wry smile. "I appreciate your taking the time to come with me."

Becky shrugged. "It's really not a problem, Pete. I needed to pick up some birthday presents for Tina before next week, anyway."

She parked in front of Dillingham's Dry Goods. A jangling bell announced their entrance, and a moment later, Linda Dillingham, the owner's twice-divorced daughter, came out of the storeroom. She wore a slim-fitting denim skirt with a bright red blouse, chunky gold jewelry and chic, high-heeled boots that had never seen a barnyard. Becky glanced down at her own clothes and suddenly felt dowdy as hell.

Linda's perfunctory smile brightened by at least a thousand watts when she caught sight of Pete. "Good morning," she said, fluffing her shoulder-length black hair with one hand. "I haven't seen you in a long time, Becky."

Becky didn't like the predatory gleam in Linda's eyes one bit. Of course, she'd never liked Linda much when they were high school classmates, either. Even back then, Linda had been fixated on attracting males. On top of that, she was a vicious gossip. Knowing there was no way to avoid it, Becky introduced the woman to Pete.

Linda batted impossibly long eyelashes up at him while she offered her dainty, manicured hand. "How long will you be staying, Pete?"

Pete shook Linda's hand, gave her a friendly smile and patiently answered her questions. Becky's dislike of the woman grew with every flirtatious remark, and Pete's ready responses irked her even more. Good Lord, would the two of them never run out of chitchat?

"Excuse me, but we're in kind of a hurry," Becky interrupted at the first opportunity. "Pete needs some work clothes."

"Oh, I see," Linda replied, shooting him a coy smile. "What can I help you with?"

"I'll help him find what he wants." Becky grabbed his arm and tugged him toward the back of the building.

When they were out of Linda's hearing, he tapped Becky on the shoulder. "Wasn't that a bit rude?"

"Look, I haven't got all day. You wanna talk or shop?"

"I want to shop, of course, but—"

"Then let's get on with it."

To Becky's surprise, unlike Sam and Hank, Pete seemed to enjoy shopping. He chose his new wardrobe with care, asking her opinion of the fabric, style and color. The hard part came when he emerged from the dressing room wearing a chambray shirt similar to the one she was wearing and a pair of jeans, and asked her to check the fit.

Her breath caught in her throat and she barely prevented her mouth from dropping open in admiration. Now *that* was more like it, she thought, her earlier irritation with him forgotten. The shirt delineated the breadth of his shoulders and fit smoothly down his sides, giving his torso a lean, rangy look that was definitely appealing. And the jeans hugged his body in a way that forced her to gulp and made her fingertips itch. The man had darn cute buns.

"What do you think?" he asked, holding his arms out at his sides self-consciously.

Becky wasn't about to repeat what she thought. "They look, uh, just fine, Pete."

"Don't you think the pants are too long?"

"You won't be wearing them with sneakers."

"Oh, that's right. Maybe I should keep them on while I try on boots." He eagerly scanned the store before taking off for the appropriate display.

Becky grinned at his boyish enthusiasm. She retrieved his other clothes from the dressing room, figuring that from the expression on Pete's face, he'd want to wear his new jeans and shirt home. When she caught up with him, Linda had attached herself to his side like a wood tick and launched into a sales pitch for a fancy pair of dress boots.

Becky sighed, then waded in to save Pete from making an expensive mistake. It took some doing, but she finally convinced him to buy a pair of plain black ropers that cost half as much and would last twice as long. By the time that argument was settled, and Linda had practically molested the man in the process of getting him properly fitted, Becky's supply of patience was nearly spent.

It wasn't because Pete had turned out to be another male sucker for Linda's come-hither looks and manner, she told herself. Becky Dawson wasn't the jealous type, and she had no claim on Pete anyway. But, if he wanted to make time with the town floozy he could damn well let *her* help him pick out the rest of his duds.

She dumped his chinos, sweatshirt and sneakers in his lap and muttered, "Don't forget to buy a hat." Then she walked over to the children's department before she said something she might regret later. God, how could such an intelligent man stand that woman's simpering?

Slowing her pace, Becky found a rack of summer clothes in Tina's size. She stroked the soft fabrics and admired the bright colors, finally settling on a sunshine-yellow pair of shorts with a matching tank top. Then she picked out gifts for her niece from Sam and Grandma D, as well.

She arrived at the cash register to find Linda busily ringing up Pete's purchases. It looked as if he'd bought enough clothes to last at least two weeks. Sporting his new jeans, shirt, boots and a hand-tooled leather belt, he dug a credit card out of his wallet. Becky eyed his stuff for a moment, then turned to him with a resigned sigh.

"You'll need a hat."

"I hate hats," he replied, smiling at her.

"It'd be a shame to cover up hair like his," Linda put in, glancing up from her work long enough to wink at him.

Pete smoothed one hand along the side of his head and puffed out his chest like a damned rooster. Becky bit the inside of her lower lip before trying again.

"Pete," she said, using a patient tone that sometimes worked when Tina decided to be stubborn, "there's a reason cowboys wear hats. You really ought to get one."

"Becky," he answered in an equally patient tone, his mouth curved up in a teasing grin, "I'm not going to buy one. I'd never wear it."

"Suit yourself," she said with a shrug. Thinking, *Okay, buster, it's your sunburn,* she wandered over to the women's section of the store.

All right, maybe she was a *little* jealous, she admitted to herself, gazing at a frilly, mint-green sundress. It was just the kind of garment Bob Hartman, her one serious boyfriend in college, would have pushed her to buy. The color and style might even look good on her, but she'd feel like an idiot wearing the thing.

Pete's deep voice boomed from directly behind her in a terrible John Wayne imitation. "Well, little lady, ya reckon I can pass for a cowboy now?"

Becky quickly turned her back on the dress and faced him. He'd added a denim jacket to his outfit, which made him look broader across the shoulders and chest. She swallowed a sigh of admiration for the picture he made, then chuckled when she noticed the straw Stetson pulled low over his eyes.

"You'll do, Sinclair," she answered. "I like that little feather in your hatband."

"Why, thank you ma'am," he answered, making her laugh out loud at his exaggerated drawl. "I decided it was silly not to take your advice about that."

"Smart man. Ready to go?"

"Sure." He leaned to his right and nodded at the clothing rack behind her. "That's a nice dress you were looking at. Aren't you going to try it on?"

Becky cast a quick glance over her shoulder. "It's all right, I guess, but it's not really my style."

"Why not? I think it would look great on you." He reached around behind her and snatched the dress from the rack, holding it up in front of her, judging its size.

She shook her head, trying not to cringe when she heard Linda's high heels clicking across the floor toward them. "I'd never wear it. Put it back."

"I've finished ringing up your things, Becky." Linda stopped beside Pete and raised her eyebrows as she took in the scene before her. "Did you, uh, want something else?"

"No, that's fine," Becky said gruffly. "Let's go."

"I think you should try this on," he insisted.

A high-pitched giggle escaped from Linda's scarlet lips. Becky, her face burning, batted the dress and Pete out of her way and stalked back to the cash register.

"Oh, my," Linda said breathlessly. "I'm sorry. It's just that, well, if Becky Dawson ever showed up in a dress, half the town would pass out." More giggles erupted.

Becky grabbed the receipt sitting on top of the sack containing Tina's birthday presents. She looked at the sum and scribbled out a check, biting her lower lip until she tasted blood as she heard the two of them approach her. She ripped the check out of its book, slammed it onto the counter and marched out of the store.

Chapter Four

Ignoring Linda's invitation to "Call me sometime, Pete," Peter grabbed his own bags and hurried after Becky. He barely made it into the pickup before she took two deep breaths, gunned the engine and pulled away from the curb.

"I'm sorry," he said quietly. "I didn't mean—"

"Shut up, Sinclair," she hissed. "Just shut the hell up."

Though he didn't completely understand what had just happened, Peter decided this might be a good time to do as he was told. They made quick stops at the bank, a saddle shop and the farmer's co-op. To Peter's relief, Becky's good humor quickly returned as she dealt with the local merchants, who greeted her with the respect due an old friend.

"Want to stop for a hamburger before we head home?" she asked, when they'd carried the supplies Sam wanted back to the pickup.

"That sounds good."

"All right. You're in for a treat."

She drove down Pine Street toward the east end of town. Peter studied Pinedale's main drag with interest, counting at least three bars, four or five gift shops, a triangular chamber of commerce building, an enormous grocery store and a handful of restaurants and motels.

It was a typical little Western cow town, he supposed, but the businesses were well kept, and he liked the way the people stopped and talked with one another on the street, waving at friends driving by. From the size of the courthouse and the library, he suspected Pinedale had a fairly decent tax base.

Becky slowed for a left turn in front of another triangular-shaped building painted with vivid, vertical stripes in pink, yellow, green and blue that reminded him of a circus tent. A small trailer, decorated with horizontal stripes in the same primary colors was off to the left, and a row of equally bright picnic tables had been set under an awning to the right.

Peter looked up at the Pepsi sign atop a pink pole out front and read the words beneath it out loud. "King Cone. Home Of The Road-Kill Burger!" He turned to Becky. "It's a joke, right?"

She gave him an innocent smile he didn't trust for a minute, then shrugged and parked in front of the tables. "Who knows? You're not squeamish, are ya, Pete?"

He inspected another sign on the side of the building. It featured a picture of a dazed moose, whose head and all four legs stuck out of a hamburger bun, along with lettuce, an onion slice and what he thought was supposed to be a tomato. The same grisly slogan surrounded the sandwich.

"Hey, I'm a doctor," he said, climbing out of the truck. "Of course, I'm not squeamish."

Becky shot him an amused, knowing glance, led the way to the window and placed their order. They sat at one of the picnic tables to wait for their food.

"I really am sorry I embarrassed you this morning," Peter said, setting his new Stetson on the bench beside him.

Becky shrugged and turned her face toward the highway. "Well, Linda was right. Half the town probably *would* pass out if I ever showed up in a dress."

"Maybe you ought to wear one sometime, just to shake everybody up." His suggestion earned him a wry, lopsided grin.

"Yeah, maybe I should. But I don't have the time to mess with all that . . . female stuff."

"You sound as if maybe you'd like to change that."

She propped her chin on the heel of one palm and observed him thoughtfully for a moment, then wrinkled her nose at him. "Nah. I'd just feel silly and everybody else would laugh. I'm not a very feminine woman, Pete."

A voice boomed over the drive-in's loudspeaker. "Your order's ready, Becky."

Before Peter could get his feet under him, Becky was off the bench and striding over to the building. He studied her trim, yet curving hips, her narrow waist, her delightfully rounded buttocks encased in tight jeans, those wonderful, long, long legs, the fat braid that made his fingers itch to undo it and see all that glorious, cinnamon-colored hair down around her shoulders again, and he snorted with laughter. Not a very feminine woman? Hah!

She returned, carrying a white paper sack and two large cups of Pepsi. Peter made it a point to inspect the front of her as thoroughly as he'd just inspected her back. Her full breasts looked feminine enough to please any man who didn't have some kind of deviant mammary fixation. Her graceful neck led to an oval face with features that were more striking than beautiful, but undoubtedly female and undeniably attractive. And what about those tiny gold earrings winking at him in the sunshine?

"What's the matter?" Becky asked. "Have I got dirt on my nose or what?"

"I was just trying to figure out why you don't think you're feminine."

"Aw, you know," she grumbled, her cheeks turning a delightful shade of pink. "I look like a circus clown in makeup, and I've never been able to wear nylons for more than five minutes without getting a run, and—"

"Being feminine isn't about what you wear or don't wear."

"Oh, yeah? Tell that to Grandma D, will ya?"

"Well, it isn't," Peter said. "It's a state of mind."

She sorted out the food and settled back onto the bench across from him. "That's an interesting attitude. But when you've been a tomboy your whole life, you start to wonder.... Oh, fiddlesticks. Let's change the subject."

Peter wished he could coax her to finish that sentence, but the defensive tilt to her chin told him it would be better to wait. Instead, he eyed the thick hamburger in front of him.

"What do you suppose is in this?" he asked, picking up the sandwich with both hands. "Deer? Antelope? Moose?"

"Could be. But it might be skunk or raccoon or coyote. Take a bite and see if you can guess," she said, her eyes taking on a challenging twinkle.

Reminding himself that Wyoming must have health inspectors just like any other state, Peter followed her suggestion. A delicious flavor assaulted his taste buds when he bit into the juicy meat. He held it on his tongue for a moment anyway, confirming his initial impression that it really was beef.

Becky laughed. "Had you wonderin' there for a minute."

Peter shook his head at her and enjoyed another bite. She picked up her own sandwich, and for the next few minutes the only sounds came from the traffic on Highway 187.

"So, how did a doctor manage to get the whole summer off?" Becky asked after taking a sip from her drink.

"I haven't had a vacation in years," Peter answered. "I decided I'd better get away from the grind before I quit medicine completely."

Her eyes widened in surprise, or perhaps a better word was horror. "You might really do that? After all that education?"

Her reaction didn't surprise him. His college roommate, Evan Ross, had reacted the same way when Peter had stopped to visit him in St. Louis on the way to Wyoming. If a fellow physician hadn't been able to understand his feelings, was it any wonder Becky didn't, either? Peter tried to smile, but found his emotions toward his career were still too raw.

"I might have to," he admitted. "That's one of the reasons I decided to stay here. I need some time to think about it."

"I'm sorry." She reached across the table and touched the hand he had unconsciously tightened into a fist. "I wasn't judging you, Pete. It's just that I always wanted..." Her eyes took on a wistful expression.

"Wanted what, Becky?"

"To be a vet. It didn't work out. But if I'd made it, I can't imagine anything that would make me give it up."

"Why didn't it work out?"

"Family circumstances. But I'm not unhappy with what I'm doing now." She wadded up the uneaten portion of her hamburger in its paper wrapper and stuffed it into the sack. "Well," she said with a bright tone that didn't quite ring true, "are you finished? We oughtta be getting home."

Peter nodded his assent, and before long they were driving back through Pinedale. "Where do people go for a date?" Peter asked, hoping to lighten the mood.

"Usually the Cowboy or the Stockmen's," she answered, indicating two of the bars Peter had noticed earlier. "They both have bands on the weekends. The Cowboy's more of a working man's place. The yuppies go to the Stockmen's."

"Pinedale has yuppies?"

"Well, yuppie cowboys and tourists. McGregors Pub is a nice place for dinner, and there's a roadhouse north of Cora called The Place that's kinda fun. There's a movie theater over in Big Piney, and a lot of folks drive to Jackson.''

"How far is Big Piney?"

"About thirty-five miles. Jackson's seventy-seven."

Peter shook his head in amazement, which made Becky laugh. "Hey, we don't see distances the same way you Easterners do."

"Obviously not. Do you date much?"

"Some. I've gone out with the sheriff a few times."

"Is it serious?"

Becky rolled her eyes at him. "You sound like Grandma D. He's a nice guy and we have fun together, but no, it's not serious. How about you?"

"What about me?" he asked, trying to keep the satisfaction he felt at the information she'd just given him out of his voice.

"Are you dating anyone...seriously?"

"No. My, uh, work doesn't leave much room for a social life."

An easy silence fell over them for the next five miles as they drove north into a broad green valley surrounded by mountains on three sides. Peter admired the scenery flying past his window and felt a tension inside he hadn't been consciously aware of, beginning to relax.

"There's more development out here than I expected," he said, indicating a subdivision of ranchettes, each with its own satellite dish.

"Lots of folks think they want a piece of the Old West."

"You don't sound very happy about that."

Becky shrugged. "It's hard for me to see good range land covered with houses. But these folks don't bother me as much as the corporations coming in and buying up ranches."

"Why is that?"

"They don't always make very good neighbors and they don't understand that a ranch is more than a bottom line."

"Are you speaking from experience?"

She executed the turn onto the gravel road to the ranch and nodded. "There's one sitting on our northern boundary, where Janice's parents used to live. They call it the Executive Cattle Company, if you can believe that. A guy by the name of Marvin Castle runs it. He's offered us a big pot of money for the Circle D and he can't get it through his head that we're not gonna sell out. He thinks we oughtta be grateful for the chance to sit around on our behinds for the rest of our lives at some fancy resort."

"A lot of people would jump at an opportunity like that." He smiled inwardly at the baleful glare she gave him for that observation.

"This land's been in our family since 1896, Pete."

"So, it would be like selling your heritage. No amount of money could ever replace that."

"Exactly. And that's what Castle and his kind just don't get. They think everybody's got a price."

When they rounded the next curve, Becky slammed on the brakes. Peter's seat belt cut into his lower abdomen, and he automatically braced one hand on the dashboard to steady himself. A moment later, the dust cleared enough for him to see five coal-black cows and an equal number of calves staring curiously through the windshield at him.

Cursing under her breath, Becky switched off the ignition and climbed out. Peter followed her example and started walking over to join her. One of the calves trotted up to inspect him. He reached out instinctively and petted its glossy head, then heard an enraged bellow behind him.

He pivoted on one heel and saw a huge black animal charging straight for him. His heart raced and his mouth suddenly felt as if it were filled with dust. He tried to run, but his new boots felt awkward and his feet didn't want to move.

A hand clamped around his wrist and yanked him away from the calf. Becky stepped in front of him, waving her arms and yelling. The cow slowed to a walk. Keeping a suspicious eye on the humans, she swerved toward her calf and, after assuring herself that it was all right, herded it off to the side of the road.

"That was close," Peter muttered, wiping one hand across his forehead.

Becky grinned and patted his shoulder. "Rule number one. Don't get between a cow and her calf. That goes for any other animals you run across, including moose. If you make a lot of noise, you'll probably be able to spook 'em, but don't challenge a mother's protective instincts if you can avoid it."

"I'll remember that," Peter assured her, feeling incredibly stupid. "What do we do now?"

"We get 'em back inside the fence and find where they got out." She pointed up the road. "There's a gate up there about a quarter mile. I'll push 'em on foot, and you can drive the pickup. Stay behind me and over to the left side of the road."

While Peter climbed into the driver's seat, Becky let out an ear-piercing whistle and whacked one of the cows on the rump. The cow moved off in the right direction, her calf and the other animals following. As he watched Becky work the small herd, Peter began to see why the Dawsons weren't fat. She walked back and forth between the road and the barrow ditch, breaking into a jog now and then to shoo the stragglers along. By the time she had the errant animals safely back inside the fence, she wasn't even winded.

At her request, Peter turned the pickup around and drove slowly along the fence until she told him to stop. She jumped out of the truck again when he'd parked, went around to the back and dug out some tools and a pair of heavy leather gloves.

"I don't understand this," she said as they approached the spot where the barbed wire sagged to the ground. "Hank and I rode this whole section yesterday."

She handed him the tools and pulled on the gloves before marching over to the fence post. "Would you look at that?"

"What is it?" Peter asked, moving closer to her.

"Somebody's pried the staples out of this post."

"Maybe the wood rotted and they just pulled out."

"It's a new post. See those marks there? Some idiot took a screwdriver or something and popped the staples out."

Peter leaned down for a closer look. "You're right," he agreed, tracing his index finger across a scrape in the wood. "That's strange. Why would anyone vandalize your fence?"

"Beats me. It's a damn fool thing to do, especially right here where there's a blind curve in both directions. We're lucky nobody hit one of the cows. The last thing we need right now is a lawsuit." Becky chewed her bottom lip for a moment, then sighed. "Well, maybe it was just some kids out partyin' last night. Let's get this sucker fixed."

She was an excellent teacher, Peter thought, as she showed him how to stretch the wire tight and secure it onto the post with new staples. He smiled at the thought of any other woman he knew wielding a hammer with such confidence. He caught a whiff of a clean, soap scent as she hovered near his left shoulder to watch him attempt to fasten the next wire in place.

Perhaps Becky wasn't the kind of woman who wore perfume and other feminine trappings, but out here in the pasture carpeted with grass and sagebrush, and that cloudless blue sky overhead, she fit. Her complexion was smooth and lightly tanned, and the sunshine reflected off the reddish highlights in her hair in a way no hairdresser could ever reproduce. Mascara would have been overkill on the thick, curling lashes that fringed her intelligent green eyes.

Her sincere, unaffected manner was another facet of her beauty he enjoyed immensely. She didn't need any more adornment than nature had already given her. Peter wished she could see that.

"That'll do it," she said, stripping off her gloves and heading back to the pickup. "You learn fast, Pete."

He laid the tools in the truck's bed. "Thanks. You've done this a lot, haven't you?"

She chuckled. "You could say that. We usually get three or four feet of snow in the winter. When it melts off, just about every piece of barbed wire on the place is on the ground. When we move the herd up onto our forest permits at the end of June, we have to fence off all that land, too."

They chatted about the ranch operation until they reached the house. Becky insisted he bring his new jeans inside to wash the starch out of them and handed him a laundry bag. "If you'll put your dirty clothes in this, I'll pick it up on Mondays."

"You're planning to do my laundry?" he asked in surprise.

"Would you rather take it into town to the Laundromat?"

"Of course not, but I don't expect—"

"Don't worry about it," she said with a wry grin. "I do everybody's laundry. Grandma D'll iron your shirts if you want while she watches her soaps."

Grandma D called them into the kitchen. She served iced tea and chocolate-chip cookies still warm from the oven, while Becky shared what tidbits of gossip she'd picked up in town. Then they drove the pickup over to a storage shed and unloaded the supplies.

"How about a riding lesson?" Becky suggested. "If you're coming on the roundup tomorrow, it'll help you to get acquainted with your horse now. We'll get your saddle adjusted and save ourselves some time in the morning, too."

"All right. Have you got a quiet old nag for me?" he asked hopefully. Her low, husky laugh sent a warm, curling sensation to the pit of his stomach.

"Why would you want one?"

While they walked to the barn, he told her about Hank's performance earlier that morning.

"He was just showing off," she assured him. "Everybody likes to tease a new hand, so don't let 'em get to ya. Our horses have more get-up-and-go than you'll find at a riding stable, but they're not really dangerous."

She grabbed a halter and led the way to the horse pasture. As they'd done the night before, the animals trotted to the fence to greet her. Becky lavishly doled out affection and told Peter their names. Then, telling him to stay put and watch this time, she slipped through the gate and approached Whiskey, a big gelding named for the color of his coat.

Whiskey made a few halfhearted attempts to dodge Becky, but he couldn't resist her low, crooning voice and eventually submitted to the halter. Peter didn't blame the animal. If she ever called to him that way, he'd come running in a second. He accepted the halter rope when she brought Whiskey over to him and tentatively held out his free hand for the horse to sniff.

"Hang on just a sec, Pete. I want to check Misty while we're here," Becky said.

She approached the black horse with the spotted rump and performed the same procedure of checking its belly and looking under its tail that he'd seen her do before.

"I saw you do that last night. Is there something wrong with that one?" Peter asked, scratching Whiskey behind his ears.

"She's pregnant," Becky replied with a grin. "She probably won't foal for a couple of weeks, but it could happen any time."

She joined him on the other side of the fence and they walked Whiskey back to the corral. Explaining the proper procedures and the reasons for them, she saddled and bridled the animal. Though he had no trouble understanding what she wanted him to do and had a nearly photographic memory, Peter couldn't resist playing dumb in order to keep her standing close beside him, their shoulders brushing, her hands gently guiding his through the intricate process.

After going over each step with him three times, she stripped the animal down again and told him to try saddling and bridling the horse on his own. Her smile of ap-

proval when he accomplished the task gave him as much
satisfaction as he'd felt at receiving his college diploma.

While Becky was a patient teacher, she was also a demanding one. She made him mount and dismount until his
right leg swung over the horse's broad rump in a smooth,
continuous motion. She corrected his posture and the way
he held the reins, and had him guide Whiskey around and
around the corral at different gaits until he started feeling
sympathy for carousel horses.

By the time she called a halt and let him climb down, Peter's legs felt rubbery and sweat plastered his shirt to his
back. Then she had Peter put away the tack and give the
horse a good rubdown before turning him loose in the pasture again. They watched Whiskey lie down on his back and
roll from side to side in a patch of dirt.

"My dad used to say a horse was worth a hundred dollars for every time he rolled over like that," Becky said, a
faraway look in her eyes.

"If that's true, Whiskey's worth a fortune."

She nodded, then smiled up at Peter and started back toward the barn. "He's a good horse, all right. I think you'll
get along fine with him. You did real well for a beginner,
Pete."

"Thanks, Becky. I feel a lot more confident after that
lesson."

"Just don't get too confident," she cautioned him. "If
you don't know something or understand something, admit it and you won't have many problems. Why don't you
go in and get cleaned up for supper? I've got a few things to
do out here, but I'll be in shortly."

An irresistible urge washed over Peter. He cheerfully gave
in to it, bending his head and planting a warm, friendly kiss
on her smiling mouth. Heat flooded his body when her lips
trembled and then parted ever so slightly in response to the
brief contact. God, she was sweet.

He straightened away from her before the temptation to
take it further got the better of him. Her surprised gaze flew

to his face. It was all he could do to feign a nonchalant attitude, as if he went around kissing women every day, but he managed it.

"Thanks again, Becky," he said, turning away. "I'll see you at supper."

Becky watched Pete walk toward the house, so stunned by that quick kiss, she didn't hear the rhythmic clopping of hooves when Hank and Sam rode into the barnyard a moment later. She raised one hand to her tingling lips and exhaled a deep, shuddering breath. He hadn't meant anything by it, she was sure; it was probably just one of those casual city rituals to him, kind of like a handshake. But, Lord, had it ever been nice!

"Hey, Becky," Hank singsonged from behind her, startling her half out of her wits.

She whirled around and groaned at the sight of both brothers wearing broad, devilish grins.

"Was that dude gettin' fresh with ya, sis?" Sam asked.

"Of course not," she muttered, striding briskly to the barn door. "He was just thanking me for a riding lesson."

"That must have been *some* lesson," Hank observed dryly. "You ever thank anybody that way, Sam?"

"Not me. Looked like it might be worth a try sometime."

"I'll say," Hank agreed. "Did he thank ya like that after ya took him shoppin', Beck?"

Doing her best to ignore them, Becky marched into the tack room. Unfortunately, their voices carried quite well through the doorway that opened onto the corral.

"He must be quite a kisser," Sam said.

"Yeah. Ol' Beck was all goofy-eyed when we rode up. Looked like a lovesick calf."

"We'd better keep an eye on that boy," Sam suggested. "Can't have him sweet-talk her into somethin' she's not ready for."

"Ya mean don't let him have free milk or he'll never buy the cow?"

"Damn right."

Becky couldn't stand one more remark from either of them. "Both of you knock it off!" she hollered, stomping outside to glare from one brother to the other. "Just mind your own damn business, will ya?"

Hank threw back his head and laughed before turning to Sam. "Whooee! Sounds like she's in love to me. Maybe you'd better have a little talk with Pete tonight, Sam."

"Yeah, looks that way."

"If either one of you says one blessed word to Pete, you can baby-sit him yourselves during the roundup," Becky said with such quiet conviction that their teasing grins faltered. "And then I'll scrub the toilets with your toothbrushes."

With that, she stalked off to the house, her head held high and her shoulders straighter than a marine's at attention. Hank hooted with laughter. Sam waited until the screen door of the mudroom banged shut before turning a frown on his younger brother.

"I think we'd better let up on Becky, Hank."

"Aw, come on. She'd never use our toothbrushes to—"

"Of course, she wouldn't. But maybe she really likes this guy. I'd hate to see her back off from something special with him because we're givin' her such a hard time."

"You think she'd do that?"

"When was the last time you saw her light up like that around a man?"

"Not since she went away to college," Hank answered, thoughtfully rubbing his chin. "Man, I'd love to get my hands on the SOB who hurt her."

"So would I," Sam agreed. "So let's not mess things up for her with Pete. All right?"

"Yeah. But I'm gonna have to bite my tongue clean off to keep from teasin' her," Hank grumbled.

Chapter Five

After supper that night, Becky pressed the dryer's start button, stuffed a load of towels into the washer and carted the basket full of warm jeans to the folding table. She hung up the first pair, turning when she heard footsteps coming down the basement stairs.

"Good Lord, Becky," Janice said, smiling as she crossed the room, "are you still at it?"

"Laundry breeds around here, Jan. What brings you to the dungeon?"

"I got lonesome. The men are out looking at Pete's car and Grandma D's giving Tina a bath."

Becky nodded toward one of the bar stools sitting beside the table. "Have a seat. How are the wedding plans coming along? Gonna be ready by August?"

"We should be. I'm planning to run over to Idaho Falls next week and do some shopping."

"Have you heard from your folks lately?"

Janice glanced away. "Yeah. They're looking forward to coming to the wedding and seeing all their old friends."

"How do they like Montana?"

"All right, I guess. Mom said Dad's selling a lot of feed, but he hates being a salesman." Janice gave Becky a wobbly smile. "I wish they hadn't sold the ranch."

"They didn't have any choice," Becky said gently.

"I know. Anything was better than bankruptcy. But it doesn't seem fair for them to have to struggle so hard now. If ECC would have paid my folks what they've offered you guys for the Circle D, Mom and Dad would be sitting pretty."

The resentment in the younger woman's voice whenever she mentioned ECC's offer for the Circle D made Becky uneasy. She didn't blame Janice for feeling the way she did. In fact, Becky's heart wrenched with sympathy for her former neighbors; the thought of ever losing the Circle D was enough to make her stomach ache. Still, she wished her future sister-in-law could accept the fact that the sale was over and done with, and had been for the past year.

"Your folks are survivors, Jan. They'll be okay."

"You're right." Janice straightened her shoulders and put a determinedly cheerful expression on her face. "Let's talk about something else." She tipped her head to one side for a moment, then gave Becky an arch look. "What do you think of Pete Sinclair?"

"Not you, too," Becky said with a groan.

"C'mon, Becky. Don'tcha think he's handsome?"

"Hey, I'm not blind."

"He seems awfully nice," Janice continued enthusiastically, "and Grandma D says his grandpa was richer than sin and Pete probably inherited most of his money."

"I thought you were in love with my brother," Becky said in a dry tone.

Janice laughed. "Of course, I am. But Pete's a pretty neat guy. I think he's interested in you, Becky."

Becky's heart fluttered at that remark, but she maintained an impassive expression. "What makes you say that?"

"He watches you all the time when you're not looking. And he gets these sweet, funny little smiles on his face."

"He's probably never met a grown-up tomboy before. Linda Dillingham practically slobbered all over him at the store today and he didn't seem to mind."

"Oh, her." Janice dismissed the other woman with a sniff and waved one of her small hands. "You could blow her right out of the saddle if you even halfway tried."

"Don't start with that fix-yourself-up stuff, Jan," Becky warned. "I'm not good at it and I don't have time."

"It wouldn't take that much time. I could give you a few makeup tips and show you some different ways to do your hair. Lord, I wish I had your hair."

"Oh, yeah?" Becky asked.

"Yeah. We could do a lot more with it if you'd get about four inches cut."

"Aw, forget it."

Janice patted Becky's shoulder, then jumped off the stool when the back door banged shut upstairs. "At least think about it, Becky. Sounds like the men are back. I'll see you later."

Shaking her head, Becky hung up the last pair of jeans and reached for a basket of underwear she hadn't folded yet. Honestly, at the moment she was sorry Pete Sinclair had ever darkened their door. You'd think the man could walk on water the way the whole dang family had gone nuts over him.

Sure, she liked him. Sure, she felt attracted to him. Sure, she'd enjoyed that quick kiss this afternoon and ever since, had wondered what it would be like to *really* kiss him.

But was that any reason to chop off her hair and start painting her face every day? Wasn't it a tad late for that? He'd already seen her at her worst—well, maybe not her absolute worst, but close enough. Wouldn't it be just a little too obvious that she was interested in him if she suddenly started messing with the way she looked?

Becky snorted in disgust. Hank and Sam would tease her without mercy. Grandma D and Janice would give her endless, unsolicited advice on how to run a romance. After their conversation at the King Cone today, who knew what the heck Pete would think? God, she'd feel like a desperate old maid, ready to do anything to finally get a man.

At this very moment, Linda Dillingham was probably enthroned on a stool at the Stockmen's Bar, telling everyone who would listen that poor, pathetic Becky Dawson had her sights set on a gorgeous hunk from back east. Becky's earlobes burned and she shuddered at the thought of people talking about her, and then laughing. Dammit all, she'd been a laughingstock once. Once was more than enough.

She was *not* a desperate old maid. Her life was fine and dandy the way it was, thank you very much. She didn't need Pete Sinclair or any other man to make her happy. She had work she enjoyed and people she loved who loved her in return. She had a dream of her own, and had been saving money religiously in order to make it come true.

If a man ever came along who could accept and love her the way she was and share in her dream without trying to take it over, well, then maybe she'd be willing to share her life with him. But if having a man meant trying to change Becky Dawson into a lady—God, how she hated that word—she would cheerfully be a spinster for the rest of her days.

Her mind made up, Becky smacked the neat piles of underwear back into the basket. If Pete showed any more signs of being interested in her, she would set him straight pretty damn fast. They could be good friends this summer, but that was it. If he wanted a romantic fling, he'd have to look elsewhere. Better a little ache in her chest now, than heartbreak and humiliation later.

Peter saddled Whiskey under Becky's watchful gaze the next morning, wondering what had gone wrong in their relationship. He'd thought she was acting a bit more reserved around him last night, but had chalked it up to her busy schedule. While he'd been relaxing with Sam, Hank and Janice, Becky had been whipping around the house, doing laundry, cleaning and taking care of Tina. She'd still been going strong when he left for his own quarters at nine o'clock.

Unfortunately, this morning, he felt an even greater distance between them. She was polite and pleasant, but her easy banter and the cute grins he'd enjoyed so much the day before had been replaced by a brisk, efficient manner that reminded him of a head nurse who had intimidated him when he'd been a new intern.

Stepping in front of him, she tested the saddle's stability with two sharp tugs on the horn and walked around Whiskey to check Sioux's rigging, as well. After leading the blue roan out of the corral, she waited for Peter to follow with Whiskey and closed the gate. Then, with a fluid motion that Peter envied, she mounted Sioux.

"See if you can get on without anyone holding him," she said with a smile that didn't quite reach her eyes.

Peter raised his left foot to the stirrup and started to put his weight on it. Whiskey took two steps forward, forcing Peter to hop along on his right foot.

"Easy boy," Peter muttered, feeling incredibly foolish.

Whiskey blew out a loud snort in reply. The gelding took another two steps forward when Peter tried again. He looked to Becky for advice, but she didn't offer any. He patted the animal's neck and talked quietly to him between attempts, finally swinging his right leg up and over Whiskey's back on the fifth try. He shot Becky a broad grin.

"Let's go," she said without so much as a nod, nudging Sioux's sides with her knees.

The blue roan took off at a walk, but Whiskey broke into a bone-jarring trot, nearly bouncing Peter out of the saddle. He grabbed the horn in time to save himself, pulled back on the reins and the animal settled down. Peter remarked on the weather and asked a couple of questions about the roundup. Becky answered in clipped sentences.

He gave up on starting a conversation and settled uneasily back in his saddle. As the sun climbed the eastern sky, the land came to life. Insects buzzed the tips of the grass and the occasional clumps of sagebrush, their tiny wings snapping and popping in the cool morning air. Birds dive-bombed after them in search of breakfast.

Whiskey's rhythmic steps gradually lulled Peter's jitters. Today he was simply along for the ride. No one expected him to be an expert here. He might look silly if he made a mistake, but nobody would die because of it. He wouldn't have to make agonizing decisions or try to give grieving relatives answers he didn't have.

The journey out to their assigned area must have had a similar effect on Becky. She remained silent, but the lines of tension around her eyes and mouth slowly eased, leaving a serene, if somewhat sober expression on her face. He'd give a month's salary to know what was going on in her mind at that moment, but he didn't quite have the courage to ask.

When they reached their destination, Becky indicated the center of the field. "We'll push 'em all into the middle there and drive 'em over to the branding pens. Stay here while I bring in the first bunch. Then you can try it."

"All right."

Whiskey sidestepped, bobbed his head and blew out an impatient snort when Sioux took off without him. Peter reined him in and patted his mane. "I know how you feel, boy," he murmured. "I want to go, too."

Becky and Sioux circled behind a group of black Angus cattle grazing near the fence. The blue roan approached the placid beasts at an eager trot. Becky waved a coiled rope and shouted at them, startling the calves into flight. A few of the cows mooed in protest, but slowly they began to move in the right direction.

Woman and horse moved with grace and speed, darting after a frisky calf here, a recalcitrant heifer there. They made it look so easy and fun, Peter couldn't wait to join them. Evidently Whiskey agreed; his hide shivered with excitement and an accidental tightening of Peter's knees sent the gelding bounding forward in a beeline toward Sioux.

The cattle took one look at the horse bearing down on them and scattered in six different directions. Becky looked up in surprise at the sound of Whiskey's hooves pounding across the turf. Scowling, she went after the ones who'd gone to the right.

Whiskey lowered his head and executed an abrupt, ninety-degree turn to head off the others. Peter grabbed for the saddle horn, missed it, then experienced an all-too-brief moment of flight before his backside hit the ground. Air whooshed out of his lungs on impact, his hat fell off and the next thing he knew, he lay flat on his back.

Before the clear blue sky overhead stopped spinning like a carnival ride, Becky knelt beside him. He tried to sit up, but she firmly pushed him back down.

"Take it easy there, Pete. Hurt anywhere?"

"I don't think so." He shook his head, clearing his vision.

"Okay, sit up nice and slow, then." She passed one arm beneath his shoulders, supporting him as he obeyed.

In the moments it took for his equilibrium to return, Peter became pleasantly aware of the warmth of Becky's breasts pressed against his right arm. The low, soothing tones of her voice rippled along his nerve endings and brought images of a darkened bedroom to his mind.

"All right now?" she asked anxiously.

Peter couldn't remember a time when he'd felt much better, but he closed his eyes and laid his head on her shoulder, drinking in the clean fragrance of soap on her skin. "I'm still dizzy," he lied.

Becky gently combed the fingers of her free hand through his hair. Peter bit his lower lip to hold in a sigh of pleasure.

He'd never thought of his scalp as an erogenous zone before.

"I don't feel any bumps," she said. "Did you bang your head on a rock?"

"I don't remember." He faked a moan and moved his head restlessly, bringing his lips closer to the side of her neck.

"Just rest for a minute, then." She shifted to a sitting position with her legs curled up to one side. Her free hand moved along his left shoulder, down his arm and across his chest. "Lord, I hope you didn't break any bones."

Blood rushed to Peter's groin at her innocent exploration. "I really messed up, didn't I?" he asked in an attempt to distract himself.

"Yeah, well," she grumbled, a hint of a smile lurking at the corners of her mouth, "it happens. You don't take orders worth a damn, Sinclair."

"Yeah, well," he answered, perfectly mimicking her drawl, "I'm used to giving orders, not taking them."

Becky shook her head and chuckled, stroking his hair off his forehead. "That's obvious. Feel better yet?"

Knowing the swelling in his jeans would give him away any second, he nodded. She loosened her hold on him, but before she could move, Peter wrapped his left arm around her waist and held her in place while he nuzzled the satiny skin beneath her ear, then reached for her mouth. God, she was sweet and warm....

Becky lurched out of his embrace as if she'd been stung by a wasp. She jumped to her feet, clamped her hands on her hips and glared down at him. "You were faking!"

Peter slowly pushed himself upright and dusted off the seat of his pants. "Only a little."

"Dammit, I was scared to death you were really hurt."

"I'm sorry." Smiling, he reached for her, but she slapped his hands away. "Come on, Becky, don't be angry."

"Angry? There's an understatement. Get this through your head, Sinclair. That wasn't one damn bit funny."

"Becky, I'm not hurt."

"What if you had been? We're almost eighty miles from the nearest hospital. It takes twenty-seven minutes to get from our house to the clinic in Pinedale when you're drivin' like hell, and at least another hour and a half to get an airplane from Jackson to Pinedale and back to Jackson again. And God only knows how long it would have taken me to get you to the house."

"Are you angry about that?" Peter asked, quietly. "Or because I was trying to kiss you again?"

Becky stiffened, then glanced away. She inhaled a deep breath, as if to calm herself before facing him again. "Look, my dad had an accident with the tractor and died from internal bleeding while we were trying to get him to the hospital. So pardon me all to hell if I get riled over that stunt you just pulled."

"I apologize. I promise I won't ever do it again." He studied her rigid stance, feeling like an absolute jerk before continuing. "But you didn't answer my question. Are you upset with me for kissing you?"

She shrugged, as if kissing him had turned her on about as much as kissing a buffalo. "I've been kissed before, but don't make a habit of it. C'mon, let's get back to work."

His pride stinging, Peter rammed his hat onto his head and made it onto Whiskey's back with only three attempts this time. He looked expectantly at Becky, and was surprised to find her almost smiling at him. He didn't care for the sympathy in her eyes, but he'd take what he could get.

"Do you know why Whiskey dumped you?" she asked.

"I'm not sure. He changed directions so fast...."

"He's trained to work cattle, Pete. When a cow or a calf breaks away from the herd, Whiskey knows he's supposed to go after it, and he'll do it without waiting for a signal from you."

"How should I handle that?"

"Just let him have his head and stay as loose in the saddle as you can. Watch the cows and try to anticipate where hey'll go next. When Whiskey's head goes down, expect a sharp turn and try to lean into it."

"That doesn't sound too difficult."

"It isn't, once you've got the hang of it."

"How long will that take?"

She tipped her hat back and studied him for a moment. 'Oh, I'd say you'll catch on after about three more falls."

Peter's mouth dropped open in dismay, and his left hand automatically clamped onto his bruised rear. "Three more?" he asked, seeking confirmation of the unbelievable.

Becky whooped with laughter, then reined Sioux around to go after the cattle again. "Who knows? If you're lucky, you'll learn faster than I did."

They worked the perimeter of the field, flushing the cattle out of the brush. Peter managed to stay in the saddle for the rest of the morning, but his thighs ached from continually gripping Whiskey's sides, his butt felt as if it had been pounded into hamburger and sweat rolled off him as profusely as if he'd been in a sauna for hours. Still, he felt he'd acquitted himself reasonably well, and valiantly stifled a whimper of relief when Becky finally called a break.

Walking as if he'd aged fifty years, he led Whiskey over to the willow tree where Becky was spreading out their lunch. Every muscle shrieked in protest when he squatted beside the small creek to wash his hands and face. Then he flopped down on the grass beside Becky and gratefully accepted a thick roast-beef sandwich and a can of Coke.

"Well, whaddaya think of being a cowhand now, Pete?" she asked.

"I think it may kill me."

"It won't be so rough when your muscles get used to riding all day."

"I usually jog for an hour every morning. I thought I was in pretty good shape."

"You use a different set of muscles when you're riding."

"No kidding," he grumbled. "I probably won't be able to move tomorrow."

"You know, you don't really have to do this," Becky said quietly.

"You sound like you're trying to fire me. Was I that bad?"

"Not at all," she assured him. "In fact, you did better than I expected. But ranching's not for everyone."

"Would you rather I left the Circle D, Becky?"

Her cheeks turned red. "Of course not. What kind of a fool question was that? Why, Grandma D would—"

"I didn't ask about your grandmother. I asked about you. Would *you* like me to leave?"

She suddenly appeared to find the toes of her boots extremely interesting. "Not unless you want to go. I didn't mean to be rude to you this morning, Pete."

Peter hooked an index finger under her chin and forced her to look at him. "I deserved your scolding. You've been extremely kind to me, Becky, but I'm getting the impression that I make you uncomfortable. Am I right?"

"Are you always this blunt?" she asked, pulling away with a self-conscious laugh.

"I've been told it's one of my more annoying faults," he admitted with a grin.

"Well, I guess there's not much profit in beating around the bush."

"I'm glad you feel that way. So tell the truth, Dawson. Do I make you uncomfortable or not?"

"Sometimes."

"Why? Don't you like me?"

Her green eyes took on a teasing glint. "Sometimes."

Peter chuckled and yanked her hat down over her face. "Thanks a lot."

"Hey, you wanted an honest answer."

"So give me another one. Did you really hate it when I kissed you?"

"No."

"Does that mean you liked it?"

"Sorta."

Peter threw his hands up in mock-disgust and flung himself flat on his back. "You laconic westerners drive me nuts." He lay there for a moment, listening to the music of Becky's laughter. Then he rolled onto his side facing her and propped himself up on his elbow. "Do you think you could manage more than a one-word answer?"

"Maybe." She chuckled at his fierce scowl before relenting. "What's the question?"

"I think I'd better tell you something first. The truth is," he said, choosing his words carefully, "I'm attracted to you, Becky. I enjoyed kissing you yesterday, and I'd like to do it again. Would you like me to or not?"

"Lord, you *are* blunt," she muttered.

"It's not a difficult question."

"It's more difficult than you think." She grabbed a long strand of grass and yanked it out of the dirt, twisting it around and around her index finger.

"Why? Do you think I'm repulsive?"

"Of course not. You're a handsome man and you know it, Sinclair."

"Then what's the problem? Is it your family? You're afraid of more pressure from them?"

"Partly, but..."

"But what? Don't go laconic on me again, Dawson."

Laughing in exasperation, she threw the blade of grass at him. "You want the truth? All right. The truth is, I'm attracted to you, too, but that doesn't mean I'm some naive rancher's daughter who'll jump into bed with you."

"Who said anything about bed? The subject was kissing."

She blushed furiously and quickly repacked her saddlebags. "Yeah, well, kissing does lead to other things, so keep your lips to yourself. It's time to go back to work."

Peter groaned at the thought of climbing onto that horse again, but he couldn't help smiling with satisfaction over

Becky's admission that she thought he was handsome and that she'd "sorta" liked his kiss. He'd have to kiss her again and see if he couldn't change that "sorta" into a "really."

When they headed back to the house late that afternoon, Becky found herself sneaking glances at Pete and struggling with ambivalent emotions every time she did so. He had to be exhausted by now, and was probably sore as hell, but he hadn't complained once. What he lacked in experience, he made up for with grit, determination and enthusiasm. If he stuck it out, she figured they'd be a darn good team by the end of the month.

He caught her looking at him and gave her a sexy wink. She turned her head to hide a smile. No sense puffing up his ego any more than she already had. She couldn't believe she'd actually told him she was attracted to him.

But dammit all, she *liked* the man. So he was a flirt. So he'd fooled her into holding him in her arms this morning. Once her fear had passed, she'd found his little trick... flattering. When she was with him, she forgot to worry about what other folks might think and it felt good.

Though some people might fault his bluntness, she respected his honesty. She admired the way he could laugh at his mistakes and apologize when he'd been wrong. She liked the way he treated her grandmother and the way he'd naturally fit himself into her family.

Still, all those things she'd told herself last night were still true. He'd said he was only talking about kissing, but she wasn't dumb enough to believe that was where it would end. There was enough chemistry between them to lead them into bed. Much as she hated to admit it, she was downright tempted to crawl in between the sheets with him.

Lord, an affair with Pete would be exciting. It hadn't been any hardship being celibate all these years because she hadn't met a man who could turn her on. In a way, it was a relief to know her sex drive hadn't shut down forever after that disaster with Bob Hartman back in college. Why not grab a little happiness while she had the chance?

Because you'd be stupid enough to fall in love with him, her conscience chided her. *Hell, Becky, you're already half in love with him now.*

Fear rose in her throat like acid. It hurt to breathe, and the fine hair on the back of her neck and arms tingled and stood on end. She glanced at the man riding so confidently beside her. He gave her a broad, friendly smile and her heart lurched as if on cue.

Temptation and trouble went hand in hand, she grimly reminded herself. But, merciful heaven, resisting his charm wasn't going to be easy.

Chapter Six

"Aunt Becky, I need two dozen cupcakes for school," Tina announced that night at the supper table.

"When do you need them?" Becky asked.

"Tomorrow."

Becky gasped. "Tomorrow? Why didn't Mrs. Johnson send a note home with you?"

"She did, but I lost it," Tina admitted with a sheepish grin. "I'm sorry I forgot to tell you."

"That's okay, honey. I think I've got a cake mix in the pantry."

Hank wore a grin to match his daughter's. "Uh, Beck?"

"What?"

"It's my turn to bring treats for the co-op board meeting tomorrow afternoon. While you're in the kitchen tonight, would you mind bakin' some brownies for me?"

"Land sakes, you could give a person a little more warning about these things," Grandma D scolded. "My favorite show's on tonight and I've got a bridge game tomorrow, but I guess I'll get to it somehow."

"No, Grandma, I'll take care of it," Becky said firmly. "You've done enough for one day."

"So have you, Rebecca Anne," Grandma D retorted. "I'm not so old I can't manage this kitchen."

"Nobody said you were, Grandma," Sam put in diplomatically. "I'm sure Jan will be glad to help Becky."

"Jan rented a movie for us to watch tonight," Hank protested. "We've been waitin' to see it for months."

"It's all right," Becky replied. "I'll enjoy doing a little baking for a change. Grandma, would you put Tina to bed after your program?"

"Be glad to." The old lady sighed, then pushed herself to her feet. "Guess I am a little tired at that. I'll be in the living room if anybody needs me."

Peter frowned. After the day they'd put in, he felt absolutely wiped out. Though Becky was more used to working that hard than he was, she had to be exhausted, too. Couldn't these people see that? Evidently not.

"Speakin' of food, sis," Sam said a moment later, "you're plannin' to make potato salad for the branding barbecue on Saturday, aren't you?"

"I don't think I'll have time, Sam."

"But it's a tradition, Becky. Why, it won't seem like branding day at all without your potato salad," he coaxed, giving her a hangdog look.

"Maybe Grandma will make it for you."

"You make it more like Mom used to. Grandma always puts in too much mayonnaise."

Becky exhaled an exasperated sigh, but she smiled and reached across the table to ruffle Sam's hair. "All right, ya big baby. I'll make it for you."

"Thanks, Beck." Sam pushed back his chair and walked over to the coffeepot. "Oh, nuts."

"What's the matter?" Becky asked, getting up to clear the table.

"There's no coffee. I've got some paperwork to do, and I thought I'd take a cup with me."

"Go on ahead and get to it," she answered. "I'll make some fresh and bring it in to you."

Hank and Janice left to watch their movie. Tina scampered off to find Grandma D. Struggling against stiff muscles, Peter got to his feet and carried a stack of dishes to the sink. When he brought over another load, Becky glanced up at him and smiled.

"Thanks, Pete, but you don't need to help."

"I don't mind," he assured her. "It sounds as if you could use a little help tonight."

Becky switched on the coffeemaker, then shrugged. "It's always crazy around here. But you must be tired. Why don't you go in and put your feet up with Grandma D?"

"When are you going to get a chance to put your feet up?" he asked.

"Probably next winter," she answered with a chuckle.

"In that case, I'm doing these dishes. You start the baking."

"But—"

"No buts, Rebecca Anne," he insisted, sounding exactly like Grandma D when she was putting her foot down. "I know how to do it. Besides, I don't want a cranky boss tomorrow."

Her eyes dancing with amusement, Becky stuck her nose in the air. "I'll have you know, I'm never cranky."

"Good. Let's keep it that way. Get to work, Dawson."

"Yes, sir. Anything you say, sir."

As if by magic, a mixer appeared on the counter, along with a cake mix, measuring cups, cupcake pans and papers and a carton of eggs. The mixer whined, the beaters whirred and the cupcakes landed in the oven in five minutes flat. The instant the coffeemaker stopped dripping, Becky dashed into the den with a cup for Sam, then ran back into the kitchen and started the brownies.

Peter began to feel as if he'd been locked in the room with a low-flying jet. The woman's stamina and organizational skills amazed him. He'd worked with some extremely efficient nurses over the course of his career, but Becky could have taught even the best of them a few things about saving wasted motions.

When he'd finished the dishes, Peter offered to stay and help, but Becky shooed him out of the kitchen. His conscience bothered him about leaving her, but he had to admit the thought of a hot shower was irresistible. He said good-night to Grandma D and Tina and walked the half mile to the foreman's house.

Becky lifted the pan of brownies onto the cooling rack and wiped her forehead with the back of one hand. Whew! She could check Misty while the brownies cooled and stir up a batch of frosting when she got back. She glanced at the clock and grimaced when she saw it was already eight. If Pete hadn't done the dishes for her, she'd still be frosting the darn cupcakes at ten. She wondered if he had any idea how much she appreciated his help.

Sniffing enthusiastically, Grandma D entered the kitchen. "Smells good in here." She walked to the counter and inspected Becky's handiwork. "They look radical, Becky."

Becky chuckled at her grandmother's use of Tina's favorite phrase. "Thanks, Grandma. How was your program?"

"It was a damned old rerun. Tina claims I snored through the last half hour," the old lady grumbled. "You got these done pretty quick."

"Pete did the dishes for me."

Grandma D's eyes twinkled behind her red-framed glasses. "He's a nice boy, isn't he?"

Though she'd never be able to think of Pete as a boy, Becky nodded. "I think he'll be a good hand."

"You must have worked him pretty hard today. He sure was movin' slow when he said good-night. Maybe you oughtta take him some liniment."

"Good idea. I'll do it when I check on Misty."

"You better do it now," Grandma warned. "He looked about ready to drop in his tracks."

"All right." Becky retrieved the liniment bottle from the pantry and paused before heading out the back door. "Go on to bed, Grandma. I'll frost that stuff when I get back."

The old woman leveled an innocent stare at her grand-daughter, waited for the screen door to bang shut, then pushed up the sleeves of her sweatshirt and went to work. Becky heard a metal mixing bowl rattle against the counter and sighed with resignation. At least Grandma had taken a nap after supper.

Becky trudged out to the pasture, her tired muscles complaining. Lord, it had been a long day, and tomorrow wouldn't be any shorter. Misty's welcoming neigh brightened her spirits. The waxy drops on the mare's nipples, indicating she would foal within the next week, banished all thoughts of weariness from Becky's mind.

"It won't be long now, girl," she crooned, scratching behind the horse's ears.

Misty snorted and rubbed her head against the woman's chest, demanding more attention. Becky gave it gladly. After waiting eleven and a half months, she was every bit as eager as the mare for this baby to arrive.

When the horse was finally satisfied, Becky picked up the liniment, crossed the pasture and climbed through the fence, fifty yards from Pete's front door. The lights were still on, thank goodness, but she suddenly realized how isolated the foreman's house was from the rest of the ranch. The ambivalent emotions she'd experienced that afternoon returned, slowing her steps.

Pete answered her tentative knock wearing only a pair of jeans. Confronted with his broad, naked chest, Becky felt her mouth dry out. Her eyes followed the tapering pattern of hair over a hard, flat belly to the button at his waistband. God, his navel was an innie, just right for...

She forced her gaze up to his face and encountered a warm smile of invitation that made her throat constrict with an audible gulp.

"Come in," he said, holding the screen door open for her. "Did you finish your baking?"

Baking? Who cares about baking? she thought a trifle hysterically, sidling gingerly past him to avoid direct contact. Her nose twitched at the pleasant, shower-fresh scent of his skin. His black hair gleamed with dampness in the room's dim light. Her fingers ached to touch it so badly, she tightened them around the liniment bottle's neck in a strangling grip.

"What can I do for you, Becky?" Pete asked.

The laughter dancing in his eyes told her she was gawking at him as if she'd never seen a man's chest before. Feeling a blush race up her neck, she thrust the liniment at him and cleared her throat to speak.

"Grandma thought you might need this."

He accepted the bottle with a deep, rumbly chuckle. "Thanks." He unscrewed the cap and sniffed the contents, immediately jerking his head back. "Boy, that stuff reeks."

"You get used to the smell after a while. Of course, you don't have to use it, if you don't want to, but it really does help." Damn, was that her voice, so high and breathless, rattling away at the speed of light?

Pete casually draped an arm around her shoulders and ushered her into the center of the room. "Then I'll have to try it. Would you mind putting some on my back for me?"

His calm, even tone made the request seem perfectly reasonable, but every hormone she possessed screamed, "Red Alert! Red Alert!"

"Oh, well, I, uh... I really should be going, Pete. I still have to frost Tina's cupcakes and Hank's brownies."

"Please? What's a little back rub between friends?"

"I don't think your back's where you really need the liniment," she said dryly.

Pete laughed and clapped both hands against his backside. "Hey, I'll take what I can get."

He lowered himself to the floor with a groan and stretched
out on his stomach. Propping himself on one elbow, he held
the liniment out to Becky with a pleading look.

Her hand automatically reached for the bottle. Pete
crossed his hands on the floor and laid his chin on them,
then closed his eyes and exhaled a tired sigh. She knelt beside him and gazed at the broad expanse of his back, rubbing her sweaty palms on her thighs.

Sitting on her heels, she thought, Oh, my, where to start?
At his neck and work down to that cute little mole in the
small of his back? Or at his waist and work up to those
broad shoulders? Was that a bruise on his right shoulder
blade? It sure was, and it looked like a nasty one, too. He
must have gotten it when he fell off Whiskey.

She unscrewed the bottle's cap and poured the oily liquid
into her hand. The pungent odor made her eyes water and
cleared her brain of the fanciful, erotic images trying to
form there. *Get a grip, Dawson,* she ordered herself. *After
all, what's a little back rub between friends?*

Holding her breath, she rubbed her palms together and
laid them both flat against the center of his spine. His muscles tensed at the sudden contact, then gradually relaxed as
her hands slid over his back, spreading a generous layer of
liniment across his swarthy skin. A couple of days working
without a shirt and he'd have a tan to die for.

Pete let out a soft moan—a mixture of pleasure and pain.
Smiling, Becky straddled his hips and went to work in earnest, kneading the bunched-up muscles in his neck and
shoulders into submission, sweeping long, soothing strokes
from his shoulder blades to his waist, massaging each bony
vertebra with her thumbs.

Lord, but he had a beautiful back. Her palms grew hot
from the liniment and the friction of skin against skin. Her

breathing became light and erratic. Her heart beat in a slow, throbbing rhythm, and those fanciful, erotic images crept back into her mind. She had to fight a compelling urge to let her firm touch soften into a caress.

"That feels wonderful," Pete murmured.

Her fingers trembled at the low, husky tone of his voice. The temperature soared. Her breasts felt heavy and full. Her inner thighs tingled where they brushed the sides of his hips. If she didn't get away from him in the next thirty seconds, she would do something extremely foolish, but her hands refused to leave his smooth, warm flesh.

He raised up on one elbow and looked at her over his shoulder. His eyes were slumberous, his face flushed, his mouth curved ever so slightly in a sensuous smile. Becky couldn't move, couldn't breathe, couldn't look away from the desire in those dark, mesmerizing eyes.

Shifting slowly, as if he feared he might frighten her away, Pete turned over and pulled himself into a sitting position. He cupped the sides of her head with his hands; his thumbs caressed her temples. His minty breath warmed her face, and then his lips closed over hers.

His kiss was everything she'd ever imagined, everything she'd ever wanted a kiss to be. Though his body was hard and taut with restraint beneath her, he nibbled at her mouth and fondled the sensitive skin behind her ears with gentle fingertips, wooing a response rather than demanding one. Wanting more, she tipped her head to one side and swiped his lower lip with the tip of her tongue, delighting in his answering groan.

He dropped one arm to her waist and settled her onto his lap. Even through two pairs of jeans, there was no mistaking the extent of his arousal. The intimate contact shocked her and yet she couldn't turn away from the sweet, teasing kisses he coaxed from her lips or the caresses, soft as dandelion fluff, he trailed down the sides of her neck with his free hand.

His exquisite gentleness made her feel fragile and frustrated and unbearably excited, all at the same time. God, it had been so long—too long—since she'd felt this delicious hunger. If he wouldn't give her what she needed, she would take it. Her left hand gripped his shoulder for balance; her right hand plunged into the thick, glossy hair at the back of his head, holding him still. She deepened the kiss, sighing with satisfaction when his tongue plunged into her mouth.

The world tilted in a dizzying rush as he lay back, bringing her with him. His arms wrapped tightly around her, flattening her breasts against his chest. His heart thundered in time with hers; his ragged breathing filled her eardrums. And still the kiss went on, infecting them both with a contagious excitement.

No longer gentle, his hands explored her back and sides, hips and waist, thighs and buttocks. His lips moved along her jawline and down her neck. His tongue dipped into the hollow above her collarbone. She shivered with delight.

"Mmm, you smell like chocolate," he murmured, nuzzling the first pearl snap on her shirt.

"Grandma says I smell like a damned old horse."

His laughter vibrated the length of her body. His arms tightened around her, rubbing the aching tips of her breasts against his chest. He sniffed the side of her neck, then nibbled on her earlobe. "She's right, but it suits you."

Bracing her hands on the floor on either side of his head, she pulled away slightly and smiled down at him. "Is that supposed to be a compliment or an insult?"

He grabbed her braid and tugged her back down within kissing range. "Definitely a compliment. It's a nice...earthy smell."

Then his lips claimed hers again. It felt so natural, so wonderful to be held and caressed like this, she wanted to sink right into his bones. There was passion—a rich, simmering passion that filled her with need. And yet, there was affection and respect in his touch, a patient willingness to savor whatever she chose to give without rushing her to keep up with him.

Wanting to return the pleasure she was receiving, she gently rocked her hips against his and stroked one hand down the side of his bare chest. He moaned in response and rolled on top of her. Her elbow brushed against something, she heard a muffled thud, but she was too entranced with the deep, drugging kisses they shared and the wonderful weight of his body resting on hers to pay attention to whatever it was.

Resting on one forearm, he released the first snap on her shirt and went on to the second and the third. His pupils dilated as he gazed down at her breasts, swelling above the plain cotton cups of her bra. He inhaled a deep, shuddering breath, then choked and gave his head a violent shake.

Becky reached for him instinctively, but he lunged away from her, one long arm stretched out toward something. When she turned her head to see what it was, an acrid odor seared her nostrils. She bolted to a sitting position, choking and sputtering as Pete had done.

He set the liniment bottle upright before racing to open the windows. She ran for the roll of paper towels in the kitchen. They worked side by side, sopping up the mess, breathing through their mouths.

Free of the excitement she'd found in Pete's embrace, Becky felt her common sense return. She glanced at the spot they'd occupied a moment earlier and cringed at the thought of what would have happened if they hadn't been overpowered by liniment fumes. So she wasn't some naive rancher's daughter who would jump into bed with him, was she?

If he'd ever believed that before, Pete would never believe it now. She couldn't blame him for that—she didn't believe it herself. No, from the way she'd behaved, the man no doubt figured she would eagerly take right up where they'd left off.

She mashed the wad of towels down harder against the rug, lowering her head so he wouldn't see her flaming cheeks. The front of her shirt gaped open to her waist at the movement. She refastened the snaps with one hand as surreptitiously as she could, but each snick sounded like a pistol shot in the silent room.

Damn her hide, maybe she *was* a pathetic, sex-starved old maid, after all. From the very first kiss, she hadn't tried to resist him, hadn't even wanted to. Hell, after about three whole seconds, she'd participated with enthusiasm and egged him on at every opportunity. A few more minutes, and she'd have been yanking his jeans off and begging him to take her, and she wouldn't have given a rip about getting pregnant, either.

She hadn't shown any more sense than a kid playing with matches beside a gasoline tank. At her age she ought to know better, but around Pete Sinclair she obviously didn't. The attraction or lust or whatever it was between them, was too raw and explosive for her to handle.

"What's wrong, Becky?" he asked quietly.

"Nothing," she replied, testing the rug for soggy spots with trembling fingertips.

He grasped her chin and tipped her head up, silently demanding that she look at him. Her heart contracted at the tenderness in his gaze. She climbed to her feet to escape his touch, fearing she would throw herself into his arms again.

"You're regretting what we just did."

She nodded, then balled up the paper towels in her hand and carried them out to the trash can in the kitchen. Pete followed, blocking her path when she would have returned to the living room.

"Why do you regret it?" he demanded, reaching for her shoulders.

"I don't want to talk about it."

"Well, that's too bad, because I do." Hurt flashed in his eyes, but he softened his tone. "I've never enjoyed kissing anyone more than I did kissing you, Becky. I thought you were enjoying yourself, too. Did I do something that offended you?"

"No." She stepped away from him and shoved her hands into her pockets.

"Then what's upsetting you?"

"I told you to keep your lips to yourself this afternoon, remember?"

He grinned at her. "Because kissing leads to other things?"

"Yeah. And it darn near did, didn't it?"

"Would that have been so awful? We're both consenting, responsible adults."

"Which one of us was gonna be responsible for birth control, Pete? Do you keep some on hand all the time, just in case the opportunity presents itself?"

His face flushed. "Uh, no. But I'll take care of it before—"

"Don't bother. It's not going to happen again."

"Come on, Becky. You don't really believe that."

"Oh, yes, I do. I don't want it to happen again."

"You can lie to me all you want, but you'd better not lie to yourself." He pointed toward the living room. "What we shared in there was...magic. Why are you trying to convince yourself you don't want to feel it again?"

"All right, maybe I do," she admitted, "but that doesn't mean I have to let myself do anything about it. You'll be gone by Labor Day. I'm not modern enough or liberated enough to be a summer fling."

With that, she brushed past him and stalked to the front door. He grabbed her arm before she could swing it open, releasing her when she turned on him with a glare.

"What makes you so sure you'd only be a summer fling?" he asked. "How can you know that if you won't give our relationship a chance to develop?"

She sighed and shook her head, then gave him a bittersweet smile. "Think about it, Sinclair," she said softly. "I was born to be a red-necked cowgirl. I couldn't fit into your life if I died tryin'. I haven't had all that much experience with men, but I've had enough to know you're way out of my league.''

''My God, Becky, are you still a virgin?''

''That's none of your damn business.'' Her spine straight and stiff, she marched across the porch and down the steps.

Peter watched her disappear into the darkness outside, then turned back to his living room. It still reeked of liniment, but his emotions were in such turmoil, he barely noticed. He felt like a jerk for asking her such a personal question, but he still wished she'd answered it.

He went to the kitchen and grabbed a beer from the refrigerator. Resting one hip against the counter, he twisted off the bottle cap and lobbed it at the trash can. Two points.

It didn't make any difference to him whether she was a virgin or not, except that if he ever did make love to her, he wouldn't want to hurt her unnecessarily. His groin hardened painfully at the image of burying himself to the hilt in her body. He swallowed an icy gulp of beer, but it didn't cool him off much. Certainly not enough.

Damn. He wanted her so fiercely it hurt. He'd never had a woman respond to him so eagerly, so honestly. Not even his ex-wife.

He'd never doubted his masculinity, never felt a need to prove it by treating women as conquests, but Becky made him feel like a . . . well, like a macho stud. And, he had to admit, he loved feeling that way. It was funny, now that he thought about it.

Karen, his ex, had been a petite, delicate, ultrafeminine woman who should have brought out all of his protective, caveman instincts. But it hadn't worked that way. Her clinging helplessness and constant whining about the time he spent at the hospital had made him withdraw from her. His reaction to her demand for a divorce had been relief.

In comparison, Becky was tall and robust and it wouldn't surprise Peter in the least if she could beat him at arm wrestling. She was extremely competent and self-sufficient—it would never occur to her to ask for help changing a flat tire.

She was a woman other people naturally depended on, the glue that held the Dawson family together.

He'd never met a woman who needed him less, and yet, he found himself wanting to hold her in his arms and protect her, share her burdens and lighten her load. He'd loved hearing her soft whimpers of pleasure when he'd kissed and caressed her. He'd almost lost control of himself when her hands had touched him with such obvious enjoyment.

Was she still a virgin? He didn't think so. Her responses had been too hungry, as if she'd known sexual pleasures before and had missed them. There had been real anguish in her eyes when she'd told him she wasn't liberated enough to be a summer fling, as if someone had used her that way before.

Peter's gut knotted at the thought of any man taking Becky's virginity and then hurting her. He wanted to kill the creep, whoever he was. He slammed his beer bottle onto the counter, splashing the contents onto his hand.

Are you any better, Sinclair? his conscience demanded. *Are you ready to make her any promises?*

Remorse smashed him in the face. Yes, he wanted Becky Dawson. He could probably have her, too. But she deserved more than his lust, more than his selfish needs. She deserved nothing less than a lifetime commitment from her mate, and his life was so messed up, he couldn't give her one.

Even if he knew what he wanted to do about his career, the differences in their backgrounds would make a lasting relationship between them difficult, if not impossible. Perhaps those differences could be worked out in time. But until he *was* ready to make a commitment to her, he would keep his hands, his lips and the rest of his anatomy to himself.

Chapter Seven

The next morning, Becky decided that facing Pete Sinclair again ranked right up there with the three most embarrassing moments of her life. Since he avoided meeting her gaze and sounded more laconic than any Westerner she'd ever met, she figured he must feel pretty much the same way. Damn sex for spoiling what could have been an enjoyable friendship.

They rode out in silence to the area Sam had assigned them. Becky hated it. Sulking about a disagreement had never been her style; she preferred to get a problem out into the open, talk it over and be done with it. Unfortunately, every time she glanced at Pete's stern profile, her courage evaporated like drops of water sprinkled on a hot griddle.

The deep lines around his nose and mouth made her wonder how much physical pain he was suffering from the saddle sores he'd earned yesterday. Dark circles of fatigue under his eyes told her he hadn't gotten any more sleep than she had. He'd hardly touched his breakfast. She wouldn't blame him if he announced he'd changed his mind about staying on at the Circle D.

Her heart ached with regret at that thought. Grandma D would be awfully disappointed if he left, and she wouldn't be the only one. Despite all her reservations about getting involved with Pete, all her rational and irrational fears, Becky still wanted more time with him.

He was...different from the men she was used to. He was more sensitive, more willing to treat her as an equal, softer in some ways than, say, Sam or Hank, but he was still very much a man. Maybe more man than she could handle. But she'd felt more alive in the two days she'd spent with him than she had in the past ten years, and, dammit, she didn't want him to walk out of her life now. Not yet.

If only they could take things more slowly. Be friends for a while. Really get to know each other without all this confusing, man-woman stuff between them. Maybe then she'd feel more comfortable about physical intimacy with him.

Her experience with the sex act hadn't convinced her it was worth shouting all that much about. After last night, however, she had to wonder if it might not be different with Pete. Was there more to it than she remembered? There certainly seemed to be in the romance novels she read, but she'd always chalked that up to literary license and the writers' kinky imaginations.

She felt like an idiot for not knowing at her age, but damn, she was curious. If Pete left, she might never know. But what could she do about it? Walk up to him and say, "Oh, by the way, I've changed my mind and I might like to have sex with you, after all?" Right.

Well, she thought, sneaking one more glance at him when she opened the last gate, she didn't have time to worry about it now. There were too many cattle to round up if they wanted to be ready for branding tomorrow morning.

Now that Pete knew what he was supposed to do, the job went faster. They worked steadily until ten-thirty without speaking more than two sentences to each other, then Becky called for a break. She counted the cows and calves while Pete went off into the bushes for a few minutes.

Nuts. According to the tally Sam had given her, they were one cow and four calves short. She asked Pete to count them when he came back, and made her own trek into the brush.

Since his numbers matched her own, there was nothing else to do, but ride the field again and find the darn critters. Becky sent Pete along the southern fence line and took the northern one herself. A small creek, whose banks were choked with willows, cut across the northwest corner of the pasture. She suspected the missing animals were hiding near the water.

Sure enough, ten minutes later, she heard a soft bawling coming from a clump of willows straight ahead. The creek had overrun its banks, turning the ground into a marshy bog. Becky let Sioux pick his own way through the thick underbrush, and groaned in dismay when she spotted the calf, buried halfway to his belly in the black, gooey mud. His mother stood guard, shaking her head at the horse and rider.

"Easy, Mama," Becky crooned, uncoiling her rope, "we'll get your baby out of there for ya."

"Becky?" Pete's voice called from off to her right. "Where are you?"

"Over here. We've got a little problem."

The cow bellowed and shook her head again when Pete rode up beside Becky.

"What's wrong?" he asked.

"The calf's stuck, and his mama's not gonna let us get near him."

"What do you want me to do?"

"Ride up on her right side, nice and slow, and distract her. I'll come at her from the left and rope her while she's goin' after you. Don't get too close."

"All right." His eyes shining with excitement, he grinned at her. "But answer one question first."

"What's that?"

"Are you any good at roping?"

Becky mashed her hat down hard onto her head and smiled at him. "That cow's so damn mad, you'd better hope so."

Chuckling, he nudged Whiskey into a walk and went off to follow her instructions. Her rope ready, Becky and Sioux circled around to the other side. Pete flapped his arms and shouted rude remarks at the cow. As if she'd understood and taken immediate offense, the cow charged him.

Becky gave the rope three hard swings, then tossed it overhand at the cow's head. It settled cleanly around the animal's neck. She dallied the other end of the rope around her saddle horn and reined Sioux to the right.

When the loop tightened around the cow, and the horse had trotted her for a hundred yards, she lost her will to fight. Becky tied her to a fence post and went back for the calf. Pete stood at the edge of the bog, talking softly to the frightened animal.

"You must have some bedside manner, Doc," Becky teased him as she dismounted.

"Nice roping," he replied with a wry smile. "Are you always that accurate?"

"Everybody misses sometimes."

"I'm glad you didn't tell me that before you made me provoke that cow. Are you planning to rope the calf to get him out of there?"

"I'm afraid he's too weak to handle that much stress. Ever try mud wrestling?"

"I'm afraid not."

"Well, c'mon," she answered, wading into the muck. "Here's your chance."

Pete put a headlock on the calf while Becky pulled its front feet out of the gumbo. The animal bawled and struggled, whipping his tail back and forth.

"Hold still, ya mangy little varmint," Becky muttered.

She moved to the calf's rear end. One hoof came up with a loud, sucking pop. When she freed his other hoof, all hell broke loose. The calf kicked back with both hind feet, catching Becky squarely in the ribs and knocking her flat on her backside. Then he thrashed his way out of Pete's hold, pulling the man off balance with enough momentum to send him sprawling facedown in the goo.

With a final kick of his heels, the calf made it to solid ground. He turned, stared at the humans struggling in the sticky mud and let out a long, loud bawl before trotting off into the brush in search of his mother.

"I'll enjoy turning you into a steer tomorrow," Becky called after him, feeling the wet, slimy muck ooze through her jeans and underwear.

Pete pushed himself onto his knees and dug clumps of mud out of his eye sockets. He shook his head, sending the black stuff flying in every direction, then floundered to his feet. Gunk dripped off the brim of his hat, his eyebrows, his nose, chin and chest.

Becky took one look at him, plopped back onto her fanny and roared with laughter. "You remind me of a mud monster in one of Hank's old comic books."

Curving his long fingers into claws, Pete raised them beside his head and shambled toward her, making grunting noises deep in his throat. His grin painted a white slash across his blackened face as he loomed over her.

"How's about a little kiss, baby?" he asked, waggling his eyebrows at her.

"Get away from me," she cried, giggling and scooting back as fast as she could.

"Not nice to laugh at mud monster," Peter growled. He reached down and grabbed her hands, pulling her to her feet and into his arms. "Mud monster wants mud woman."

Unable to stop giggling, Becky fought against his hold and succeeded only in smearing the mud on the front of his shirt onto the front of hers. It soaked right through to her skin. She twisted her head back and forth as his mouth pressed gloppy kisses down the side of her face and neck.

"Stop," she cried, gasping for air. "God, that's awful."

Pete let her go. A deep, booming laugh erupted from his throat when he saw Becky trying to wipe off her neck with her muddy hands.

A challenging glint lighting her eyes, she bent down and scooped up a handful of gumbo. "So, ya think it's funny, do ya?" she asked, advancing on him.

He held up both hands in front of his face and backed away from her. "Now, Becky, you laughed at me first."

"Tough. This is war, Sinclair."

She took aim and fired the mud ball at his chest. He ducked and tried to turn away, but it caught him beneath his left ear. He scraped it off and tossed it right back at her, hitting her square in the chest. In seconds, the fight degenerated into a laughter-filled, mud-slinging contest that ended only when a deep, amused voice drawled behind them.

"Havin' fun, kids?"

Sitting astride his big gray gelding, Smokey, Sam grinned down at them. Becky felt about ten years old and two feet tall.

"Oh, uh," she stammered, shaking clumps of mud off her fingers, "we were just, uh, rescuing a calf that got bogged down."

"Where is it?"

"He's around here somewhere," Pete answered. He offered Becky his hand, and together they struggled to higher ground. "I guess he must have wandered off."

"Must have." Sam tipped his hat back and studied them for a moment, his lips twitching. Then a more sober expression crept over his face. "How'd your count come out on this field?"

"We're still three calves short," Becky told him.

"Two," Pete corrected her. "I found another one before I came over here to help you."

"Damn," Sam muttered.

"What's going on?" Becky asked.

"Unless you find those two calves, we're missing twenty-five head."

"Think we've got rustlers?"

Sam shook his head. "If we do, they're damned clever. They usually cut open a fence and grab whatever cattle they can. But we're missing a calf or two out of every pasture."

"Could it be predators?" Pete asked.

"The coyotes might have gotten one or two, but not that many when the calves are this big," Becky told him. "Besides, we haven't found any carcasses, have we, Sam?"

"Nope."

"It's kind of like that fence we found down when we came back from town the other day," Becky said thoughtfully.

"What fence?" Sam asked.

She explained what had happened, ending with a shrug. "I didn't think much about it at the time, but now I wonder if somebody's trying to give us a hard time."

Sam sighed. "Let's not get too paranoid, sis. We're gonna go back and search every pasture again. Maybe we'll find them." He reined Smokey around. "Bring this bunch you've got here over to the main herd and then you two better go back to the house for some clean clothes. Tell Grandma we'll be late for supper."

They watched him ride away before turning to look at each other. The mud had started to dry and crack around Pete's nose and mouth. Becky grinned and a shower of dirt rained onto her chest.

"I hope you know we're never gonna hear the end of this," she warned him.

"I don't care," Pete answered, returning her grin. "I haven't played like that in years."

Chuckling, she rubbed both hands over her face and neck, and Pete followed suit. When they'd scraped off as much as possible, they mounted up and went back to work. The morning's tension had been erased, and they spent the rest of the day talking and joking as if nothing unpleasant had ever passed between them. Though her skin itched unbearably in a few unmentionable places, and she was concerned about the missing calves, Becky smiled every time she thought about that mud fight.

Supper was a hurried, strained affair, the lost calves the main topic of conversation. Only two had been found during an intensive search. When Becky explained that each animal represented a six- to eight-hundred-dollar loss to the ranch, depending on the price of beef when it was sold, Peter understood why everyone was upset.

While he sympathized with his hosts, however, he felt a warm glow in his chest every time Becky turned one of her sweet, easygoing smiles in his direction. He'd been miserable from the minute she'd left him the night before until they'd shared that ridiculous fight in the mud. Seeing her smile at him again was like finding a letter from your best friend at the bottom of a stack of bills.

Neither of them had spoken a word about what had happened at his place the night before. If Peter had his way, they never would. During the dark, lonely hours of the night, he'd feared Becky would ask him to leave the Circle D.

He didn't want to do that. Where would he go? What would he do with himself for the next three months? In spite of his aching muscles and occasional feelings of inadequacy, he was happy here. It felt wonderful to be connected to other people, especially people like the Dawsons.

Yes, he still wanted Becky. In Washington, it seemed that his whole life was hurry, hurry, hurry. If he wanted something, he'd better grab it, because there might not be time later. But he needed to remember he wasn't in Washington now. It was difficult to change his mode of thinking, but wasn't that the reason he'd taken a leave of absence in the first place? To get a new perspective on his life?

If he stayed at the Circle D for the whole summer, there wasn't any need to rush into a sexual relationship. He would see Becky every day, work with her every day. Considering how much they enjoyed each other's company, he had every reason to hope their friendship would eventually grow and deepen into something more meaningful. All he needed to do was relax, be patient and spend time with her.

Peter put that thought into immediate action. After supper, he ignored Becky's protests that he must be exhausted and helped her with the dishes again. It took some talking, but he finally convinced her he was capable of peeling and chopping potatoes, onions and hard-boiled eggs for the potato salad. He used professional curiosity as an excuse to tag along on her nightly visit to Misty.

Becky didn't appear to mind. In fact, when they found the mare pacing and sweating amid several small piles of manure, signs of imminent birth, Becky seemed glad to have him with her. Her eyes glowed with anticipation and excitement. All signs of fatigue vanished. She talked nonstop in a quiet voice while they led the horse into the foaling stall in the barn.

"Aren't you going to call a veterinarian?" he asked, watching Becky carefully wash the mare's udder and vagina.

"Not unless there's a problem. She did just fine the last time."

After removing the halter and giving Misty a final, affectionate pat, Becky left the stall. She organized her supplies on a nearby table, then led Peter to a stack of hay bales far enough away to give the mare some privacy, but close enough to monitor her labor.

"This could go on for hours," she said, sitting on one of the bales. "You don't need to stay if you're tired."

"Are you kidding?" he asked. "I delivered human babies when I was an intern, but I've never seen a horse born. I wouldn't miss this for anything."

Misty pawed at the clean straw, lay down and rose again repeatedly. Milk dripped from her udder, and she deposited more little piles of manure. Becky leaned back against a bale behind her, then shifted forward for a better look, every bit as restless as the mare.

"Do you always get this excited?" Peter asked.

"Always," she admitted with a grin. "There's something about a new life that makes all the hard work worthwhile. And Misty's special because I delivered her and trained her myself. If this foal is as good as her first one, I may start my own business."

"Would you leave the Circle D?"

"Maybe someday. I'd like to have my own place."

Her answer and the wistful note in her voice surprised Peter. "Why don't you do it now?"

She shrugged, then looked down at her hands. "Grandma's getting on in years and Tina's still pretty little."

"Won't Janice take over with Tina when she marries Hank?"

A worried frown creased Becky's forehead. "I hope so for Tina's sake, but they haven't been getting along too well. Janice is so busy with the wedding plans right now, she doesn't have much time, and I guess Tina's probably jealous because Hank's paying so much attention to Janice. I imagine it'll all work out sooner or later."

As if she couldn't sit still another second, Becky jumped to her feet, walked over to the table and rearranged her supplies. Misty stuck her head over the side of the stall and snorted. Becky patted the mare's neck, crooning soft reassurances until Misty pulled away and lay down again.

"You've got a pretty good stallside manner," Peter said as Becky walked back toward him. "It's too bad you didn't go to vet school."

She stuck her hands in her pockets, then sat beside him. "Yeah, that would have been nice. What about you? Have you done any more thinking about leaving medicine?"

Peter leaned forward and clasped his hands between his knees. When he didn't speak for a few moments, Becky laid a hand on his shoulder and gave it a gentle squeeze.

"You don't have to talk about it, if you don't want to."

"It's not that," he answered, shaking his head. "I still don't completely understand what I feel, myself. I'm not sure anything I say will make sense to you."

"It doesn't have to make sense to me. Sometimes it just helps to think out loud. I do it all the time with Misty."

He couldn't resist the opportunity to tease her. He raised an eyebrow, as if he doubted her sanity. "You talk to your horse? Does she ever answer you?"

"Hey, that's the beauty of it," Becky told him with a laugh. "She doesn't talk back or give me advice I don't want, or tell anyone my secrets. She just listens."

"The perfect confidante."

"She's as close as they come."

"You'd do that for me?"

"What are friends for, Pete?"

What indeed? he thought. Becky turned sideways and put her back against the door of an empty stall, then raised her knees and wrapped her arms around them. Her big, serious green eyes focused on him with interest, but no demand, and, suddenly, the words poured out of him.

"I was such an idealist when I went into medicine. I chose oncology as a specialty, because I thought I could really make a difference. I knew I'd lose a lot of patients, but I thought I could handle it." He sighed and shook his head.

"That would get to anyone after a while, Pete."

"Yeah, well, it wasn't supposed to happen to me. I completely lost my objectivity and became too involved with my patients. It got to the point that I hated my colleagues who could be objective and told myself they didn't care enough. A lot of them refused to be called in when a patient went bad in the middle of the night. I always elected to be there, even though I knew there really wasn't anything I could do to help, other than console their families."

"I'll bet their families appreciated that," Becky said quietly. "I know I would."

"Oh, they did," Peter agreed, "but every time, it took another piece of my soul, Becky, until there just wasn't anything left for me to give. I'd get so angry."

"Angry at what? Your patients?"

"Sometimes. Especially if they'd noticed symptoms and waited to see their doctors out of fear. Sometimes I'd be furious at the disease itself. There are forms of cancer, like pancreatic and ovarian, that are so quiet, there aren't any symptoms until it's usually too late to do anything. And then, the treatments. God..."

"What about them?"

"They'd make my patients so sick and cause them so much pain. They'd work for one person, but not another, for no particular reason anybody could understand. It was like flailing around in the dark, trial and error."

"Sounds frustrating."

"That doesn't begin to cover it. I was sad to lose the old people, but they'd lived their lives, accomplished what they wanted to. But the kids, and the young mothers whose kids still needed them..."

His throat closed up, and he had to choke down the lump before he could continue. Becky reached out and took his hand, comforting him without speaking.

"They really broke my heart. And the young fathers... Their families desperately needed their paychecks. The cost of care can beggar a whole family. And for what? A chance to suffer a little longer?"

"No. A chance to live, Pete. That's the best thing you can offer anyone. You saved some of them, didn't you?"

"Not enough, Becky. Not nearly enough. For a lot of those people, it wasn't much of a chance to begin with."

"That's not your fault. Without you, they wouldn't have had any chance at all."

"Yeah, well, now they don't, at least not from me. They're so brave sometimes, and to watch them fight and fight and still loose... I just can't face it anymore."

"You did what you could, Pete. Don't be so hard on yourself. Everybody has a breaking point."

"I sure found mine. I just don't know if I can ever put myself back together again."

"Give yourself some time to heal."

"That's what I'm trying to do, but every time I think about it, I break out in a cold sweat and my hands shake like a wino's. I wouldn't want to be my patient."

"Are there other areas of medicine you could get into? Something where you wouldn't have to confront death on such a regular basis?"

He shrugged. "I guess I could go into general practice. I might need to take some refresher courses, but I volunteered one night a week at a free clinic, so I've kept up my basic skills better than most oncologists."

Misty grunted. A moment later, they heard what sounded like several gallons of water gush onto the straw. Peter turned to Becky, but she was already halfway to the stall.

"Come here, Pete. Quick."

He hurried to Becky's side. She grabbed his hand and held it while they looked inside the stall. The mare lay on her side, breathing heavily.

"She'll rest for a little bit now, but the contractions should start soon," Becky murmured.

Ten minutes later, they did. Misty lifted her tail when a contraction started, and one tiny hoof appeared at the entrance to her womb. Then it disappeared until the next contraction started.

"Damn, where's that other hoof?" Becky muttered, tightening her grip on Peter's hand. "Oh, look...there it is! Come on, Misty, you're doing fine, sweetheart."

Peter found himself swept up in Becky's excitement, holding his breath when the mare strained, feeling a growing sense of awe and delight when he could finally see the foal's nose and then its head. With one last mighty push, the shoulders emerged from the birth canal and the rest of the foal slid onto the straw, encased in a membrane.

Becky entered the stall and crouched beside the foal, stripping the membrane away from its nose and clearing its nostrils. The little animal started breathing. Becky sent Peter a triumphant grin that warmed him down to the soles of his feet. Then she stroked the exhausted mare's neck and rejoined Peter, immediately taking his hand again.

When Misty raised her head and nuzzled her baby, Becky led Peter back to the bales to give the animals a few minutes of privacy.

"That was amazing," he said quietly. "Thanks for letting me stay."

"I'm glad you did. It isn't always that easy. For a minute there, I was scared to death that other front leg was caught on the rim of Misty's pelvis," she answered, craning her neck toward the stall.

"I hate to sound ignorant, but is it a boy or a girl?"

She chuckled. "I couldn't see. We'll find out when it stands up. I'm hoping for a colt—that's a boy—but a good, healthy filly wouldn't be bad, either. Tina's gonna go nuts when she sees it."

They fell silent for a while then, and Peter decided that simply being with Becky Dawson in the quiet barn and holding her hand was probably better therapy than any psychiatrist could give him. He sent up a fervent prayer of thanks that he hadn't destroyed their friendship last night and leaned back against the bale behind him with a tired, but satisfied sigh.

Becky rested her head on his shoulder as naturally as if it had always belonged there. "I'm sorry you got interrupted. Did you want to talk anymore?"

"No. This should be a happy moment. But it helped to talk. You're a good listener, Ms. Dawson."

"Anytime, Pete. Anytime."

Her voice was so soft and dreamy, he thought she might be falling asleep. But half an hour later, rustling noises came from the stall and Becky was on her feet in an instant. Peter followed her, amazed at how quickly her energy level renewed itself.

Misty stood in the center of the stall, now, and the foal was making endearingly awkward efforts to rise. Becky bounced up and down on the balls of her feet, as if to encourage the little animal, then turned and threw her arms around Peter's neck in an exuberant hug.

"It's a colt!" she cried.

He cheerfully returned her hug and kept one arm around her shoulders when she went back to watching the horses. The colt managed two wobbly steps, lifted his head to his mother's udder and began to nurse vigorously. The mare looked at the human audience, every inch the proud mama.

"Oh, isn't he a dandy?" Becky whispered, her eyes glistening with unshed tears.

"That sounds like a good name for him," Peter replied.

"Dandy," she said slowly, before turning back into his arms and hugging him again. "You're right. That's perfect. We'll call him Dandy."

Though he felt his groin responding to her nearness, Peter accepted Becky's embrace for what it was—a sharing of joy at Dandy's safe arrival. She pulled back a moment later and looked up into his eyes, and suddenly the atmosphere between them changed.

She went absolutely still for the space of a heartbeat. Then her fingers caressed the back of his neck and moved up into his hair, gently, but undeniably pressing his head toward her. Her eyelids fluttered shut as their lips met, parted and met again.

How could a simple kiss express so much? he wondered. Happiness, sympathy, understanding, passion, affection— they were all there. His hands splayed over her back, holding her to him as if her loving touch held everything he needed to heal his wounded spirit and make life worth living again. The only thing he knew for certain in that unbearably sweet moment, was that he never wanted to let her go.

Chapter Eight

Becky groaned, rolled over and pulled the pillow over her head when a brisk knock sounded on her bedroom door at six o'clock the next morning. She felt as if she'd barely had an hour's sleep and she'd been having the nicest dream about Pete....

"Becky? You all right?" Sam's deep voice called.

"I'm fine," she answered, burrowing deeper into the covers, hoping she could recapture that dream.

The door opened with a squeak. Boots clomped across the hardwood floor. A hand lifted the pillow off her face.

"What are you still doin' in bed?" her brother demanded.

"What does it look like? Go away, Sam."

"Are you sick?"

"No." She yawned and rubbed her eyes. "Misty had her foal last night. I didn't get to bed until three-thirty."

"Hey, that's great." He sat on the side of the bed, stretched out his long legs and crossed his feet, as if he intended to stay a while. "Was it a colt or a filly?"

Becky raised up on one elbow and glared at him. "Go look for yourself. They're in the barn. Now, can I *please* go back to sleep?"

Sam laughed and ruffled her hair. "You can sleep tomorrow, sis. It's branding day. We need you."

"Oh, Lord, I forgot." She slumped back down on her pillow. "All right. I'll be down in a few minutes."

"Take your time." He stood and walked to the door. "I'll milk Gertie and feed your calves."

"Hey, Sam? Don't tell anyone about the foal. I want to see Tina's face when I tell her."

"Okay. But I'm gonna look at it, since you won't tell me what it is."

She watched the door close behind him, then dragged her tired body from the bed. A quick shower revived her somewhat. She hurriedly dressed, but found herself dawdling in front of the mirror. Should she put her hair in a ponytail today? Or maybe pull it to one side before she braided it? Which way would Pete like it best?

Her eyes widened in dismay as that thought registered. Had he really become so important to her in less than a week? Evidently he had.

She set the brush down on the dresser and touched her lips with trembling fingertips, remembering the way they had felt when she'd kissed Pete last night. Oh, yeah, she couldn't blame him this time. It had been an instinctive gesture, a need as compelling as her need to breathe.

His grim story had made her ache for him. He thought he'd failed, somehow, that he'd been weak. She thought he'd shown incredible strength in tolerating the situation for as long as he had. She'd wanted to console him, erase his painful memories, show him that his honesty hadn't diminished him in her eyes, and she'd done it the way women have been comforting their men for centuries.

There was nothing wrong with what had happened last night. He'd let her go, they'd tended to Misty and Dandy and gone off to their separate beds. But something had changed during that brief kiss. Something important.

When she'd looked into his eyes, she'd realized Pete was every bit as vulnerable to her as she was to him. Until then, she'd been so concerned about protecting herself from heartbreak, she hadn't thought about his feelings. He needed the simple human contact she'd taken for granted her whole life—warmth and understanding, hugs and affection.

Pete needed those things more than he needed sex, although he might argue the point with her, she thought with a wry grin. It would be difficult for her to give him one without the other when the chemistry between them was so blasted strong, but she wouldn't run anymore from a relationship with him.

She considered Pete's pouring his heart out to her that way, an act of trust and friendship. By listening, she had formed a bond between them she couldn't betray. From now on, she would be there for him. That's what friendship was all about.

Unfortunately, now that she understood his dilemma, she felt it was even more important to keep their friendship platonic. He had a big decision ahead of him. He needed to be able to make it for himself, without feeling obligated to anyone else.

When she'd first met him, she'd thought he was handsome and sexy, and that he probably had women lined up a mile long. She'd feared he would use her and toss her aside at the end of the summer. But she'd been wrong. Dead wrong. Last night, after hearing the depth of his emotion for and commitment to his patients, there wasn't a doubt in her mind that if they made love, he *would* feel obligated. She couldn't do that to him, or let him do it to himself.

For Pete's sake, she would have to be strong enough to resist the sexual attraction they both felt. It sure as hell wasn't going to be easy.

Sighing, she twisted her hair into its regular old braid and hurried to the kitchen. Hank, Janice and Tina sat at the table. Grandma D stirred a kettle of baked beans sitting on the stove's back burner. The screen door on the mudroom slammed, and an instant later, Pete walked into the room.

His eyes lighted up and a warm smile spread across his face when he saw her standing in the opposite doorway. Her heart promptly sent her pulse into overdrive. No, she thought, returning his smile, it wasn't going to be easy.

"Well, it's about damn time you guys showed up," Hank said, propping his elbows on the table.

"Good morning to you, too, Hank," Becky replied calmly.

She took plates from the cupboard, handed one to Pete and lifted the lid from a skillet at the front of the stove. They helped themselves to the bacon and scrambled eggs inside, then sat beside each other at the table. Grandma D brought the coffeepot and a plate of toast.

Hank's teasing grin appeared. "Seems kinda funny you'd both sleep in today. Do anything...interesting last night?"

Becky studied her brother thoughtfully for a moment. He'd been awfully restrained with his wiseacre remarks the past few days, and she'd enjoyed it. If he thought he could start in again, it was high time she gave him a dose of his own medicine. She put a dopey expression on her face, turned to Pete and batted her eyelashes at him.

"We sure did," she said in a simpering voice. "Didn't we, honey?"

Pete choked on his eggs, but recovered quickly when she nudged him under the table with her knee. His eyes dancing with mirth, he looked soulfully down at her. "We sure did, sweetheart."

Lord, his voice sounded as if he'd just crawled out of bed after a satisfying night's romp. Feeling unusually warm all of a sudden, Becky sighed and forced her gaze back to her brother.

Hank sipped his coffee and eyed them both warily. "I didn't hear you come in last night. Where'd you go?"

"Oh, we were out in the barn. There's lots of nice, soft hay out there, you know? And it's so...private."

Tina looked at Becky as if she thought her aunt had suddenly gone wacko. Janice giggled. Grandma D came over and sat at the head of the table. Hank's eyebrows lowered into a scowling V.

"Are you tellin' me you did it in the barn?" he demanded.

"Did what, Daddy?" Tina asked.

Becky bit her lip to keep from laughing at the disgruntled expression his daughter's question produced. "Yeah, Hank, did what?"

Glaring at Becky, Hank subtly nodded toward Tina. "You know damn well what. Now, didja or didn'tcha?"

"That's none of your business," Becky told him with a sugary smile. "I don't ask you what you and Janice do when you're alone."

He slammed his coffee cup onto the table and leaned forward, his dark eyes practically shooting sparks. "That's not funny, Rebecca Anne. Janice and I are engaged. It's not the same thing at all."

Lord, smoke would roll out of his nostrils any minute. If she'd known how much fun it was to provoke Hank's temper instead of losing her own, she would have done it years ago. Since he wasn't getting anywhere with her, he turned his wrath on Pete next.

Thumping his index finger against the table, he came up out of his chair ranting. "Now look, Sinclair, you'd better not be messin' with my sister, or you'll answer to me. And Sam'll be standin' right behind me."

Pete smiled at him, calm as you please, but Becky decided things had gone far enough. "Relax, Hank."

"I'll be damned if I will."

"We delivered a *f-o-a-l* last night," she informed him, shooting a significant glance at Tina. "That's why we were in the barn so late."

Hank's mouth dropped open, then slammed shut with an audible snap. Becky couldn't stand it any longer. She threw back her head and howled with glee, and everyone but Hank and Tina joined in.

Grandma D slapped her knee. "Well, I'll be. She finally gotcha, Hank."

"Daddy, what's goin'. on?" the little girl whined.

"Never mind, honey," he said with a reluctant grin. "Your Aunt Becky just played a joke on me."

Tina tipped her head to one side, closed her eyes and repeated the letters Becky had spelled out for Hank. "That spells foal!"

She jumped out of her chair and ran around the table to her aunt. "Misty had her baby last night. Didn't she?" She grabbed Becky's hand and pulled with all of her six-year-old might. "C'mon! I wanna see it!"

Laughing, Becky allowed the little girl to pull her to her feet. The rest of the family followed them out to the barn. They crept inside and found Sam standing beside Misty's stall. Dandy was nursing again.

Sam picked Tina up to help her see over the high stall door more easily. Becky moved to the rear of the group, feeling like a proud parent as the others complimented the colt's conformation. Then a warm, strong arm closed around her shoulders, and when she looked up into Pete's smiling face, her happiness was complete. Aw, to heck with all of her worries. It was going to be a great day and she intended to enjoy every blessed minute of it.

Five pickups carrying friends and neighbors arrived when the Dawsons left the barn. Grandma D grabbed Peter's hand and introduced him around the group as if he were a long-lost grandson. After catching up on the latest news, several of the women carried cakes and pies into the house. Everyone else went out to the branding site.

Peter stayed close to Becky, helping wherever he could and enjoying the congenial atmosphere while the portable corral was set up and the branding irons heated. Then the group divided into teams and the work began.

Hank and one of the Circle D's hired hands roped the calves and brought them over to the two wrasslers. The wrasslers released the rope, flipped each calf onto its side and held it down while one person branded it, another vaccinated it, another attached an ear tag, and if it was a bull calf, another castrated it. Then the animal was sent bawling back to its mother, and the entire process was repeated with the next one.

Noise, dust and the stench of burning hide filled the air. At first, Peter thought he'd never seen so much chaos, but as the morning wore on, he began to appreciate the precision and rhythm of the operation. Everyone knew his or her job and did it. Becky encouraged him to try each task, and while he had to accept a lot of ribbing, he found the other members of the team more than happy to teach him.

By the end of the afternoon, he was hot, tired and filthy, but he was proud of his new skills and delighted that he'd become an accepted part of the crew. He rode back to his house in Becky's battered pickup, sharing a companionable silence. With a smile and a wave she dropped him off, and he watched her drive out of sight before heading inside for a shower.

After changing into clean clothes, he walked down to the main house, deep in thought. The Dawsons worked harder physically than anyone he'd ever known, but he could understand why they chose to live the way they did.

Here, a person felt valued for what he could contribute to the group's effort, no matter how small that contribution might be. There was a great deal of satisfaction in learning to do a job well, and the people were generous in their praise

and encouragement. Business managers could learn a lot
about motivating employees here.

Lawn chairs decorated the Dawsons' backyard. A row of
picnic tables, groaning with food, formed a buffet line next
to the house. Peter accepted an ice-cold beer from Sam and
exchanged greetings with his new acquaintances, searching
the crowd for Becky all the while. She appeared at the back
door a moment later, carrying the huge bowl of potato salad
they had made the night before.

She set it on one of the tables, then paused, scanning the
yard as if looking for someone. His breath caught in his
chest when her gaze turned in his direction and a warm,
sweet smile spread across her lips. God, she looked wonderful.

Her jeans were new and crisp, her lavender, Western-cut
blouse soft and feminine. She'd fastened the sides of her
hair away from her face with combs, exposing dangling gold
earrings. The rest of her hair hung free, almost to the small
of her back. Fiery highlights reflected the rays of the setting sun as she stepped out into the gathering to greet her
guests.

He wanted to go to her and stroke those glossy strands,
but didn't quite have the nerve. Though she'd kissed him last
night, and they'd shared a joke on Hank and an intimate
moment in the barn while the family admired Dandy, her
attitude toward him had undergone a subtle change. He
didn't completely understand what that change entailed, but
he knew he didn't like it much.

On the surface, everything seemed fine. Becky couldn't
have been more friendly and helpful during the branding.
She'd smiled at him readily and often, coached him and
traded wisecracks with him, just as she had with everyone
else. That was the part he didn't like—being treated as if he
were merely a casual friend, or worse yet, another brother.

Granted, he'd decided there was no need to rush into a
sexual relationship with her. He'd even done his best to ease
up on the flirtatious remarks and glances in order to give her

more space and time to get to know him. However, there was a limit to how far he was willing to back off.

Yet, here she came, taking her time, winding her way through the crowd and giving every male whose path she crossed that same, perky smile she'd given him. More than one of those men cast a wistful glance at her as she passed by, but Becky continued on, blithely unaware of the masculine admiration she received.

Peter's fingers tightened around the beer bottle until his knuckles ached. So that was it—at least part of the answer to the question that had been nagging in the back of his mind ever since he'd met her. Namely, why had a woman as warm and giving as Becky Dawson never been married? He'd been wondering if the guys in the area were blind or stupid.

But it wasn't that men weren't interested in her. He'd already counted at least five, married or not, who'd looked as if they wouldn't mind getting close to her. Damn close. It was incredible, but without offending them in the least, the woman gave them absolutely no encouragement whatsoever.

She talked to them, laughed with them, looked at them as if she were their mother or their sister, and the hope died out of their eyes in about ten seconds. Peter suspected Becky wasn't even conscious of the technique she used to keep men at a distance. It certainly was effective. But now that he understood the dynamics, she was about to confront a male who would ignore those subtle hands-off signals.

Skirting clusters of guests, Peter found Becky talking to Sam, Hank, Janice and a couple he hadn't met before. He insinuated himself into the group beside Becky, placing his left hand at the back of her waist while he leaned forward to shake hands with Skip and Darlene Thomas. Becky shot a quick glance at him and sidled a half step to her left.

Pretending he hadn't noticed, Peter sidled right along with her and let his hand slide around to rest on her hip in a casual, yet possessive gesture. She sent him a what-the-hell-do-you-think-you're-doing? look, then shifted her weight as if she would move again. He tightened his grip and gave her the most sensual smile he could muster.

It must have been a good one. Her pupils dilated. Her cheeks flushed a delicate shade of pink. Her respiration quickened, and her tongue darted across her lower lip.

There was a distinct pause in the conversation, as if the others had become aware of the sudden tension between Becky and Peter. He tore his gaze from hers and asked the Thomases a polite question while he nudged Becky even closer to his side. She resisted the pressure of his hand, but didn't pull away completely, and Peter contented himself with that small victory for the moment.

Then Grandma D announced it was time to eat. Everyone moved toward the picnic tables. Peter turned to follow. Keeping his hand on the curve of her hip, he brought Becky along with him. She lifted one hand to the side of his chest and pushed against it, but he didn't release her.

"I'd, uh, better see if Grandma needs me," she said with a nervous little laugh.

"She's got plenty of help," he replied, indicating the women scurrying around on the other side of the buffet with a nod of his head. "You've worked hard enough for one day, Becky. Take a night off while you've got the chance."

"I shouldn't, Pete—"

"I don't know these people very well," he interrupted, lowering his voice to an intimate level. He raised his hand to the back of her neck, sliding it under that thick, soft mane of hair to massage her nape. "And I feel a little...out of place. Stay and eat with me. Please?"

She inhaled a shallow breath, her eyes intently searching his for a moment. Then she pulled out of his grasp, let out a shaky sigh and nodded. "All right."

He let her go this time, but remained close beside her as they moved with the line. "That's a pretty blouse. The color brings out the green in your eyes."

"Thank you."

She looked away, but not before he caught a glimpse of her deepening blush. He smiled to himself and flicked the edge of one of her earrings. "I like these, too."

She whipped her head around, sending both earrings dancing in the air. "Stop it, Pete."

"Stop what?" he asked, raising both eyebrows in surprised innocence.

"Stop acting like we're on a date or something. Everybody'll think we're a . . . couple."

"Maybe I want them to think that." He allowed a wounded tone to creep into his voice. "But if you're ashamed to be seen with me—"

"Of course I'm not." She sniffed in exasperation. "But people talk around here, you know?"

"Are you afraid it'll get back to the sheriff?"

"Don't be a dope. I told you that's not serious."

"Then what's the problem? Last night I felt close to you, Becky." He put his arm around her shoulders and gave her a quick hug. "I thought we were friends."

"We are, but . . . look, do we have to discuss this here?"

Since they'd finally reached the tables, he handed her a plate and gestured toward the food with his other hand. "Why don't we eat?"

She shot him a disgruntled look and made her way along the line. Peter stayed as close as he dared, chuckling inwardly when she led him to a large group including Sam, Hank and Janice, sitting in the shade of a big cottonwood tree in the middle of the yard. So she thought there would be safety in numbers, did she?

He laid his plate on the grass beside hers and went to get them both a beer from a big metal tub filled with ice. Then he sat beside her and dug into his dinner. When his hunger had been assuaged, he returned to the offensive.

As if they were indeed a couple, he snatched a pickle from her plate and popped an olive from his own plate into her mouth when she opened it to protest. He did his level best to charm her, teasing her and letting his eyes glow with admiration every time he looked her way. At first, she was stiff and self-conscious, as if she feared someone might remark on his behavior. Gradually, however, she relaxed and appeared to enjoy herself.

Toward the end of the meal, Peter speared a piece of meat that had been dipped in batter and fried. He'd thought they were chicken livers at first, but the texture and flavor weren't quite right for that. Still, they were tasty, and he raised his fork to his mouth with relish.

"Like those oysters, do ya, Pete?" Hank asked.

"Oysters?" Peter lowered his fork and studied the morsel impaled on it. It didn't look like any oyster he'd ever seen. He shot Becky a doubtful look. "Is that what it is?"

"They're Rocky Mountain oysters, Pete," she said with a chuckle.

Others in the circle laughed, as well, watching him with wide, expectant grins. Peter knew he'd heard that term before. It was some kind of a delicacy.... Then he remembered Tina and one of the other kids moving from team to team during the branding, carrying a plastic ice-cream bucket, collecting the testicles that had been removed from the bull calves. Well, he'd eaten squid and octopus.

"Oh. Interesting flavor," he answered, and popped the "oyster" into his mouth without a second's hesitation.

"Ya know, Sinclair," Hank drawled, his broad shoulders shaking with laughter, "for a city boy, you're not half-bad. I didn't figure you'd last two days, but you've done all right."

Peter shrugged, then smiled at Becky. "I've had a good teacher."

"Yeah, well, good help's hard to come by these days," Hank continued. "Maybe you oughtta think about stayin' on permanently."

Never taking his eyes from the woman beside him, Peter answered. "The thought has crossed my mind, Hank."

One of the women tittered. Elbows nudged. Whispers buzzed around the group. Becky's gaze dropped to her plate like a bird shot out of the sky.

Tina ran across the yard to Becky's side a moment later, a gang of children trailing behind her. "Will you take us to see Dandy, Aunt Becky?"

Becky scrambled to her feet, an expression of relief crossing her strained features. "Of course, I will, honey."

Concerned that he'd gone too far, Peter frowned as he watched her hurry off toward the barn. He picked up their plates and rose to his feet, starting when a hand landed on his shoulder. He turned to find Sam Dawson at his side.

"Let's take a little walk."

The suggestion sounded more like an order. Peter nodded and handed the dishes to one of Grandma D's assistants. They stopped at the beer tub and both of them grabbed an icy bottle. Then they strolled around to the front of the house and sat on the steps.

Sam stretched out his long legs, crossed one booted foot over the other and for a long moment gazed at the mountains in the distance. "What's goin' on between you and Becky, Pete?" he finally asked, his voice low and gritty.

"Nothing serious. Yet."

"But you'd like it to get serious."

Peter smiled. "She's an amazing woman. Surely you realize that."

"Yeah, I do, but . . ."

"But you're wondering what my intentions are?" Peter finished for him.

"Somethin' like that."

"She's a grown woman, Sam."

"I know. Normally I'd mind my own business, but you're different from the guys she's used to."

"In what way?"

Sam snorted, then shook his head. "In lots of ways. You know it as well as I do. The main thing I'm concerned about is that you'll be leavin' in a few months."

"And you're afraid I'll leave her with a broken heart."

"That about covers it. Do you really care about her, Pete? Or is she just kinda...entertaining to ya, 'cause she's handy?"

Peter considered taking offense at those questions while he sipped his beer, but decided Sam had a right to ask them. "You're underestimating your sister," he said quietly. "I care about her a great deal."

"Enough to marry her?"

"You know I can't answer that. I don't know her well enough yet. It's definitely possible."

"Well, until you decide, Sinclair, keep your pants zipped."

"I think Becky's old enough to make her own decisions, Dawson," Peter said evenly, meeting the other man's hard gaze head-on.

Sam's mouth quirked at the corners for an instant before he looked away. "Yeah, I reckon she is. But let me tell you a little story before you do anything you might both regret."

"All right. I'm listening."

"Becky never dated much in high school. She got asked to her proms and the important dances like that, but she never had a steady boyfriend. It didn't seem to bother her a whole lot, but she liked guys well enough, and she could be quite a flirt when she wanted to." He smiled, as if at a particularly fond memory. "She always had a helluva lot of grit for a girl."

"And then," Peter prompted him.

"And then she went to college down in Laramie. When she'd come home, she'd chatter about one guy or another, and it was plain to see that she was havin' a good time playin' the field like college girls are supposed to do. During her sophomore year, though, we kept hearin' about this one dude—I think his name was Bob or Bill or something

like that—and I figured she was pretty serious about him."
Sam's lips tightened into a grim line and he fell silent.

"What happened?" Peter asked after a moment.

"I don't know for sure," Sam said slowly, "but she came home for Christmas that year actin' like a whipped pup. She wouldn't say a word about what was botherin' her, but I'm damned sure that Bob, or whatever the hell his name was, hurt her pretty bad. Mom had her stroke then and Becky never went back to school, but I doubt she'd have gone back in any case. At least not as long as that guy was still around."

"And she hasn't let a man get close to her since," Peter said thoughtfully.

"That's right. Until you came along."

"She hasn't let me get all that close, Sam," Peter admitted.

"Maybe. But she wants to. I can see it in her eyes every time she looks at you. And I'll be damned if I'll sit back and watch her get hurt like that again."

"You sound like Hank did this morning. You knew he already warned me?"

Sam shrugged. "We love her, Pete. She's got nobody else to protect her."

Peter accepted that statement with a nod of understanding, and they finished their beer in silence. Finally he asked, "Do you want me to leave?"

"Nope," Sam answered immediately. "Then she'd be left with a lot of what-ifs to wonder about. All I'm askin' is that you don't hurt her."

"That's the last thing I want to do. But relationships don't come with guarantees, Sam."

"I understand that. And, like you said, Becky's a grown woman and she's got to make her own decisions. Just be honest with her and don't promise her anything you don't mean to carry through on."

"I never intended to do anything else."

"I'm damn glad to hear it. I didn't really think you would, but I'd hate to have to beat your brains out." Sam gave him a wolfish grin, then offered his big hand to Peter.

Chuckling, Peter took it and gave it a firm shake. "I don't imagine I'd enjoy that much, either. And don't worry. I won't abuse your hospitality."

"All right." Sam unfolded his big frame to a standing position. "Let's go back to the party."

"Wait a minute," Peter said, rising beside him. "What if Becky breaks my heart? You know, that's a distinct possibility."

"You're right about that," he answered with a sympathetic grin. "But I'll tell ya somethin', Pete. I think she's worth the risk."

Becky led the children out of the barn and furtively studied the crowd in the yard. Thank God, Pete was nowhere in sight. After telling Tina she had some work to do in the kitchen, she hurried to the house and snuck in the back door. Then she breezed through the kitchen with a smile and a wave for the women putting away food and washing dishes, and dashed up the stairs to the privacy of her room.

She shut the door and leaned against it, heaving a sigh of relief at having accomplished an escape from the questioning eyes of her friends and neighbors. She walked to the bed on wobbly legs, plunked herself down and felt a wave of exhaustion wash over her. Lord, what a day, she thought, tugging off her boots.

Flopping onto the comforter with her hands beside her head, she muttered, "Damn the man, anyway."

All day long, she'd struggled to keep her attitude toward Pete friendly, but...impersonal. He'd acted pretty much the same way toward her. She had thought he was picking up on her hints just fine, and they could both ease back into a nice, simple friendship without either one of them losing face.

And then what did that idiot have to go and do, but practically announced to half of Sublette County that he had the hots for her! For cryin' out loud, hadn't he figured out people talked about such things in a small town like this? And her family—shoot, Grandma D was probably already planning the wedding.

Becky moaned and pulled a pillow over her face, wishing she could curl up under it and never come out. She'd like to wring his fool neck, beat some sense into his hard head, tell him what she thought of his highfalutin intelligence. Honestly, when it came to people, the man didn't have the brains of a damn pinecone.

Tears of frustration stung the backs of her eyes, but she blinked them away and bounced the pillow off the opposite wall. Dammit, she wanted to do what was best for him. But, God, when he gave her those sizzling looks and touched her as if he had every right to, her insides turned to mush and her common sense galloped off like a racehorse at the sound of a starting gun.

How much of what she'd been feeling had shown on her face? Did he know how much she wanted him? Did everyone else? How the hell did she get herself into these things? Better yet, how the hell could she get herself out?

When she heard a soft rapping at her door, Becky sat up, wiped her eyes and sucked in a deep breath before calling, "Come in."

Grandma D slipped inside the room, took one look at her granddaughter and came over to sit beside her on the bed. "I figured you'd be upset," she said softly, taking Becky's hand between her palms.

"Was I that obvious?" Becky asked, hating the way her voice quavered and rose on the last syllable.

"Only to the folks who love you."

Becky patted her grandmother's gnarled fingers. "Yeah, I know what you mean. I'm just so confused...."

"And I'm damn glad you are."

"Well, thanks a whole chunk," Becky said dryly. "I always knew I could count on you for sympathy."

"Now, stop that, Rebecca Anne. Right now. I just meant I'm glad you're feelin' something for a man. And it don't hurt my feelin's none that he's a good man like Pete, either. Why, you could have a wonderful life with him—"

"C'mon, Grandma, get real. The most I could have with him would be a summer affair."

"So, have it!"

"Just like that?"

"Why not? What are you savin' yourself for, anyway? I'd rather see you get out there and live a little than hide at home and dry up into an old prune."

"I can't believe you're sayin' this."

"Well, I am. And I guess it's about damn time I told you the truth about me."

"What's that supposed to mean?"

"It means you don't know everything you think you do." The old woman pulled herself up straight and scowled at Becky. Then her eyes took on a faraway cast.

"Your grandpa wasn't the only man I ever loved. Bart Dawson was kind and gentle, and I'll never regret the years I had with him, but there was somebody else before him—a man I never forgot."

"Jonathan Sinclair?" Becky guessed.

"That's right."

"What was he like, Grandma?"

"Oh, he was a handsome fella. Looked a lot like Pete, as a matter of fact. We got into all kinds of scrapes when we were kids, but he was a good friend until we grew up."

"What happened?"

Grandma D smiled and shrugged. "Our hormones got to actin' up, and we fell in love. He asked me to marry him."

"If you loved him, why didn't you do it?"

"I wanted to, Becky, but I was scared to death."

"Did he have a bad temper?"

The old lady sniffed and shot her a droll look. "I'd like to see the man who could ever scare me with his temper."

"I get the point," Becky said with a chuckle. "Why were you afraid of him, then?"

"Well, I guess you'd have to know about my mama to understand. Ya see, she was a fragile kind of woman, a real clingin' vine. When my daddy died, she was so dependent, she couldn't make it without him. She just kinda faded away."

"What does she have to do with Jonathan?"

"He was such a strong, forceful man, and I loved him so much, I was afraid I'd end up just like her. I told myself I wasn't ready to settle down, but the truth is, I ran off to visit some cousins in Kansas City like a scared rabbit. Six months later, I came to my senses and was ready to go back to him, but I found out he'd already married someone else."

"Oh, Grandma, that's awful."

"Yeah, it was. But I'd hurt him bad, and there was nothing either of us could do except stay friends. I was always grateful for that."

"Then you married Grandpa on the rebound?"

"That's right. He'd come to Kansas City with his dad for a stock show."

"Did he know about Jonathan?"

"Yeah, I told him. And he loved me and trusted me enough to let me stay in touch with Jonathan. That's what kind of man he was. They don't come any better than Bart."

"Wow," Becky murmured, shaking her head.

"Don't get me wrong, now, Rebecca Anne. I didn't spend my life pinin' for Jonathan. Your grandpa and I had a good life together. But I never felt the passion and the fire with him that I did with Jonathan. I don't want you to miss out on that if you've got the chance with Pete."

Grandma D rose stiffly and lovingly smoothed a strand of hair away from Becky's face. Then she walked slowly to the door, for once showing every one of her eighty-five years. She opened it and looked back over her shoulder at Becky.

"I know you got hurt pretty bad once, and I don't blame you for bein' cautious. But will you remember one thing for me?"

Unable to speak, Becky nodded.

"When you get old, it's not the things you did that you regret. It's the things you didn't have the guts to do."

Chapter Nine

During the next three weeks, the work load at the Circle D increased, but the tension between Becky and Pete settled down to a low simmer. Becky pondered her grandmother's advice regularly, and, more often than she liked to admit, thought about taking it. But for some reason, Pete must have changed his mind. Since the branding barbecue, it was as if someone had turned off the man's libido.

He was friendly as could be, even affectionate on occasion. They got along extremely well together, but he had definitely retreated from pursuing a sexual relationship with her. Becky stifled a sigh and, though she didn't believe it for a second, told herself it was for the best.

Since it was already the middle of June, Sam and Hank were fencing the land they'd acquired for summer pasture through Forest Service permits. They would move the herd at the end of the month.

Becky and Pete had harrowed the meadows at the ranch, breaking up the cow manure to fertilize the hay crop. Yesterday, they'd finished repairing the irrigation system. It had been no small task getting the sixty-five head gates in working order while keeping track of the cows at the same time. Luckily, Pete was turning into a darn good hand.

He worked hard, listened to instructions and wasn't afraid to get dirty. The only problem for Becky was that his chest and shoulders were filling out to impressive proportions from all the heavy labor he'd been doing. To make matters worse, the weather had gotten warmer and he'd started working without a shirt in the afternoons. His chest and back were turning a deep, golden brown—as if he hadn't been sexy enough to start with!

She enjoyed his company, loved having him for a friend. But dammit, nobody'd turned *her* libido off, and it was starting to get to her in a bad way. She'd never felt so itchy, so restless, so... lustful in her whole life. At night, her dreams about the man would shock a vice cop. Her thoughts weren't a whole lot better in the daytime.

And now he didn't want her anymore. Men! For the life of her, she would never understand what went on inside their heads.

But it wasn't only the sex thing that drove her crazy. Being with Pete day after day, she'd gotten to know a lot about him. He'd never had much contact with his parents. He'd taken figure-skating lessons when he was a kid and played basketball in high school and college. He liked the same kinds of movies she did, despised spinach and peanut butter and inhaled spy novels.

He was easy to talk to, quick to laugh and stubborn as hell when he thought there was a better way to do something. He could also be moody, even downright disagreeable, but it didn't seem to bother him to apologize. All in all, she was fascinated with him. Shoot, she was already three-fourths in love with him, not that it mattered now.

"Well, there's no use whinin' about it," she muttered to herself as she headed downstairs.

At least today they would get a break from their routine. Sam needed salt and mineral blocks, and she and Pete were going to Pinedale to get them. As usual, everyone else had given them a list, as well. He met her at the pickup, wearing what he called his cowboy clothes.

Damn, but he looked good.

Smiling through gritted teeth, she climbed into the truck and they headed off to town. Having developed an interest in country music, Pete switched on the radio. Becky settled back, relieved that she wouldn't need to talk to him.

They finished their errands at eleven-thirty, and, though it was early, Pete insisted on taking her to lunch at the Sweet Tooth Saloon. He led the way to a table in the back of the nearly empty restaurant. Becky sat on one of the old-fashioned, ice cream-parlor chairs with a weary sigh.

After ordering their lunch at the counter, Pete returned to the table. "You haven't said much today. Is something wrong?"

Becky shook her head. "No, I'm just a little tired."

"That doesn't surprise me. You work too hard, Becky."

"Is that your professional opinion, Doc?" she asked with a cheeky grin.

He frowned thoughtfully for a moment before answering. "As a matter of fact, it is. I'm worried about you."

"No need to be. I'm tough. We've got a lot to do this time of the year."

"But you don't have to do it all yourself."

"Everybody else is working as hard as I am," she argued, wondering what had put this particular wasp under his Stetson.

He shook his head and frowned again—directly at her this time. "No, they're not, Becky. I've been watching you all for a month now. Everyone else takes a little time off in the evening, but you keep going until you're ready to collapse."

"I like to keep busy."

"It's more than that. You're your own worst enemy."

"What's that supposed to mean?" she asked tartly.

"You do things for your family that they could easily do for themselves. You wait on them hand and foot and spoil them rotten."

"I do not."

"Yes, you do. You're so busy anticipating their needs, they don't even have to ask you for what they want half the time. You let them take advantage of you."

"I think you've slipped a gear, Doc."

"You want an example? Why is it your job to do the dishes every night? Why doesn't someone else take a turn?"

"Grandma and Janice cook the meals. It's only fair that somebody else does the dishes. Besides, Grandma's exhausted by suppertime. It's the only way I can get her to go rest."

"Number one, I think your grandmother's in better shape than you give her credit for. And number two, you're exhausted by that time, too, because you've been working your butt off all day outside. What about Janice and Hank and Sam? What about Tina? They could all take a turn."

"Tina's too little. Jan and Hank need some time together before the wedding. Sam has paperwork to do almost every night. And if I let him or Hank in the kitchen, they'll break every dish we own."

"They could learn, if you gave them a chance. And what about the laundry?"

"What about it?"

"Why do you do it for everyone? I could do my own. So could everyone else except Tina."

"I don't mind doing it. Besides, it wastes water and detergent to do a bunch of little loads all the time."

He shook his head. "The least you could do for yourself is make everyone haul their dirty clothes downstairs for you and take the clean ones back to their own rooms."

"What do you think we are, Sinclair? A hospital staff? We're a family. I enjoy taking care of people, and I don't do anything most mothers wouldn't do."

"But you're not their mother. If you're not afraid to do a man's work all day, I don't see why your brothers shouldn't help with the housework. Does anyone but you ever push a vacuum or clean a bathroom or scrub a floor? You've let your family turn you into a maid."

An obscene retort hovered on the tip of her tongue, but their order was ready and Pete went to fetch it. Becky inhaled short, choppy breaths, trying to calm herself. She couldn't remember ever feeling this angry before. When he returned and set a turkey sandwich in front of her, her stomach revolted and she had to shove the plate away or risk disgracing herself right there in the restaurant.

"Becky, I'm sorry," Pete said, immediately contrite. "I wanted us to have a nice lunch today. I didn't mean to upset you."

"Well, you did. I've been called a lot of things before, but never a drudge."

"I didn't call you a drudge."

"You might as well have."

He raked his fingers through his hair, then laid his hands palms-up on the table. "Look, the only reason I noticed all this is that I did the same thing to myself."

"Oh, right."

"I did. I thought I was indispensable, that I was the only one who could make sure everything was done right. I could have delegated more, but I didn't. I burned out as a result. It's an easy trap to fall into, and I'd hate to see you get caught in it."

"I'm fine, Pete."

"You might be, for now. But you've got circles under your eyes, and you've lost a good ten pounds since I came to the ranch. Everyone's got a breaking point."

The husky note of tenderness in his voice brought sudden tears to her eyes. Looking away so he wouldn't see them, Becky swallowed at the lump in her throat. Then she folded her hands into fists.

"My family loves me, Pete Sinclair," she whispered fiercely. "Maybe they take me for granted, but they need me, and they love me."

He reached across the table and covered one of those fists with his hand. "Of course, they do, Becky. I've never doubted that for a minute. Both of your brothers have threatened to beat me to a pulp if I ever hurt you."

She yanked her hand away in surprise. "They did?"

"You yourself heard Hank do it," he reminded her with a crooked grin, retreating to his own side of the table. "Sam let me have it the night of the branding barbecue."

"Oh." Cripes, she could imagine that scene with no trouble at all. Hank had been bad enough, but when Sam went all beady-eyed and stern, he was one mean-looking dude. Poor Pete. No wonder he'd backed off. Thank you, big brothers.

"I only brought this up because I care about you, Becky," Pete continued. "I care a lot. And believe me, when I look at you, I don't see a drudge."

"What do you see, then?"

"A woman who has a ton of love to give. A woman who gives it without asking for anything in return. A woman who's too busy caring for people she loves to take care of herself. She's rare and she's beautiful, inside and out."

She couldn't look away from his big dark eyes, so filled with concern and admiration. For her. The tight knot of pain in her abdomen, brought on by their argument, slowly unraveled, replaced by a warm glow of pleasure.

"You know what else I see?" he asked softly.

Becky shook her head.

"I see a woman who sacrificed her dreams. I'd like to see her do something about getting those dreams back."

"Aw, I never had any dreams that were all that important."

"Oh, yeah? What about being a vet? You wanted that, didn't you?"

She shifted uncomfortably on her chair, then started fiddling with the salt and pepper shakers. "I…yeah, I did. But when Mom had her stroke, Grandma was still grieving over losing Grandpa and she wasn't doing too well. Hank was still on the rodeo circuit and Sam had his hands full with the ranch. I couldn't leave."

"Of course, you couldn't. But how did you become responsible for everyone?"

"It just kind of happened, Pete. Mom needed a lot of care for a long time. Somebody needed to take over, and I was the only one available."

"What about after your mother died? Couldn't you have gone back to school then?"

"I thought about it. We all had a rough couple of years after Mom died. By the time everybody was functioning again, Hank brought Christine home. She was already six months pregnant, and she hated the ranch from the minute she laid eyes on it. I could see that things weren't going to work out too well."

"So you stayed."

"That's right. Then Tina was born and Christine took off." Becky shrugged. "Grandma wasn't up to taking care of a tiny baby. Hank was pretty bitter, and he didn't have any idea of how to take care of Tina."

"I admire your loyalty, Becky. But what about now? Wouldn't you really like to breed your Appaloosas? Perhaps have a husband and children of your own?"

"That might be nice," she admitted with a shrug. "I can hear my biological clock ticking, but I've never met a man I cared enough about to change my life for him. I'm gettin' too old and set in my ways to change it, anyway."

Pete chuckled and rolled his eyes at her. "I think you've got a *few* good years left."

"All right. So what's the point of all this, Pete? What is it you think I should do? Pack up and get out of everybody's hair?"

"I think your whole family would go into shock if you did that. You might want to ease them into independence with smaller steps at first."

Becky considered his suggestion, and found that it had merit. Now that her emotions were under control again, she figured he had a point. The family *did* take advantage of her sometimes. "How would I do that?"

"Hey, I'm the one who packed up and left," he answered with a wry smile. "I don't think I'm qualified to tell you what to do, Becky."

"C'mon, Sinclair, you've *always* got some ideas."

"You don't like that about me?" he asked quickly. Then his face flushed, as if he'd revealed something he hadn't intended to. "I mean, I know I can be overbearing sometimes, when I don't intend to be."

Becky laughed and patted his hand in reassurance. "I like hearing your ideas, Pete. I don't always agree with them, but I don't mind hearing them."

"Oh. Well, that's all right, then." He drummed his fingers on the table for a moment. "You know, sometimes your family offers to help you, and you usually smile and say, 'No, that's all right. I can handle it,'" he said slowly.

"I do that?" she asked, sincerely surprised.

He nodded. "They expect you to say that. Most of the time they start walking away before you've even finished the sentence. If I were in your position, I would simply take them at their word and turn the job over."

"That might be interesting." Imagining the shocked reactions she'd get if she ever did that, Becky grinned. "What else have you noticed?"

"You don't say 'no,' and mean it. Everyone knows they can wheedle you into giving them what they want, even if it's really inconvenient for you."

"Give me an example."

"The potato salad for the branding barbecue. You didn't want to make it, but Sam got to you with nostalgia for your mother. Do you really think anyone would have missed potato salad with all the other food that was served that night?"

Chagrined, Becky stared at him. "No. You're right. Boy, was I ever a dope."

Pete shrugged. "You just wanted to make him happy. The trick is in realizing that you don't need to make everyone happy all the time."

"So, I'd only do that kind of stuff when I really wanted to?"

"It would be a start, Becky. You could save some time for yourself that way. And then you could gradually encourage them all to do the things they're perfectly capable of doing for themselves."

"You've given this a lot of thought."

"I'm not as close to the situation as you are . . ." He hesitated, as if he would say something more.

"Out with it, Pete," Becky demanded with an encouraging smile. "What were you gonna say?"

"It's, uh . . . I don't think it's any of my business."

"So what else is new? Say it anyway. You've made a lot of sense so far."

"All right. It's about Tina."

"What about her?"

"She looks to you as her mother."

"I've raised her since she was three weeks old."

"You've done a wonderful job, too. But she has a father, and she's going to have a stepmother soon. Don't you think she needs to form a stronger bond with them?"

Becky frowned, then slowly nodded. "Yeah, I guess she does. But what are you saying? That I'm getting in the way of her doing that?"

"Well . . . yes. You put her to bed every night, get her ready in the morning and wash her clothes. Your grandmother does it, too, but Tina comes to you first when she needs something. Shouldn't Hank and Janice be handling her now?''

"They haven't shown much interest."

"Why should they when you're right there to do it for them?'' he asked gently.

"I can see what you're saying, but I . . .'' Her throat constricted and she couldn't go on.

"But you love her as much as if she were your own. It won't be easy to let go, will it?''

Becky shook her head, but she knew he was right. Oh, damn. She'd only wanted to help. Had she actually hurt Tina instead? And Hank, too? Had she denied him the chance to be a real father with her interference?

"Hey, you haven't done anything wrong,'' Pete said soothingly, reaching across the table to take her hand again. "You've given Tina the love and attention every child needs and deserves. All I'm saying is that maybe it's time to turn some of the responsibility over to her parents."

She gulped. "Yeah. You're probably right about that. And I'll think about everything else you've said, too. Let's get out of here.''

Peter followed Becky from the restaurant, mentally kicking himself. Dammit, when would he learn not to push so hard? He should have stopped while he was ahead, but, like the tactless idiot he was, he hadn't.

He offered to drive. She shot him a sharp look, then climbed into the driver's seat without speaking, her expression telling him further conversation would not be welcomed. She drove carefully, but he could practically hear the self-recriminations echoing inside her head. God, he felt as guilty as if he'd tortured a defenseless animal.

Whatever Becky had done for or to her family, she'd done with a loving, generous spirit. Who was he, a man who had no experience with that kind of love, to criticize? His motives for starting the conversation had hardly been selfless.

Over the past three weeks, he'd taken to heart Sam's warning about not hurting Becky. He wasn't afraid either of her brothers would do him bodily harm, but he knew it was the right thing to do for himself and for Becky. Though it had cost him sleepless nights and countless frigid showers, he'd ruthlessly controlled his sexual urges and concentrated on getting to know her as a person.

Day after day, he'd watched her give of herself until she had nothing left to give, and he resented the love she lavished so freely on people who didn't always appreciate her efforts. He wasn't sure he was really in love with her, but he would admit that he was jealous. He was even jealous of the attention she gave her horses, for God's sake.

The truth was, he didn't want to free Becky from her responsibilities to give her time for herself. He wanted her to have more time and energy for *him*.

He sneaked a glance at her when she turned onto the gravel road winding up into the mountains to the ranch. Her eyes were dry. Her lips were compressed. Her jaw was set with grim determination. A gunslinger out of the Old West wouldn't have looked any tougher. Only a faint quivering in her chin betrayed the stormy state of her emotions.

Sighing, he looked out the window, automatically reading the sign for the Bar Z ranch. From here on, the road became rougher, the inclines higher, the curves tighter. Becky drove with confidence, as if she'd driven this road so many times that she could do it blindfolded.

Peter rested his head on the side window and shut his eyes against the afternoon sun's fierce glare. He heard the engine strain as they crested a long, steep hill. They started to coast down the other side, their speed increasing with every rotation of the tires. The road curved. Becky stiffened beside him and muttered a short, explicit curse.

Straightening up, he saw an immense Hereford bull standing crosswise in the middle of the road at the bottom of the hill. Becky's hands tightened on the steering wheel. She stomped on the brake pedal. It clunked against the floorboards and lay dead. The pickup gained momentum. She pounded the horn, but the animal just stood there, looking calmly at them, swishing his tail as if his only immediate problem were an irritating fly.

"You damn stupid bull, get out of the way," she muttered, yanking the emergency brake.

Smoke poured out around the wheels and the truck skidded to one side, slowing for a few moments. Then they were rolling again, faster and faster down the steep grade. The engine roared in protest when Becky shifted down. The truck slowed again, but not enough. Not nearly enough.

"Tighten your seat belt, Pete," she called. "That's Jack Zorn's prize bull. We're headin' for the ditch."

Peter obeyed her instinctively, bracing both feet against the floorboards. They bounced violently as the truck slid into the brush. The muscles in her forearms standing out in bold relief, Becky fought for control.

Silently cheering her on while his head snapped back and forth, Peter thought they were going to make it. She yanked the steering wheel hard to the left, trying to avoid the fence running parallel to the road, and suddenly they were airborne. The sky tilted at a sickening angle, then disappeared. A deafening crunch of metal being crushed filled his ears with the next jolt, and the sky reappeared through the rain of glass shards falling from the shattered windshield.

He thought he heard Becky cry out as they rolled the second time, but the sound was obliterated when they smashed into the fence and came to an abrupt, shuddering halt. The engine died, leaving his head ringing in the sudden silence. Peter spat out a mouthful of dirt, then looked over at the unconscious woman slumped over the steering wheel.

Fear clawing at his gut, he fumbled with his seat belt, murmuring, "Oh, damn, Becky," over and over. He finally got it off and forced himself to take several deep breaths before touching her neck in search of a pulse. Thank God, she had one.

It wasn't as strong as he would have liked, but it was there, he assured himself, gently laying her back against the seat. Forcing himself to remember the training he'd received as an intern, he examined her. A thick coating of dust covered her face and hair. Blood seeped from a rapidly swelling laceration in the center of her forehead. She had a concussion, but he couldn't find any other injuries.

Since the passenger door was blocked by the fence and he didn't want to crawl over Becky, Peter climbed through the opening once occupied by the windshield. He sniffed the air for leaking gasoline, but couldn't smell any, then surveyed the debris scattered along the ditch. The cooler filled with perishable items they'd picked up at the grocery store lay open on its side, fifteen yards away.

He hurried toward it, his legs threatening to wobble out of control. He dumped mashed peaches from a plastic bag, dropped several chunks of ice from the bottom of the cooler into it and started back to the truck. Then, shaking his head in disgust, he reversed directions and wet his handkerchief in the water left by the ice that had already melted.

At a quiet moan from the pickup, he raced back to Becky. Her eyelids fluttered as he tenderly bathed her face. When he pressed the makeshift ice pack against her forehead, she flinched and tried to push it away.

"It's all right, sweetheart," he said hoarsely, profound relief tightening his chest and throat. "You're safe now. You're going to be just fine."

She groaned, opened her eyes, then closed them again, as if the light hurt. "What the hell happened?"

"You tried to fly the pickup."

"Damn stupid bull."

"That's right," he told her with a shaky laugh. Had a cranky voice ever sounded so wonderful?

"You okay?" she asked, struggling to sit up.

Though her eyes were more focused now, Peter restrained her. "I'm fine. Take it easy, Becky. Where does it hurt?"

"Just my head. Damn stupid bull. Jeez, my teeth taste like dirt."

"Mine, too."

He stroked the dusty wisps of hair at her temples. Finally, unable to restrain himself another second, he gathered her carefully into his arms. She snuggled against his chest, laying her head on his shoulder. They sat quietly for a few minutes, drawing strength from each other.

Then she sighed and opened her eyes. "Try the CB."

He gently released Becky, leaning her against the door, then followed her somewhat garbled instructions for using the radio. He couldn't even raise static.

She muttered, "Damn stupid bull," three more times before murmuring something that sounded like, "Battery."

"What about the battery, Becky?" he asked anxiously, fearing she was drifting back into unconsciousness.

She grimaced, but didn't open her eyes. "Battery. Wire came loose. Damn stupid bull."

Peter climbed out of the truck, forced the dented hood up and peered inside. He didn't know much about engines, but he knew what a battery looked like. He jiggled it and tightened all the wires before crawling back inside the cab. He tried the radio again and a moment later Janice's voice crackled in the air.

"What's up, Pete?"

He briefly explained their situation.

"Sam and Hank just came in," she replied. "They're on their way."

"Tell them to get the medical bag out of my car and call an ambulance," he said.

"Will do."

Heaving a sigh of relief, Peter turned his attention back to Becky. The next fifteen minutes felt more like fifteen years as he kept her talking and held the ice pack to her forehead. Finally a cloud of dust appeared on the horizon, and the Dawson men arrived a moment later.

Becky opened her eyes at the sound of their voices. Sam reached in through the window and stroked her hair.

"How ya doin'?" he asked softly.

"Damn stupid bull," she told him. "Head hurts."

"I'll bet it does. Hang on. Help's comin', sis."

Hank handed Peter the medical bag. After speaking briefly with Becky, he went to get the "damn stupid bull" off the road. By the time the ambulance arrived and they wheeled Becky into the Pinedale clinic, Peter painfully understood why Becky had been so furious with him when he'd faked an injury.

At the free clinic, he'd treated accident victims with cool competence and professional detachment. His feelings for Becky changed all of that. He felt her pain as if it were his own, and he desperately wanted to heal her.

Despite her confusion, he believed she would be fine in a few days, but he couldn't trust his judgment in her case. However, the prospect of losing her had clarified one thing. He loved Becky Dawson. Deeply and irrevocably. From the instant he'd seen her unconscious at the steering wheel, he'd run out of patience.

He wanted a permanent, loving relationship with this woman, and he wanted it now. Whatever it took, he would find a way to convince her she belonged with him.

Chapter Ten

Bright sunshine bathed every corner of the room when Becky woke up the next day. Her head ached as if she'd been on a four-day drunk—not that she'd ever gone on one, but she figured that's how much it would hurt if she ever had. She tried to lift her right hand to rub her eyes, but her arm muscles felt as if someone had beaten them with a crowbar.

Moaning, she opened her eyes to half-mast and gingerly turned her head, surveying her surroundings. She was in her own room, but couldn't remember getting there. And why was Tina sitting in a chair shoved next to the bed, watching her with that sad, anxious expression on her little face?

"Hi," Becky croaked through her dry throat and mouth, and flinched when the little girl ran out into the hallway, shrieking, "Grandma! Daddy! She's awake!"

Becky clutched her head with both hands, ignoring her sore arms and shoulders. Footsteps pounding up the stairs echoed the bass drum in her skull. She blinked in confu-

sion, then groaned when it all came back to her. The wreck.
The ambulance ride. Pete's worried face hovering over her.

She struggled up on one elbow. "Damn that stupid bull."

"You still sayin' that?" Hank asked, hurrying through
the doorway with Sam, Grandma D and Tina hot on his
heels.

"Oh, *please,* be quiet," Becky begged, pushing herself to
a sitting position.

"Take it easy, there, sis." Sam squatted on his heels beside the bed as he rearranged the pillows for her. "How do
you feel?"

"Like a train ran over me."

"Do you remember what happened?" Grandma D whispered.

"Most of it, I think. Is Pete all right?" Becky asked.

"He's fine. Sleepin' in my bed," Sam told her.

"What time is it?"

"Quarter after one. Hungry?"

Becky shook her head and instantly regretted it. When the
pain died down to a bearable level, she flipped the sheet and
blanket out of the way, intending to get up.

"Where do you think you're going?" Hank asked, flip-
ping them right back.

"I've got work to do. Wouldja get outta my way?"

"You're takin' the rest of the week off," Sam said firmly.

"Don't be silly. I can't lay around all day." She leaned
forward, but Hank pushed her back against the pillows.

"Try that again, ya little twerp, and I'll tie you to the
bed," he warned without the slightest trace of teasing in his
smile. "You scared the bejesus out of all of us. Pete says you
need rest, and that's what you're gonna get."

"But I hafta go to the bathroom and I need a shower,"
she protested weakly.

"I'll stay with her, boys," Grandma D said. "Bring her
in when I've got the water started."

Tina crept closer to the bed. "I'm sorry you got hurt,
Aunt Becky."

"I'm fine, sweetie," Becky said, giving the little girl a smile though her head still ached something fierce.

For the next hour and a half, her family fussed over her and pampered her until Becky thought she would have a fit. Sam carried her to the bathroom. After Grandma D had helped her bathe and wash the dirt out of her hair, Hank carried her back to bed. Tina brought her magazines, and Janice delivered a tray set with a lacy napkin, the good china and a daisy in a bud vase. It seemed like a lot of work for tea and toast, but Becky was touched by the gesture.

She finally dozed off in self-defense and they left her alone. At suppertime, however, it all started up again. She couldn't lift a finger to scratch her own nose without someone offering to scratch it for her. Good Lord, they all acted as if she were a fragile porcelain doll, or as if they felt guilty about something.

An hour later Pete walked into the room, moving slowly and carefully, as if his muscles hurt as much as hers did. His hair was damp from a shower, and he wore his Redskins sweatshirt with a pair of jeans. He gave her a lopsided grin that said he knew how funny he must look.

"Movin' mighty slow there, Pete," Becky teased as he eased himself down beside her.

"I think I know what it feels like to go fifteen rounds with Mike Tyson," he retorted with a chuckle.

"Need some liniment?"

His eyes twinkled wickedly at that. His gaze roamed from her face to the lacy bodice of her summer nightgown and back up to her face. Becky felt her neck and cheeks flush. He hadn't looked at her that way since...

He picked up her wrist and took her pulse, which immediately sped up, much to her chagrin. Then he leaned close enough for her to sniff the crisp scent of soap and aftershave on his skin, and briefly lifted her eyelids with his thumb while he inspected her pupils.

"Does your head still hurt?" he asked, his lips barely an inch away from hers.

"A little," she answered, hardly daring to breathe, much less move. Actually, now that he was here, so close, her headache seemed like a minor inconvenience.

He braced one hand beside her hip and raised the other to gently stroke her hair. She hadn't been able to braid it, and he combed through the long strands with his fingers, playing absently with the ends.

"You have beautiful hair," he murmured, his gaze caressing her lips. "I love seeing it loose like this."

"Thank you."

They studied each other for a long, breathless moment. Then he leaned back and Becky had to bite her lower lip to hold in a sigh of disappointment.

"Well," he said briskly, obviously striving for a more professional tone, "with a few days of rest, I think you'll be fine."

"I'm not gonna lay around for days, Doc."

"Yes, you are. You've had a serious injury."

"I've got work to do."

"You've been out of commission for over twenty-four hours. The house is still standing and nobody's died, so I think your family can survive without you for a few more days. They agree with me, by the way."

"What did you say to them?" she asked, her eyes narrowing with suspicion.

He looked down at his hands. "I just pointed out a few things about the work load you've been carrying."

"What things?"

"We talked about it at lunch yesterday."

"So that's what got into them," she muttered. "I was supposed to have a chance to think it over."

Pete shrugged, then finally met her gaze. "It was too good an opportunity to pass up, Becky. They handled it very well. In fact, Sam's talking about hiring someone to help with the cleaning and laundry. What's the big problem?"

"I'll go crazy layin' around here like a slug. That's the problem. And who's gonna keep an eye on Grandma D?"

"I will. Although I don't think it's really necessary. She's having a ball ordering everyone around. They're all coping just fine."

"I see." Becky drew her knees up to her chest and wrapped her arms around them.

"What do you see?"

"That you've gone and fixed it so nobody needs me anymore."

He reached for her hand, but subsided when she glared at him. "Look, the minute you're back on your feet, they'll all return to business as usual. Nobody willingly gives up the kind of service you've been giving them."

"I thought you liked my family."

"I do, Becky. That's just human nature. They're worried about you now, as well they should be. But it won't last unless you start setting some limits."

"Dammit, Pete, you had no right to interfere."

"Maybe I want to have the right."

She sniffed. "What's that supposed to mean?"

His dark eyes had been glittering with anger to match her own. Now they gentled, and he caressed her cheek with the backs of his fingers.

"Maybe I want to be the man you'd care about enough to change your life for," he said quietly. "But there's got to be some room in your life for me."

"Pete—"

"No, let me finish. I admire your love and loyalty to your family, Becky. It's just one of the things I find incredibly attractive about you. On the other hand, I'm so concerned about how much you have to do all the time, I can't bring myself to add to your burdens by demanding attention."

She couldn't think of a thing to say. Tears puddled in her eyes. She blinked them back, but Pete must have seen them. He brushed a tender kiss across her lips, then stood and awkwardly patted her shoulder before he walked to the doorway.

"Think about what I've said, Becky. I'll see you tomorrow."

Becky stared at the empty space left by his retreating figure, and wondered what she could possibly do *but* think about what he'd said. Her emotions seesawed giddily between elation and fear. Lord, had he meant what she thought he had? What other things did he find incredibly attractive about her? Man, she wanted details!

No. She wanted Pete. She wanted him so damn bad, her teeth ached.

He made her feel things she'd thought she would never feel again. The possibilities filled her heart with hope and yearning, and her mind with terror. What if he found her as inadequate as Bob had?

Her family had been there for her before, helped her to heal and go on. She had clung to them all these years, finding security and support in their love. But Pete wanted her to let go of the lifeline they represented and take his hand instead.

Could she possibly find the courage and trust to do that?

Becky awoke at nine-thirty the next morning, feeling alert and refreshed. Considering how perturbed she had been after Pete had left, she'd managed an amazingly good night's sleep. The house was quiet and since there was no one perched by the bed, ready to give her away, she cautiously sat up and swung her legs to the floor.

Her muscles still felt sore, but they worked better than they had yesterday. She tiptoed into the bathroom, locked the door and studied her face in the mirror. A neat square of gauze covered most of the lump on her forehead. Other than that, she looked reasonably normal.

Avoiding the bandaged area, she washed her face, then brushed her teeth and hair before creeping back to her room. She stood before the closet, her stomach growling, her legs suddenly feeling weak. Instead of getting dressed as she had originally planned, Becky pulled on a robe and walked slowly down the stairs.

She passed through the living room, hearing a low rumble of masculine voices in the kitchen. Her heart beat faster in anticipation of seeing Pete, but settled back to its regular rhythm when she entered the kitchen and found Sam and Grandma D seated at the table with Andy Johnson, the sheriff of Sublette County. All three wore grim expressions.

"Are you sayin' it wasn't an accident?" Sam demanded, his eyebrows disappearing into the thick shock of hair falling over his forehead.

"That's exactly what I'm sayin'," the sheriff answered. "The brake lines on Becky's pickup were punctured so the fluid would leak out real slow."

"Who'd do a thing like that?" Grandma D asked.

"The same guy who let our cows out and stole our calves," Becky answered from the doorway.

"Rebecca Anne," Grandma D scolded, jumping to her feet, "you're not supposed to be out of bed."

"It's too late, Grandma. I'm already out." Becky walked to the table and sat beside Sam. "Hi, Andy."

Andy Johnson was a lean, rangy man who stood an inch short of six feet. He had red hair and the freckles that went with it, blue eyes and a deceptively easygoing smile. He shot one of those smiles across the table at Becky while his eyes made a thorough inspection of her face.

"You don't look too bad for somebody who dang near got her head bashed in," he drawled.

"Don't try to sweet-talk me, Johnson," Becky replied dryly, accepting a cup of coffee from her grandmother.

"Are you sure about this, Andy?" Sam asked.

"Yeah, I'm sure. What's this about your cattle?" After Sam explained what had happened, Andy thoughtfully scratched one earlobe. "You made any enemies lately, Dawson?"

Sam shook his head. "Not that I know of."

"What about Hank?"

"Nah, he's been too busy to get himself in trouble."

"What about you, Becky? Been breakin' hearts again?" Andy asked with a grin.

Becky snorted in disgust and rolled her eyes at the ceiling. "Not unless I broke yours, Andy. You're the only guy I've gone out with in the last six months."

Andy laughed and shook his head. "Well, it sounds like somebody doesn't like you folks very much."

"It doesn't make any sense at all," Grandma D said, plunking a plate of hotcakes on the table in front of Becky.

Becky smiled her thanks. "Unless," she said slowly, "it has something to do with Marvin Castle's offer for the Circle D."

"That's a little farfetched, sis," Sam told her with a laugh. "I know you don't like Castle, but he never threatened us when we refused his offer."

"He's the only one I can think of with a motive, Sam," Becky argued, "and since the ECC's sitting right on our boundary, it wouldn't be hard for one of their hands to slip across the fence and grab a calf now and then. They'd have plenty of opportunity to sabotage our fence, too."

Andy pushed back his chair and stood. "I'd better get back to work. Let me know if anything else happens. You folks watch your backs."

Sam walked him to the door and accompanied him on outside. Becky smothered her pancakes in butter and maple syrup. Grandma D carried a cup of coffee to the table and sat in Andy's chair.

"How're ya feelin' this morning?" she asked.

"Better. Headache's almost gone. A hot shower should take care of the rest."

"That's good." Grandma D sipped her coffee, then jumped up to get Becky a refill.

"You seem pretty chipper this morning," Becky observed.

"Never better," the old lady replied with a broad smile. "It's nice to feel useful again."

Guilt washed over Becky. "Oh, Grandma, I never meant to make you feel..." Her throat closed, and she couldn't go on.

"You didn't make me feel nothin' I didn't let you," Grandma D said firmly, resuming her seat. "We had quite a little talk with Pete yesterday. Got a whole lotta things cleared up."

"Yeah, he told me about it last night. He shoulda kept his mouth shut," Becky grumbled.

"You're wrong, honey. Dead wrong. This family's not worth spit if we can't be honest with each other. You've been carryin' more than your share of the load around here. It's got to stop or you'll never have a life of your own."

"Well, if I make as big a mess of that as I have of everything else, I'm not sure I want it."

Grandma D pursed her lips, then shook her head. "You stepped in and shouldered the responsibility for keepin' this family together when you were still a kid. You've done a damn fine job. It's just gotten outta hand, that's all."

"It sounds more to me like I took over everything whether anybody wanted me to or not. Tina hardly knows Hank's her daddy. You felt useless. God only knows what I did to Sam."

"Aw, stop feelin' sorry for yourself, Rebecca Anne. You're a natural leader. Why, you made everything look so easy, the rest of us forgot you had limits, too. There's no reason to beat up on yourself. If anybody oughtta feel guilty, it's us."

"But I don't want that," Becky protested.

"Then take the week off and let the rest of us do our share for a change."

"Right. And what am I gonna do? Sit around and eat bonbons while you and Janice are workin' your tails off in the kitchen? Where is she, anyway?"

"In her room makin' some phone calls." A sly smile spread across Grandma D's lips. "As for what you're gonna do, well, Pete and I've got that covered."

"I can hardly wait to hear this," Becky replied.

"You and Pete are gonna go up to the cabin for a couple of days. It's quiet and peaceful up there. You can fish and sleep—do whatever ya want. After that, you could go sight-seein'. He hasn't seen the Tetons or Yellowstone yet."

"There's only one bed up there."

"You can take a sleepin' bag and an air mattress."

Becky studied her grandmother's innocent expression for a moment, then had to laugh. "You're an old fraud, Grandma. You know darn well what'll happen."

"I know what I hope will happen," the old lady replied, her eyes twinkling with irreverent mirth. "Will you go?"

"Do I have a choice?"

"Nope."

"Then I guess I'll go."

Grandma D clapped her hands together in delight. "Get on upstairs and take your shower, honey. Pete went into town to pick up groceries and supplies. He'll be here to pick you up at noon. I'll pack a lunch."

"All right." Becky stood, walked to the doorway and turned back to her grandmother. "Don't get your hopes up too high about Pete and me, Grandma."

"Hogwash." Grandma D approached Becky, a determined set to her jaw. "If you coulda seen that boy's face when he was takin' care of you, you'd know he loves you. And if you've got any brains at all, you'll love him right back."

"It's not that easy. We still don't have much in common, and who knows how long he'll stay?"

"Don't be so dang negative. If the love is strong enough, all that other stuff can be worked out." Grandma D turned Becky around with a push and added a swat on her rear end for good measure. "Now go on and get cleaned up."

Becky obeyed, chuckling when her grandmother bellowed up the stairs after her. "Don't forget to shave your legs!"

She passed Janice's room, hesitated, then retraced her steps. Maybe Janice would give her some advice about her hair and makeup. The door was open a crack. Becky raised her hand to knock, but heard Janice talking in a low, strained tone.

"You said that wouldn't happen.... No...I don't know."

It sounded as if the conversation might go on for a while. Shrugging, Becky went into the bathroom. She could always ask Janice later.

The hot, pounding water in the shower eased her sore muscles. Becky took her time getting ready, enjoying the feminine primping ritual for once. She'd decided Grandma D was right about one thing.

She had been negative about having a relationship with Pete right from the start. She still had her doubts about whether or not they could ever get together on a permanent basis. But by golly, she would relish whatever time she had with him.

Chapter Eleven

Peter marched into the Dawson kitchen right on time. He hoped Becky would come with him willingly, but he was prepared to haul her out to the pickup Sam had loaned him, kicking and screaming if necessary. Looking up from the picnic basket she was covering with a cloth napkin, Grandma D gave him a thumbs-up sign and a broad wink. The adrenaline pumping through his bloodstream dissipated.

"You made good time comin' back from town," she said. "Get everything you wanted?"

Peter nodded. "How's Becky today?"

"Pretty good. She'll be down shortly."

"Does she know?"

"Yup."

"Is she angry?"

"Nope."

He heaved a sigh of relief, then gave the little woman a one-armed hug. "Thanks, Grandma D."

"She didn't need much convincing," she answered with a grin. "See that you take mighty good care of her, young man."

"I'll do my best."

Becky walked into the kitchen a moment later, carrying a backpack in one hand, a rifle in the other. Peter's chest tightened at the sight of her. She had brushed her hair to one side and fastened it into a ponytail that flowed over her shoulder. Gold hoops shone at her earlobes, and a small, heart-shaped locket nestled above the V neckline of her dusty rose blouse. She looked gorgeous.

She hesitated when she saw him, then approached with her smooth, long-legged stride, giving him a tentative smile. He bent down to kiss her cheek, found her shorter than usual and chuckled when he spotted an aqua-trimmed pair of white running shoes on her long, narrow feet.

"What's so funny?" she asked, abruptly pulling away.

"I've never seen you wear anything but boots before." He sniffed a subtle, floral fragrance drifting from her hair.

Her lips curved up in a self-conscious grin. He wanted to kiss those lips. They looked shiny and soft. He studied her face more carefully. A light dusting of pink covered her cheekbones, and her eyelids were tinted a delicate shade of lavender that made them look even bigger, and—good grief—Becky Dawson was wearing makeup. For him? The thought touched him deeply.

"Oh." She averted her head as if his inspection made her extremely uncomfortable. "Well, uh, are you ready to go?"

"Whenever you are," he said, adopting a brisk tone. He took the backpack from her, then frowned when he noticed the rifle. "Do you really need to bring that?" he asked, gesturing toward the gun with his free hand.

"Yeah. Come on, I'll tell you about it on the way."

Grandma D handed Peter the picnic basket. They said good-bye and drove off a few moments later with Peter at the wheel. Becky gave directions, then recounted what the sheriff had said earlier that morning.

Peter shook his head in amazement. "Do you honestly think we're in danger?"

"I don't know what to think. But the cabin is pretty isolated. I'm not about to go up there unarmed."

"Becky, could you actually shoot someone?"

"I wouldn't want to, Pete," she said thoughtfully, "but I'd do it in a minute to protect my family or the ranch."

For the rest of the trip up a narrow mountain road, they discussed possible suspects and motives for the trouble at the Circle D. They hadn't found any answers by the time Becky told him to turn off on a rutted path, but they had established a warm, easygoing rapport between them. Peter drove around a sharp bend, and the cabin appeared.

A half circle of stately pines sheltered the back of the small log structure. Sunshine glinted off the picture windows across the front. On either side of a porch complete with rocking chairs, wildflowers bloomed in beds. A stone chimney rose from the right side of the building.

Peter parked the truck and sat silently for a moment, studying the cabin. It looked snug and cozy—the perfect place to kick back and relax. Or have a romantic tryst.

The thought sent a rush of blood to his loins. He looked at Becky. She looked at him. Their gazes met and held, and a delicious tension seeped into the cab.

She knew what he was thinking. He could see it in her eyes, along with anticipation and a gut-wrenching vulnerability. He wanted to ignore the vulnerability, haul her into his arms and take her then and there.

You can't, his conscience warned. *She's too fragile right now. She needs gentleness and tenderness and rest.*

He fumbled for the door handle, forced it open and climbed out. Becky followed suit. They each gathered a load of supplies from the bed of the pickup and walked toward the cabin.

"This is a beautiful spot," he said.

"I've always liked it," she answered. "Nobody's been up here since last summer. It'll need a good cleaning."

Smiling to himself, Peter fitted the key Grandma D had given him into the lock and swung the door wide. Becky followed him inside, then halted suddenly, her mouth dropping open in surprise.

Every surface in the living room-bedroom-kitchen gleamed in the sunlight. The scent of furniture polish lingered in the room. A red-and-white gingham tablecloth covered the small, round table in the dining area. A mason jar filled with flowers sat in the center.

She turned to him, her eyes wide with questions. "Who did all of this?"

"Hank hired some of the hands' wives to come up and clean it yesterday," Peter told her.

"*Hank* did that? Are you sure it wasn't Grandma or Sam?"

Chuckling, Peter relieved her of the backpack she carried and ushered her over to the sofa. It took only a nudge to plunk her down onto the soft cushions. "I know it's a shock, but he can be thoughtful when he tries. Put your feet up while I bring in the rest of our stuff."

She started to rise immediately. He clamped a hand on her shoulder and firmly pushed her down again. "Becky, sit."

Her eyes flashed in rebellion. Then her mouth quirked at one corner and she sat back, crossed her arms, propped her feet up on the scarred pine coffee table and muttered, "Woof."

"Thank you," Peter returned dryly before heading out to the pickup.

Within ten minutes, he had the propane-powered refrigerator stocked and their luggage brought in and stowed away. Carrying the picnic basket, he walked over to the sofa, one hand held out in invitation. She accepted it with a smile, and they strolled outside together.

She led him to a shady glen beside a creek, no more than forty yards from the cabin. He spread out an old army blanket he'd found in a closet. She took off her shoes and crawled to the middle, settling with her legs tucked to one side.

Kneeling beside her, he delved into the basket and brought out thick chicken salad sandwiches, pickles, potato chips, green grapes and two cans of Coke. It was a light feast. When they'd finished eating, he cleared the mess away and stretched out on his back with his head in Becky's lap.

"Ahhh." He sighed, smiling up into her surprised face. "This is the life."

"Do make yourself comfortable," she said with a laugh.

"Oh, I am, believe me." He shut his eyes and let the quiet and serenity sink into his soul. Gradually, the tense leg muscles beneath his head relaxed. "Your grandmother said you'd tell me about the cabin."

"Dad built it himself, just before he married Mom," Becky answered. "They spent their honeymoon here."

"Did they use it often?"

"Mmm-hmm." Her fingers absently sifted through his hair in gentle, rhythmic sweeps. "Grandma and Grandpa lived with us, so my folks didn't have a lot of privacy. Whenever they could con the grandparents into watching us kids for a weekend, they'd sneak off to the cabin."

"They didn't bring you along?"

"Nope. This was their love nest. No kids allowed."

"Smart people," Peter observed with a chuckle. "They must have had a wonderful marriage."

"They had their problems like everyone else. But whenever they'd come back from a weekend up here, Dad would whistle for days and Mom would hum while she worked. They'd have these little private jokes that would drive all of us crazy."

Her soft, dreamy voice and stroking fingertips were driving *him* crazy. The images forming in his mind of the intimate activities her parents had shared in this place didn't help much, either. Hoping to distract himself, he raised up on one elbow and pulled the picnic basket closer.

"Ready for dessert? I think I saw some cookies in here." He lifted out the plastic bag, blinked at what he found under it, then flopped back onto Becky's lap and roared with laughter.

"What in the world?" Becky tipped the basket toward her until she could see inside, choked and dropped it as if it contained sewer rats.

The look of horrified surprise on her face set Peter off on another round. He clutched at his stomach and his eyes watered, but when Becky tried to get up, he rolled over and trapped her legs with one arm.

"It's not funny, Sinclair," she said, her cheeks crimson.

"Oh, Becky," he gasped, "yes, it is. I've never had a woman's grandmother provide condoms before. My God, a whole dozen. What a realist!"

"I'm gonna murder that old biddy when I get my hands on her," Becky insisted, though her lips were definitely struggling against a grin.

Peter pushed himself up to her eye level and wiped his wet cheeks with the knuckles of one hand. "No, you're not. You're just embarrassed because she wasn't very subtle about trying to protect you. You'd think it was a scream if she'd done this to Sam or Hank."

Her shoulders started to shake. Then giggles spurted out of her mouth and she collapsed onto her back, covering her face with both hands. Peter placed a palm on either side of her, trapping her between his arms.

"Subtle?" Becky sputtered between gusts of laughter. "She wouldn't know subtle if it bit her on the behind."

Peter pried her hands away from her face. "Well, I think she's wonderful," he said sincerely.

"That's because she's not *your* grandmother," Becky retorted with a giggle. Then she sighed. "I swear, one of these days she's gonna finish me off."

He shifted onto his stomach beside her, bracing his weight on one elbow. With his free hand, he traced her eyebrows, the curve of her ear and down the side of her neck to the delicate chain holding her locket.

"Just in case she does," he murmured, leaning closer, "I want to kiss you now. Is that all right with you?"

The laughter faded from her eyes and was replaced by a sleepy, sensuous expression. "Please do," she whispered, reaching for him.

Kissing her was like free-falling onto a massive feather bed. With the first touch of her lips against his, her warmth and softness enfolded him, beguiled him, pulled him down and down into swift and sudden passion. He struggled to remember gentleness and tenderness, but her responses, hesitant at first, quickly became eager, hungry, demanding, unleashing his most primitive instincts.

This couldn't be Peter Sinclair, M.D., the controlled, careful professional fumbling desperately at the buttons of this woman's blouse like a horny teenager confronting his first chance to see a bare breast. But he had to see her—all of her—or lose his mind.

This couldn't be Peter Sinclair, the restrained, thoughtful lover who patiently aroused his partner, feverishly kissing and sucking and licking this woman's lips and shoulders and neck. But he had to discover the taste and texture of her skin, infect her with the excitement raging through him—or lose his mind.

This couldn't be Peter Sinclair, the man who never let anyone get too close or see his weaknesses, frantically grinding his pelvis against hers like some randy male stripper. But he had to show her how much he wanted, no, *needed* her—or lose his mind.

She should yell at him, slap him, shove him away for his lack of finesse, his boorish haste, but her strong, competent hands rushed over him with the same desperation. Her lips and tongue kissed and tasted whatever part of him she could reach with the same feverishness. Her pelvis rocked against his in the same frantic rhythm.

Why did people have to wear so damn many clothes? Why didn't clothes just evaporate from the heat their bodies were generating? How fast could they get naked? He'd never again wear anything but Western shirts with their convenient snaps.

Ah, the relief of feeling bare skin to bare skin. The sound of her voice, calling his name in that breathless, needy tone. The pure wonder of seeing her lush curves dappled in sunlight, her eyes darkened to the shade of the evergreens beckoning to him, welcoming him.

His fingers shook so badly, he could hardly make use of her grandmother's unexpected gift. Somehow he managed. Then he knelt between her thighs, still marveling that this beautiful, precious woman would invite him so lovingly into the most intimate part of her body.

She caressed his chest and abdomen, and wrapped her long legs around his thighs, urging him closer. He leaned over her, supporting his weight on his forearms, indulging in one last gut-wrenching kiss before entering her.

Her eyes widened at the initial contact. Her breath came in ragged little gasps. Sweat broke out on his forehead. His arms trembled with the effort to move slowly, hold himself in check long enough to allow her to accommodate him comfortably. The sensations were so exquisite, he threw back his head, clenched his teeth and sucked in great gulps of air.

Then a broad, earthy smile spread across her face and she started moving her hips. His last thread of control snapped. He pulled her long, lovely legs up over his shoulders and plunged into her with deep, almost violent thrusts.

Her eyes closed. Her head thrashed from side to side. Hoarse, mewling little moans from her throat became cries of delight, and her hands clutched at his driving hips as if she wanted more, more, always more of him. Oh, *please,* God, make this last forever.

Too soon, she tightened around him. Her back arched off the blanket. A series of internal shudders triggered his own release, and he collapsed on top of her, too spent to move so much as an inch.

Her soft breasts cushioned his chest. Their thundering heartbeats echoed off each other, then gradually slowed. Her hands made soothing sweeps from his shoulders to his buttocks. Fearing he would crush her, he tried to withdraw, but her arms wrapped around him and clung for a long moment. Here, at last, was the tenderness. It filled his heart and soul to overflowing and brought a lump to his throat.

When he finally regained the strength to pull away far enough to see her face, he wanted to die. Her eyes were closed tightly. Tears leaked out from beneath her lashes, trickling down her cheeks and into her ears.

He cradled her head between his hands. "Oh, Becky, I'm so sorry," he whispered, wiping at her tears with his thumbs. "Did I hurt you?"

She shook her head, opened her eyes and gave him a wobbly smile. "No, Pete. I just didn't know it could be so...I mean, I've never..."

"Been attacked by a raving animal? I didn't mean to lose control like that. I wanted to make it good for you, and—"

"No, you big dope." She sniffled, then laughed and playfully swatted his rump. "You were wonderful."

"Then you didn't know it could be so what? And you've never what? For God's sake, finish those sentences."

Lowering her lashes, she swallowed hard, as if gathering the courage to speak. "I didn't know it could be so, uh, overwhelming. And I've never...oh, *you* know."

Hardly daring to breathe, he rolled them onto their sides, facing each other. "I'm not sure I know anything," he said quietly, caressing her cheek with trembling fingertips. "Do you mean you've never climaxed before?"

Her embarrassed nod nearly undid him. "I thought there was something wrong with me," she admitted. "That I wasn't...passionate enough."

Relief poured into him, followed in rapid succession by anger at whoever had treated her so shabbily and a strong surge of arrogant pride that she'd found fulfillment with him. And so enthusiastically, too. He laughed with delight at the thought and hugged her to him. She flattened her palms against his chest and shoved him away.

"Hey," he protested, pulling her back into his arms, "I'm not laughing at you."

"Ya coulda fooled me. What's so damn funny, then?"

He gazed into her eyes, waiting for the defiant glare he found there to fade. "I don't know what gave you that ridiculous idea," he said sincerely, "but believe me, Becky, there is absolutely nothing wrong with you. I've never made love to a more passionate woman. I'm not sure I could survive a more passionate woman."

"You mean that?"

"Cross my heart and hope to die. If you'd been any more passionate, we would have started a forest fire and had Smokey the Bear after us."

"Oh." She twirled a curly tuft of his chest hair around her index finger, a grin twitching at the corners of her mouth. "Then will you, uh, make love to me again sometime?"

Feeling a smile stretch clear down to his toenails, he rolled onto his back, bringing her over him. He wrapped her pony tail around his hand and gently pulled her head down until her lips were within kissing distance. "Just try to stop me, Dawson. Just try."

Over the next four days, Becky discovered a whole new side to her personality. For someone who had spent a good part of her life breeding animals, she'd been amazingly ignorant about her own sexuality. Pete had no such problem. In fact, he took great delight in reenacting every torrid love scene she'd ever read in a romance novel. Becky silently apologized to the many authors she had doubted over the years.

They slept and made love, ate and made love, went fishing and made love, talked and laughed and played checkers and made love. They didn't need an excuse. They didn't need external stimuli. They didn't need a thing, but Grandma D's little foil packets. When they ran out, Becky couldn't hide her disappointment until, with a wicked smile, Pete produced a box of his own.

He was inventive, insatiable and completely without modesty. If she felt a little hesitant or bashful, he would give her a droll look and say, "Come on, I'm a doctor. You can tell me anything." For the first time in her life, she felt free to say and do and be anything she wanted.

Once in a while, a little voice piped up inside her head. *This can't last,* it would say. *You know it can't.* Becky sternly told it to shut the hell up.

She loved Pete Sinclair, and would love him until the day she croaked. She could never share with anyone else the intimate thoughts and feelings and physical acts she shared so easily with him. If this was the only honeymoon she would ever have, she wasn't about to waste it.

At twilight of the fourth day, Becky stood at the big picture window that looked down on the Circle D, while Pete cooked the trout they'd caught that afternoon. She hadn't thought about the ranch since they'd arrived at the cabin, but now she found herself wondering what everyone was doing at home. Taking the binoculars that always sat on the window ledge, she focused in on the ranch yard.

There weren't any pickups parked in back of the house yet, and Janice's car was gone. Sam and Hank must have still been out working somewhere. Grandma D and Tina were probably fixing supper. Sighing, Becky set the field glasses down, frowning when they wobbled.

She picked them up again and found a silver button sitting underneath the glasses on the ledge. It had a tiny anchor embossed on the front, and looked as if it had come from a woman's blouse. Becky didn't recognize it, but automatically stuck it into her jeans pocket in case it belonged to one of the women who had cleaned the cabin.

Two large warm arms encircled her waist from behind and a chin nuzzled the top of her head. "What's so interesting down there?" Pete asked.

"Nothing much," she answered. "Just the ranch."

"You can see it from here?"

"That's why Dad chose this spot for the cabin. He had a big flag Grandpa or Grandma could fly if they ever needed him."

"Let me see."

Becky handed over the binoculars, then laid her head back against his chest.

"There's the house. And the corral. Gertie and the calves just came out of the barn. It's amazing how much you can see with these things. Hey, there's a guy coming out of the tack room, but I don't recognize him."

"Sam probably hired a new hand to help out while we're gone." She held up her hand for the field glasses. "Hand 'em over, Pete. Maybe I know—"

"Wait a second. He's pouring something on the ground. Now he's getting something out of his pocket. Jesus! He's lighting a fire!"

Pete shoved the glasses into Becky's hands. "He's running across the corral toward the trees in the horse pasture."

Becky peered through the lenses, but only caught a glimpse of a shadowy figure disappearing into the pines. "Nuts. I missed him."

Then she focused on the tack room door, praying Pete was wrong. Damn. Flames danced in the open doorway. She scanned to the left. Double damn. The main back door showed the same picture, as did the door to the grain room. Wisps of grayish-white smoke gathered under the eaves. The whole damn barn was on fire.

She raced out of the cabin in her bare feet, ignoring rocks, pine needles and stickers in a desperate rush for the pickup. She yanked open the door and grabbed the CB's mike.

Grandma D answered a moment later. While she was promising to call for help, Sam's voice came over the radio.

"Don't panic, Grandma. We're only half a mile out."

Pete charged out of the cabin, carrying Becky's shoes and a pair of socks. "Let me drive," he shouted, tossing them to her. "You're too upset."

Becky slid across to the passenger seat. Pete started the engine, turned the pickup around and roared off down the mountain road. The fifteen-minute trip, which had been so pleasant and had taken twenty-five minutes a few days before, became a nightmare of potholes and endless sharp curves.

Knowing Pete needed to concentrate on driving, Becky remained silent, battling a sick feeling of dread in the pit of her stomach. Oh, hell, all of Hank's trophy saddles from his rodeo days, and God only knew how much other tack, feed and equipment were in that building.

By the time they reached the ranch, Hank's pickup and another with the Bar Z brand stenciled on the door were parked far to the side of the driveway, leaving a broad path for the volunteer fire department's truck, should it arrive in time. But the amount of smoke billowing from the hayloft, turning black now that the asphalt shingles on the roof were smoldering, told Becky it was already too late.

Grandma D, Hank and four men from the Bar Z stood in a tight cluster watching the inferno, their shoulders slumped in defeat. His face streaked with soot and his shirt torn, Sam sat on the back steps holding Tina in his arms. The child wept hysterically and pounded on his chest with her small fists.

"Oh my God. Mittens," Becky whispered.

She jumped out of the truck the instant it stopped rolling and ran to her niece. Becky's eyes met Sam's. The misery and helplessness she saw there sank right into her soul. She stroked the little girl's hair. Tina lifted her dirty, tear-streaked face and flung herself at Becky.

"Aunt Becky," she sobbed, "Mittens had her babies last night. An' Grandma D an' Daddy an' Uncle S-Sam w-wouldn't let m-me get 'em out. An' n-now they're all b-burned up."

"That makes you feel sad, doesn't it, sweetheart?" Becky said, sitting down with the child in her lap.

"I'm n-never gonna t-talk to them again."

Becky held Tina away and forced the little girl to meet her gaze. "You know that's not fair, Tina. It wasn't their fault the barn caught on fire. They just didn't want *you* to get burned up. We can get another cat, honey, but we could never, *ever* replace you."

Her whole body shaking with sobs, Tina wrapped her arms around Becky's neck in a stranglehold. "I k-know. B-but it's just s-so awful!"

"I know, baby. I know."

Maternal rage boiling up inside her, Becky rocked the little girl and stroked her back until the sobs finally faded to sniffles. Her eyes wet with tears of her own, Grandma D appeared at Becky's side and held out her hand to Tina.

"Come on, honey. Let's go in and wash your face. It'll make you feel better."

When the back door closed behind them, Becky and Sam joined the others watching the fire. Sirens wailed in the distance, and a few moments later, the sheriff and the fire engine arrived. The Dawsons naturally drew together as the fire crew got to work, but it was obvious they wouldn't be able to save anything from the building. Becky gratefully accepted Pete's comforting, one-armed hug, then squeezed Sam's left hand with her right one.

Sam flinched and yanked his hand away. Becky looked down at her fingers and found them streaked with blood.

"What did you do to yourself?" She took her brother's hand between her own and turned it over. A deep, jagged gash stretched from the base of his index finger to the heel of his hand. "Good Lord, you'll need stitches in that."

"It's nothin', sis."

He tugged at his hand, but she wouldn't release it. "Don't you go all macho on me, Sam Dawson. That's a nasty cut and it needs attention."

"Well, that's tough, Beck." He kicked viciously at the useless garden hose lying at his feet. "I'm not leavin'."

"I'll be glad to take care of it," Pete offered. "Take him into the kitchen while I get my bag from the car."

"It can wait, Pete," Sam insisted.

"I'm a pretty fast stitcher. Ten minutes tops."

"Go on ahead, Sam," Hank said. "There's nothin' we can do, and it sure as hell ain't much fun standin' here watchin' it burn."

"Oh, all right," Sam grumbled, his expression darker than a thunderhead.

Pete proved as good as his word. Becky watched in fascination as he cleaned and disinfected the cut, then injected Novocain and stitched the ragged edges together. He kept up a relaxed stream of conversation while he worked, putting Sam at ease and coaxing one reluctant smile out of him. Given the circumstances, Becky considered that accomplishment a major miracle. It would be a real waste if Pete gave up practicing medicine.

When the three of them went back outside, the fire crew was hard at work. The only thing they could do was stand back and watch. The sheriff approached them and stood beside Sam.

"Any idea what started this?" he asked.

Sam shook his head. "Nope. The last time the insurance agent was out, we walked through the whole damn building, inspected the wiring and everything else. We had a little gasoline in the machine shop for cleaning parts, but I can't figure out where a spark woulda come from to set it off."

"So the building was insured."

"Yeah. Thank God. It's gonna be a helluva mess replacing it, though."

"It wasn't an accident," Becky said. She told them how Pete had discovered the fire from the cabin.

"Would you recognize the guy if you saw him again?" Andy Johnson asked.

Pete shook his head. "I doubt it. I didn't get a good look at his face because he was wearing a cowboy hat pulled down over his eyes." He went on to describe the man as best he could. "I'm sorry."

"You've given us a start," the sheriff replied.

"I still think Marvin Castle and his Executive Cattle Company are involved," Becky argued, ignoring Sam's skeptical frown.

"It won't hurt to check him out, and I'll call in an arson investigator from the state fire marshal's office to take a look around," Andy said. "Let me know if you think of anything else. In the meantime, all of you be careful." With that, the sheriff left.

Becky turned to her brother. "Why don't you agree with me? Remember how insistent Castle was when he offered to buy the ranch? He was downright rude."

"It's just too farfetched. C'mon, sis, this is Wyoming. Do you really think we've got corporate raiders here?"

"It's possible, Sam," Peter said. "Corporations have some interesting ways of rewarding and punishing employees. If they've given Marvin Castle orders to acquire your land, he might be willing to go to any lengths to get it."

"It could be environmentalists," Sam argued. "You know, they've been talkin' about gettin' all the cattle out of the national forests. Or it could just be some nut."

"Well, *somebody's* out to get us, Sam," Becky retorted. "And we'd better be findin' out who, pretty damn quick."

Chapter Twelve

Sheriff Johnson arrived the next afternoon, accompanied by Ron Talcott, the arson investigator from the state fire marshal's office. Talcott was a slender, congenial man, with shaggy blond hair and blue eyes, who stood close to six feet tall. Everyone gathered around the kitchen table to hear his report.

"You've definitely had an arsonist at work here," he said. "He used a mixture of gasoline and diesel to light the fire, and opened the doors and windows to provide ventilation. That's why your barn burned so fast. What I find interesting is that he let the animals out, and didn't try to hide the fact that the fire was deliberately set."

"So we've got an arsonist who likes animals," Sam muttered.

"Maybe he wanted us to know it was deliberately set," Hank suggested.

"You mean the fire was supposed to be a warning of some kind?" Grandma D asked.

"You could take it that way," Andy Johnson agreed.

"I think you're right about that," Sam said thoughtfully. "It sure was convenient that we got home just in time to watch it burn. But there's usually somebody in the barn at that time of day, either milkin' Gertie or unsaddlin' a horse or something. How did the guy know there wouldn't be anyone around yesterday?"

"Well, how did whoever stole our calves and sabotaged my pickup know when to do it?" Becky asked. "It's almost like somebody's watching us."

"Or we've got a traitor on our hands," Hank said.

"Oh, Hank, surely not," Grandma D protested. "Why we've known everyone who's workin' for us for years."

Hank patted her hand, then shook his head. "I don't like the idea much, either, Grandma, but we can't ignore the possibility. Nobody keeps a regular schedule around here. Somebody shoulda seen *something* before now."

"Well, it just makes my skin crawl," the old lady said with a shudder. "My Lord, what is this world comin' to?"

"Let's not fly off the handle," Sam said quietly. "The fire might not have anything to do with Becky's accident or anything else."

"That's true," Ron Talcott said. "Have there been any other suspicious fires in the area recently?"

"Nope," the sheriff replied, scooting his chair away from the table. "If you folks don't have any more questions for Ron, we'd better get goin' so he can catch his flight."

When the two men had left, Sam rubbed his eyes with his thumb and index finger, then exhaled a weary sigh as he looked around the table. "Until we find out exactly what's goin' on, we all need to be careful and do what we can to protect ourselves. That means lockin' the house, the buildings and the vehicles."

Hank snorted in disgust. "You think that'll stop this guy?"

"Maybe not," Sam agreed reluctantly, "but we don't hafta make it easy for him. I'll try to hire some more men to help with the herd, so we can always have somebody here at the ranch with Tina, Grandma and Janice. Everybody who knows how to use a gun will carry one. If anyone sees or hears anything even a little bit odd, I wanta hear about it.''

"Can I say something?" Janice asked, her voice barely above a whisper.

"Of course you can, honey," Hank replied. "You're part of the family."

She gave him a wobbly smile. "Almost, anyway. I just think that maybe you ought to consider accepting Mr. Castle's offer for the Circle D." Several outraged gasps went up around the table, but she raised both hands beside her head, as if to stave off angry words.

"I know you all think it's horrible of me to suggest this, but I believe somebody wants this ranch so bad, there's no telling what he might do next. Everything he's done has gotten more and more dangerous. What if somebody *had* been in the barn? They could have been killed. I don't want to be a widow before I'm even a bride."

Hank put his arm around her shoulders and gave her a hug. "Aw, Jan, you know I can take care of myself. There's nothin' to worry your pretty little head about."

Her eyes puddled up with tears and her chin quivered, but she shot him a mutinous glare. "That's easy for you to say, Hank. But I'm gonna be madder than hell at you if you get yourself killed. Please . . . just think about it."

"Now I *know* she loves me," Hank said, grinning at the rest of the family.

When everyone finished chuckling, he turned to Pete with a more serious expression. "You'd be an easy target out there in the foreman's house by yourself. Better move in here tonight. I'll bunk with Sam so you can have my room."

The meeting broke up then, and Becky went to the foreman's house with Pete. She sat on the side of his bed, watching him fold shirts and pants into an open suitcase. Though she told herself it wasn't necessarily true, she couldn't shake the feeling, almost a premonition, that the next time he packed up all of his things, he would leave the Circle D—and her—permanently.

Dammit, it wasn't fair. She was supposed to have three more wonderful days of privacy with Pete at the cabin. She wanted to take him right back up there and make love under the quilt and never come out again.

Instead, they would all be crammed into the main house together, waiting for some new horrendous thing to happen. Next time, somebody could get hurt or killed. Maybe that somebody would be Pete. Becky gasped aloud at that thought, and Pete looked up in surprise.

"What's wrong?" he asked.

"I think you should leave," she blurted before her courage could fail her.

Dropping the shirt he'd been holding, he propped his hands on his hips and stared at her. "Why?"

"Janice is right, you know," she said slowly, groping for words. "This whole situation is getting real ugly."

"I'm not afraid."

"It's not your fight. I don't want you to get hurt."

He shoved the suitcase out of the way and sat beside her. "Is that the only reason you want me to go?" he asked, taking both of her hands in his.

"I don't *want* you to go at all. But I want you to be safe, and you won't be if you stay." She closed her eyes, then shook her head. "Oh, damn, everything is such a mess."

He wrapped his warm, strong arms around her and she rested her head against his chest, loving the steady beat of his heart beneath her ear.

"I'm not going anywhere, Becky. If someone is trying to harm you and your family, it *is* my fight. Leaving you now would hurt me more than anything that might happen here. I'd go crazy wondering if you were all right."

"But you don't need all this stress, Pete."

"What I need," he whispered hoarsely, framing her face with his hands as he lowered his head to drop a swift, hard kiss on her lips, "is you."

Oh, God, she needed him, too. Her arms slid around his neck. Her lips sought his in desperation. He responded with a muffled groan, crushing her to him. Desire ignited, fierce and hot in the depths of her belly.

She moved her hands over his head, memorizing the shape of his skull, the texture of his hair, the curve of his ears. She caressed the back of his neck, the breadth of his shoulders, the little indentations made by his collar bones. As if by mutual agreement, they parted long enough to shed their clothes.

He swept the suitcase onto the floor with one smooth motion and they stretched out on the bed, facing each other, already reaching for each other. The kisses came hotter, deeper, faster, but she wanted more, needed more. Every part of him was infinitely precious to her. She had to see and touch and taste each and every one, imprint them onto her brain and her heart forever.

Grasping his shoulders, she pushed him onto his back and straddled his hips. Lord, he was gorgeous. He looked back at her with such obvious pleasure, she felt beautiful and utterly feminine.

He reached up and caressed her breasts, and she moaned, enjoying the sensations so much, she nearly relinquished control into his capable hands. But, no. This time, she wanted to show him exactly how much he meant to her.

She forced his hands to the bedspread while she kissed her way from the ridge of his jaw to his navel. Her lips and tongue and fingertips stroked and explored, lingering on the spots that made him quiver or cry out. She reveled in her power to arouse him to a state of trembling need.

Then his hands grasped her waist and their positions were suddenly reversed. "Two can play this game," he taunted, smiling down at her with a wicked gleam in his eyes that set her heart racing with anticipation.

Oh, and he played the game so well. He touched her everywhere but where she wanted desperately to be touched, building the tension within her higher and higher. In a low,

gritty voice that made her nerve endings sizzle, he murmured erotic promises of the things he would do to her. She
writhed; she whimpered; she begged without shame. Then
gradually he began to fulfill his promises, but not fast
enough. Not nearly fast enough. She grabbed his hands and
put them where she needed them.

"Yes, sweetheart," he said, panting. "Tell me what you
want."

"I want you inside me. Now."

He plunged into her, hard and hot, sucking in a hissing
breath through clenched teeth. She clawed at his shoulders,
gasping in surprise when he rolled onto his back, bringing
her on top of him, their bodies still joined. Their fingers in-
terlocked, he stretched her above him, feasting on her
breasts with his lips and tongue.

"Take what you want," he said, rotating his hips in tan-
talizing circles.

She clamped her knees against his sides and set up a
steady, driving rhythm. It was like galloping across miles of
turf on a powerful stallion, with an element of danger for
added excitement. Sweat glistened on her skin, her breath
came in shallow gulps, her muscles burned, but she wouldn't
stop, couldn't stop until he arched off the bed, his shout of
completion triggering her own.

He released her hands and enfolded her in his arms when
she collapsed on top of him. A satisfied chuckle rumbled
deep in his chest, vibrating against her ear. She smiled and
kissed his left nipple, then rolled onto her side, facing him.

"You're incredible," he said, snuggling her closer.

"I know." Tweaking his chest hair, she gave him a smug
grin. "But that's gonna have to last us a while."

"That's a horrible thought. Don't you think your family
already knows we're lovers?"

"Oh, I reckon they know," she answered ruefully, "but
it's one thing to carry on an affair in private. It's something
else to do it with a six-year-old kid underfoot. That's why
Janice and Hank have separate rooms until the wedding.

Maybe it seems hypocritical, but I don't want to set a bad example for Tina.''

"No, I understand. I could always sneak into your room late at night and we could be quiet.''

She shot him a dubious look. "Yeah, right, Sinclair. Don't forget Tina's room is right next to mine, and the kid's a light sleeper.''

"We'll find other opportunities,'' he said.

"I hope so. God, I hope so.'' She kissed him soundly, then pulled away and started to dress. "C'mon. Let's get back to the house before somebody sends out a search party.''

Despite the tense atmosphere blanketing the Circle D over the next week, Becky and Peter continued to enjoy their newfound love. Though neither quite had the nerve to come right out and say that word aloud, they communicated their feelings in other ways. Subtle glances, secret touches and stolen kisses added a spicy zest to each new day.

Sam unwittingly did them a favor when he asked them to handle the irrigation system. They clomped for miles in rubber boots, clearing weeds from the ditches, shoring up the banks and regulating the water flowing through the gates. While it wasn't exactly glamorous work, it gave them precious time alone to talk and laugh and share all the intimacies new lovers crave.

Becky had never been happier. She carried a pistol strapped to her hip and kept her eyes and ears alert for possible danger. But not even the threat of another attack against her family could rob her of the giddy excitement she found in Pete's company.

When abstinence became too great a strain to endure, they got downright devious. Who would have thought a machine shed could be so romantic on a hot afternoon? Or a basement laundry room in the dead of night? Or under a clump of low-hanging willows next to the creek in the south pasture?

Actually, she thought they were doing a bang-up job of concealing their passion for each other, until they spent several evenings helping Sam and Hank build a temporary shed to house the new tack they'd ordered. They worked until it got too dark to see what they were doing, then sat in the backyard, relaxing with a cold beer.

Janice came out to join them and perched on the arm of Hank's wooden lawn chair. "How's the shed coming along?" she asked.

"We'll finish it tomorrow if I don't murder those two," Hank answered, shooting a disgusted look at Becky and Pete.

"What did we do?" Becky demanded with a startled laugh.

"Yeah," Pete interjected. "We helped a lot. I've got blisters on my hands to prove it."

Hank's eyes took on a wicked twinkle. "Your work's just fine. It's the sound effects I can't stand. Know what I mean, Sam?"

"I sure do," Sam agreed, rolling his eyes. "Becky's hummin' all the time is bad enough, but if Pete doesn't stop that damn whistlin', I'm gonna wrap a hammer around his neck."

Chapter Thirteen

During the first two weeks of July, the Dawsons razed what was left of the old barn and prepared the site for a new one. As the days passed and nothing awful happened, everyone began to relax. On the second Sunday, the family insisted that Becky and Peter take the day off, so that Peter could see the Green River Rendezvous Pageant held in Pinedale every summer.

Becky refused to tell him anything about the pageant. When they got to town with an excited Tina strapped in the seat belt between them, his mouth dropped open in surprise. The streets were choked with people. Mountain men and "Indians" wearing leather costumes mingled with a horde of tourists.

Since they had a couple of hours before the actual show started, they wandered down Pine Street, enjoying the atmosphere. Peter had never seen anything like it. When they'd finished watching a performance by some real Native American dancers from the Wind River Reservation, he pointed to a man wearing a T-shirt bearing the slogan Meet Me On The Green.

"Okay, Dawson, what does that mean?"

Becky chuckled. "The fur trade was big out here during the early 1800s. The fur companies sent supplies to the trappers every summer, so they wouldn't have to go back east to get them. They'd all meet to trade their pelts for whatever they needed."

"In Pinedale?"

"Around the Green River, anyway," Becky answered. "The rendezvous was a party that went on for days. It's our big party every year now, too. Just about everybody participates in one way or another."

"It's wonderful."

"I'm sorry we couldn't come for the whole weekend. There's a parade and art shows and all kinds of things going on. But you'll get to see the pageant and a rodeo tonight."

As they strolled from one event to the next, Peter found himself watching other families, especially the fathers interacting with young children. He began to fantasize about what it would be like if Becky were his wife, Tina his daughter. The thought was incredibly pleasing.

Becky chose that moment to nudge him and point out one of her neighbors dressed in leather riding a spectacular horse on his way to the Rendezvous grounds. The sun glistened on the fiery strands in Becky's hair. Her green eyes sparkled with enjoyment. Her delighted smile sent blood rushing below his belt, and he had to look away or embarrass himself.

Soon. He would ask her to marry him soon. He knew there would be problems to resolve, differences in life-style to address. But she was the woman he wanted to spend the rest of his life with. Somehow they would have to work things out.

By the time they got home that night, Tina was slumped across Becky's lap, sound asleep, and Peter's head was full of plans. He would coax Becky to take a walk with him and propose out under the stars. No, that wasn't romantic enough. He should take her out for a nice dinner, maybe in Jackson Hole, and then ask her to marry him. He could buy her an engagement ring there.

Hank's head poked out the back door as they were alighting from the pickup. "Hey, Pete, you've got a phone call. Guy says he's a friend of yours. Better hurry, he's called three times and it's long distance."

"Go on," Becky said when Peter would have taken Tina from her arms, "I can carry her."

Wondering who could have tracked him down, Peter went inside. He answered the phone with a brisk, "Sinclair here," then laughed in surprise when Douglas Brewster, one of the doctors he worked with at St. Luke's, answered.

"Peter, is that really you? I was beginning to think you'd dropped off the face of the earth."

"How did you find me, Douglas?"

"I have my ways. Emily and I flew into Jackson Hole this afternoon. We've rented a car for the week, and we'd like to drive over to Pinedale and have dinner with you."

"Did Eric send you to check up on me?" Peter asked, referring to the hospital's chief administrator.

"Emily and I have been planning this vacation for months, Peter. You know that."

"But he told you where to find me."

Douglas hesitated. "Well, yes. He's concerned about you. We all are."

"I'm fine, Douglas. Better than I've been in years. There's no need for you to come here."

"Look, I won't grill you about your plans and we don't have to discuss medicine. How does Wednesday sound?"

It was Peter's turn to hesitate. Part of him wanted to keep his past life as far away from Becky as possible. But Douglas and Emily had been his friends for years, and another part of him wanted Becky to meet them. She would have to meet his coworkers sooner or later. Perhaps it would be easier for her if she could start on her own turf.

"All right. We'll meet you at McGregors Pub at seven. It's off the main street on your left. You can't miss it."

"Wonderful. Did you say 'we'll'?"

"I'm bringing someone I want you to meet."

"Someone special?" Douglas asked with a smile in his voice.

Becky walked into the kitchen at that moment. Peter grinned at her before answering Douglas. "Very special," he said. "See you on Wednesday."

"What was that all about?" Becky asked.

"Some friends of mine are vacationing in Jackson. I'm having dinner with them Wednesday night."

"That's nice." She started unloading the dishwasher. "I hope you'll have a good time."

"I want you to come with me."

She shot him a pained look. "Aw, I don't think so."

"Why not? You'll like Douglas and Emily."

"There's too much to do around here. You just go on and have fun."

Seeing she was going to be stubborn, he walked over and took a stack of plates from her. Then he gave her his most convincing smile. "Please, Becky. I'll have a lot more fun if you come with me."

Either his smile or his wheedling tone worked. Her mouth slowly curved up on one side. "Oh, all right. Will Emily wear a dress?"

"Probably. But you don't have to if you don't want to. I know what I'd love to see you wear, though."

"What's that?"

He glanced over his shoulder, as if assuring himself that there was no one else in the room. Then he leaned down and whispered his suggestion in her ear.

She giggled and pushed him away. "I'd get arrested for that, Sinclair. Now get outta here and let me get these dishes put away, will ya? Don't worry, I'll find something decent to wear.''

Peter stole a quick kiss before leaving her. He found Janice in the living room, curled up on the sofa beside Hank. His conversation with Becky had given him an idea, and upon hearing it, Janice eagerly agreed to help him put it into action.

Becky tugged off her muddy boots late Wednesday afternoon, and shot a surreptitious glance at Pete while he did the same. The man was definitely up to something. He'd been smiling to himself all day as if he had some great secret. It was getting damned irritating.

It didn't help much that she was as nervous as the last calf waiting to be branded. If they'd been going out to dinner by themselves she would have been eager for the evening ahead, but the thought of meeting his friends from back east scared her spitless. What if they didn't like her? Or worse yet, what if they found her...amusing?

Sighing, she marched into the kitchen, grabbed a brownie from a pan cooling on the counter and hurried upstairs to shower. She'd been tempted to sneak into town and buy something new to wear, but had stubbornly resisted the impulse. Pete's friends could take her the way she was or lump it. Unfortunately, now she wished she had given in.

She pushed open her bedroom door, then rocked back on her heels when she saw a large, beautifully wrapped box sitting in the middle of her bed. Her stomach knotted painfully and her fingers wrapped themselves into fists. She forced herself to cross the room. The gift had to be from Pete. Judging from its shape, it could only be one thing.

With no desire to save the paper or the fancy ribbon, she ripped the package open and confirmed her suspicions. It was the mint-green dress she had admired at Dillingham's Dry Goods. Becky picked it up and carefully laid it out on the bedspread. Underneath the dress, she found a lacy pair of panties and a strapless bra, earrings, a necklace and bracelet, sheer panty hose, a pair of delicate white sandals, a small white purse and a bottle of Obsession perfume.

"Do you like it?" Pete asked from the doorway.

Becky took a moment to erase the emotions from her face before turning to look at him. His excited expression reminded her of Tina waiting for a reaction to the Christmas and Mother's Day presents she made at school. Though resentment burned like acid inside her chest, she couldn't bring herself to tell him what she thought of his gift.

"It's, uh, very nice. Thank you."

Pete's smile slipped a notch. He tipped his head to one side and studied her. Before he could say anything, however, Janice bustled into the room carrying a cosmetic case. She shooed Pete off to get ready, then turned on Becky.

"Good Lord, haven't you even showered yet?" she demanded. "It'll take forever to dry your hair. Get going or you'll be late."

Seeing that her future sister-in-law had the bit firmly between her teeth, Becky did as she was told. She stood under the hot water, feeling her insides turning to ice.

She would not let Pete badger her into a confession of what was bothering her, because she wouldn't *let* anything bother her. She would be every inch a lady for him this one time if it killed her. No matter what happened, she would get through this damned evening with her dignity intact. But the whole situation brought back such ugly memories.

By the time she returned to the bedroom, which Janice had turned into a home beauty shop, Becky's emotions were completely under control. She even managed to smile and respond naturally to Janice's enthusiastic ministrations and advice. The woman who finally emerged from the room and walked serenely down the stairs to greet her family and her date was absolutely gorgeous.

But she wasn't Becky Dawson. Becky wondered if Pete would realize that. Or if he would care if he did.

Sam's jaw dropped open when she made her entrance. Hank's eyes bugged out, and he muttered, "Well, I'll just be damned." Grandma D beamed and dabbed at her eyes with a tissue. Tina murmured, "Oh, Aunt Becky, you look so pretty." Pete waited at the bottom of the stairs, his sizzling gaze following her every move.

He wore a navy blue blazer, a light blue oxford shirt, open at the collar, gray slacks and black loafers. His dark hair gleamed, and the whiteness of his smile set off his deep tan to perfection. He looked masculine and sophisticated, and the sight of him made Becky's chest ache. Accepting his offered hand as she descended the last three steps, she calmly returned his smile.

"You look beautiful," he said quietly.

The sincere admiration in his eyes gave her a modicum of compensation for enduring all of this hassle. She inclined her head graciously, as if she received such compliments every day. "Thank you. Shall we go?"

He nodded, and the family stepped back as though they were making room for a couple of celebrities. Becky was not surprised to find Pete's Corvette sitting outside the front door, black and shiny and sexy as sin. He held the door while she slipped inside, then walked around the back of the vehicle and seated himself.

Becky settled into the luxurious leather seat. The car had more dials and gauges than an airplane, she thought as he started the powerful engine and drove away from the house. He glanced at her with a questioning look in his eyes, and she steered the conversation away from herself by asking about the Brewsters.

With each passing mile, Pete's eagerness to see his friends became more obvious. He'd fit into life at the ranch so easily and had seemed so content, it had never occurred to Becky that he might miss his home. But he must have, more than he'd let on. The realization brought a sharp stab of misery to Becky's heart.

They arrived at McGregors Pub ten minutes early. Pete shut off the engine. Though she felt silly, Becky waited for him to come around and open her door. It wasn't that she didn't know the rules of the dating game; she just thought they were stupid. Still, she didn't want to ruin his evening since it seemed to mean so much to him.

She inhaled a deep breath for courage, plastered a smile on her face and allowed him to escort her into the restaurant. McGregors was crowded, as usual. Recognizing most of the patrons, Becky braced herself for stunned reactions to the drastic change in her appearance.

To her relief, nobody passed out when she followed the hostess to the table Pete had reserved on the outdoor deck. To her surprise, nobody seemed to notice or care that she was wearing a dress, either. She and Pete ordered drinks and opened their menus.

A moment later Pete looked up, jumped to his feet and waved to a striking couple stepping through the doorway. Becky's stomach churned as she watched them approach. Douglas Brewster was a tall, athletic man with blond hair and blue eyes. He wore a pair of pleated slacks with an exquisitely tailored sports coat the exact color of his eyes. A slender, expensive-looking watch gleamed on his wrist as he reached for Pete's hand and gave it an enthusiastic shake.

His wife, Emily, was a dainty brunette. Her brown hair was short, frosted and artfully mussed. She wore a strapless black dress that clung to her delicate curves, three-inch heels and flashy gold jewelry that should have overpowered her tiny frame, but somehow seemed just right. Laughing, she threw her arms around Pete's waist and gave him a hug and a kiss. Becky immediately wanted to deck her.

Instead, she rose to greet the couple, feeling like an Amazon and acknowledging Pete's introductions with a forced smile. When they were all seated, Becky took a long sip from her drink, hoping it would help her relax. It didn't.

The Brewsters studied her with open curiosity. They made the usual remarks strangers do when they're trying to get acquainted and asked polite questions about the Circle D when Pete told them Becky was a rancher. Douglas and Emily were nice enough people, but once they'd all talked about the weather and their impressions of Wyoming, Becky couldn't think of another thing she wanted to say to them.

She ordered another gin and tonic and contented herself with listening to the others. She'd never been any good at small talk, though God knew Bob had tried his best to teach her. Besides, she would learn more about Pete and his relationship with these people if she kept her mouth shut.

It didn't take long to discover that he was a different man with his friends than he was at the ranch. For one thing, he'd started picking up a trace of a Western drawl in his speech since he'd been in Wyoming. When he talked to Douglas and Emily, however, his diction became more precise and his vocabulary expanded.

He didn't appear to notice that they always called him Peter instead of Pete. Becky did. Had she and her family offended him by automatically shortening his name?

He seemed fascinated by a discussion of national and world events, topics he had seldom discussed with her. Now that she thought about it, he did make it a point to read the newspaper every day, something she rarely had time for. Did he find her ignorant, her views parochial?

Then they started talking about the hospital, where Douglas and Emily were both surgeons. While the Brewsters brought Pete up-to-date on patients he had treated, Pete leaned forward, his eyes bright with interest. He fired questions at them one after another, like a man used to demanding such information and getting it instantly. From what Becky could gather, he had been sorely missed at the hospital. Obviously the feeling had been mutual.

As the evening went on, she felt more miserable and inadequate. She ordered another drink, but the knot of tension in her stomach wouldn't allow her to do more than pick at her food. How could she have been so stupid? From the beginning, she'd told herself Pete wouldn't stay in Wyoming.

But had she listened? Of course not. She'd been so infatuated with the man, so flattered by his attention, she hadn't wanted to listen. She had allowed herself to dream about spending the rest of her life with him on the Circle D, raising kids and horses. Watching and listening to him now, however, she couldn't deny the truth any longer.

Pete was meant to be a doctor, and not a small-town general practitioner like Doc Miller, who was sitting two tables away from them. Pete talked about machines and procedures the way she talked about horses and cattle. He had been overworked and disillusioned, but deep in his gut he loved medicine and he loved his job.

She could love him, feed him, wash his clothes and listen to him. But never in a billion years could she speak his language the way Douglas and Emily Brewster could.

Becky started when a hand suddenly rested on her left shoulder. She looked up to find Doc Miller and his wife, Marie, standing beside her chair.

"Sorry to interrupt," he said, smiling at Becky, "but I wanted to check on one of my favorite patients, and I couldn't help overhearing part of your conversation, and—"

Marie interrupted with a chuckle. "What he's trying to say is that he's dying to talk shop with you. He doesn't get much opportunity unless he goes to a medical convention."

"Join us, by all means," Pete said immediately.

Becky's mouth nearly dropped open when Pete introduced Doc to the Brewsters as George Miller. George? He'd always been Doc to her and everyone else during the twenty years he'd been serving Pinedale.

Still, it was fascinating to hear him describe his practice and the problems he faced as the only physician in a small, isolated community. Doc's devotion to his patients was evident, but Becky had never understood the awesome responsibility the man carried or the loneliness he felt. Like everyone else, she had simply been grateful to have him there when so many small towns in the state didn't have a doctor at all.

The discussion went on and on until it became obvious the restaurant employees were ready to close up for the night. Even then, the group lingered in the street for fifteen minutes. Finally, Doc Miller shook hands with everyone.

"It's been a real pleasure. If any of you run across a good doctor who might be interested in relocating out here, let me know. There won't be the money you'd earn in a city, but the satisfaction is tremendous."

Then the Millers left, and the Brewsters followed suit a moment later. Becky and Pete got into the Corvette and headed back home. Still pumped up from a stimulating evening, Pete talked steadily until they passed the Cora General Store and turned off on the gravel road to the ranch.

Becky listened and nodded at the appropriate moments, happy for him, but heartbroken for herself. He must have noticed how quiet she had become, however, because he gradually slowed the car and shot her a worried glance.

"I guess all that medical talk must have been pretty boring for you," he said. "I'm sorry."

"It was fine. Your friends were very nice, and I know it was good for Doc and Marie. I'm glad you had fun."

"But you didn't enjoy yourself much."

She shrugged. "I don't need to be the center of attention all the time. Don't worry about it."

"I didn't think you did, but it wasn't fair to let the conversation get carried away like that."

"No problem."

"Then what *is* the problem, Becky? You're obviously unhappy about something."

Sighing, she crossed her arms over her breasts and looked out the side window. "I'm just tired, Pete. It's been a long day. Can we leave it at that?"

"Whatever you want," he answered, impatience creeping into his voice.

What she wanted was to go to her room, throw herself across the bed and have a good cry. Neither spoke again until Pete parked in front of the house. Becky got out without waiting for his assistance and hurried up the steps. Pete caught up with her on the porch.

"Wait a minute," he said, grabbing her arm when she reached for the doorknob.

"What?"

"I want to know what's really going on," he said quietly, as if he feared they might wake someone.

Desperate to escape before she broke down in front of him, she lied. "Nothing is going on."

"Becky, we've always been honest with each other. Come down to the foreman's house with me so we can talk."

"No. For God's sake, I have to get up in four hours. Now would you *please* let me go?"

He frowned at her for a long moment, then released her with obvious reluctance. "All right. I'll put the car away and we'll talk in the morning. Good night."

Giving him a terse nod, she went inside, slipped off her sandals and ran up the stairs to her room. She leaned back against the closed door, waiting for the tears to come. Unfortunately they wouldn't. Her eyes burned. Her chest and throat ached, but the pain went too deep for the relief a good crying jag would bring.

She walked over to the dresser and removed her jewelry, avoiding her reflection in the mirror. Reaching behind her, she unzipped the dress, let it fall to her feet and stepped out of it. She picked it up, wanting to tear it to shreds.

Instead, she shook it out and hung it carefully at the front of her closet. She would see it every time she opened the door, and the dress would serve as a reminder of this nightmarish evening. She might as well start getting used to the idea that she wouldn't have Pete Sinclair much longer.

Chapter Fourteen

Peter studied Becky over the rim of his coffee mug the next morning at breakfast. Watching her now, one would never guess she had anything on her mind other than helping her grandmother get the breakfast dishes done and heading out for another day's work. Unfortunately, he knew better.

Last night she had been deeply distressed. He'd seen such stark anguish in her eyes when she told him to let her go, he hadn't been able to sleep at all. Dammit, where had the evening gone wrong?

He had known she was nervous about meeting Douglas and Emily, but it had been obvious that they both liked her immediately. God, he'd been proud of her. She had looked absolutely beautiful, and he had taken immense satisfaction in knowing most of the men in the restaurant envied him the right to be her escort. So what had he or anyone else done or said that had upset her? Could something have happened when she'd gone to the ladies' room?

No, he didn't believe that was the case. She had participated in the conversation at first, but had gradually become more quiet. He should have noticed it sooner. He thumped his mug down on the table and went out to the mudroom to put on his irrigating boots. One way or another, he would find out what was going on inside that woman's head.

Peter waited until they were out walking the ditches. Becky chatted with him as though nothing had changed, but he noticed that she didn't meet his eyes when she spoke to him and she didn't mention the night before. There was definitely a barrier between them. After all they had shared over the past eight weeks, it hurt to know that she could still withdraw from him so quickly and completely.

The sun bathed them in golden heat. The endless blue sky overhead, the stately mountains on every side and the darting birds and insects made it hard to believe that anyone could possibly be unhappy on such a glorious day. Finally, Peter couldn't stand it another second.

"What happened last night, Becky?"

She glanced up from adjusting a head gate, then dropped her gaze back to her work. "Nothing happened," she said. "I told you I was tired and I was."

"You're not a very convincing liar. You were close to tears when you left me. I want you to tell me why."

Wiping her hands on the seat of her jeans, Becky straightened to her full height. "It didn't have anything to do with you or your friends, Pete. The evening brought back some painful memories for me."

That was the last thing he had expected to hear, but he couldn't doubt her sincerity when she looked him full in the face without flinching. And yet, he suspected she was still holding something back that had plenty to do with him. "Memories of what?"

"College." She shook her head and gave him a sad, crooked smile. "It was so long ago, it doesn't matter anymore. I was silly to let it get to me."

Peter dropped his shovel and crossed over to her side of the ditch. "Your feelings are never silly to me," he said, putting his hands on her shoulders. "Tell me about it."

Becky turned away and started off toward the next head gate. "Oh, you know, it was kid stuff. There was a guy I thought I was in love with, but it didn't work out."

"How did last night remind you of him?"

"The last time I saw him, we went to a nice restaurant for dinner with some of his friends and their dates."

"What was his name, Becky?"

"What difference does it make?"

"I'm just trying to help you flesh out your story."

"You still think I'm lying?"

"No, I think what little you've told me is true, but that's not all of it. Otherwise, you wouldn't have been so upset over a dinner that happened, what, ten years ago?"

She stopped walking. Her chin came up. Her eyes flashed hot enough to evaporate the water in the ditch.

"Thirteen years, seven months and about ten days. His name was Bob Hartman. And for your information, that dinner was the most humiliating experience of my life. Excuse me if I don't share the details."

"No, I won't excuse you. If I'm being punished for something another man did, I deserve to know what it was."

"Maybe you do." Becky sat on the ground and motioned for Peter to join her. "I met him at the beginning of my sophomore year. We were lab partners in a chemistry class. He was handsome and witty and charming, and I'd never met anyone like him before."

"Where was he from?" Peter asked when she looked as if she might drift off into a world of her own.

"Chicago. He was a frat rat."

"I beg your pardon?"

She chuckled. "He was a fraternity boy. Had real smooth manners, drove a hot car. You know, a big-man-on-campus kind of guy. At least *he* thought he was."

"Go on."

"Well, he started asking me out and I was flattered, so I went. I always had a good time with him, but he thought I needed a little coaching."

"What does that mean?"

"He wanted me to look and act more like the girls his fraternity brothers dated. He'd take me shopping and tell me what to buy and what to wear. And he made an appointment for me at a beauty shop and told the gal how my hair should be cut." She picked up the end of her braid and frowned at it. "He didn't like this thing much."

"And you let him do that?"

"Sure. I was in love. I wanted to please him and make him proud of me. By the time I started sleeping with him, I was convinced he was gonna ask me to marry him any day. In fact, when he told me to get all gussied up for a big date just before Christmas vacation, I thought he would do it that night."

"What happened?"

"Well, we got to this restaurant, and I found out six of his fraternity brothers and their dates were coming, too, so I figured out I wasn't gonna get a ring that night. That was okay, 'cause there was still a week before finals were over. When we were done eating, good old Bob asked me to stand up and turn around so everyone could get a good look at me."

Her chin quivered slightly and she gulped. Peter could hardly bear to witness her pain, but he forced himself to remain silent until she could go on.

"We'd all had plenty to drink and I thought it was just some kind of a joke or something, and it was. But it was on dumb old Becky Dawson. The other guys started clapping and passing Bob money. See, they'd had a bet goin' that he couldn't turn me into a lady before the semester got over, and I'd just won it for him. They had a real good laugh over how hard he'd had to work to clean up the cowgirl."

"My God," Peter murmured, "what did you do?"

A gleam of satisfaction came into her eyes and a wry smile tilted the corners of her mouth. "As I recall, I dumped his drink over his head, kicked him where I figured it would do him the most good and gave him a black eye before I walked out. I heard he had to pay all the money back."

Peter laughed at that. "Good for you." He thought back over the previous evening, trying to see what could have reminded her of Bob Hartman's vicious prank. It didn't take long to understand.

"This is about me buying you the dress, isn't it?"

Becky shrugged. "It was a little close for comfort."

"I didn't mean it that way, Becky," he protested.

"Hey, it doesn't matter. I don't blame you for not wanting to be embarrassed in front of your friends."

"Embarrassed! Is that what you think?"

She shrugged again, then yanked a weed out of the ditch bank and shredded it with her fingernails. Peter took off his hat and slammed it onto the grass before running one hand through his hair.

"Becky, don't be an idiot." He sighed and shook his head. "You asked me if Emily would wear a dress, and I thought buying you one would be a nice present. You've done so many things for me this summer, it seemed like an opportunity to repay you in a very small way. But I was *not* afraid you'd embarrass me."

"Aw, c'mon, Doc, get real. You didn't just buy me a dress. You got everything I needed from the skin out and added perfume on top of it. We drove your fancy car instead of a pickup. And you knew your friends sure as hell wouldn't wear jeans, which is all you've ever seen me in. I'm not mad at you for that. Believe me, I understand. You have a position to uphold."

Peter stared at her in dismay, then let loose a string of profanity he'd learned while patching up drug gang members at a free clinic. Becky merely raised an eyebrow at him.

"You oughtta do that for Hank sometime, Pete. He'd be downright impressed."

"Dammit, Becky, I'm not Bob Hartman." He grabbed her by the arms and hauled her up against his chest, his voice gaining volume with every word. "I don't care about impressing Hank. And I don't care about impressing Douglas or Emily or anyone else. I love you, you crazy woman. I love you whether you wear jeans or lace or nothing at all. Is that clear?"

Her eyes big as doughnuts, Becky nodded.

"Do you believe me now?" he shouted, giving her a quick shake.

Her eyes started to sparkle. She bit her lip as if trying to hold in a laugh. She nodded again.

He inhaled a deep breath, then looked at the way her shoulders were all scrunched up around her neck and loosened his hold on her. Ashamed of how rough he'd been, he set her gently back on the ground. "Did you mean that?"

She nodded for the third time, but a chuckle escaped, followed by great whoops of laughter. "God, I love it when you go all masterful, Sinclair," she said, wiping at her eyes. "And you're sooooo romantic."

Peter grinned. He'd always taken his job seriously, perhaps too seriously, although he doubted his patients would see it that way. When his job had become his whole life, he'd started taking himself too seriously, as well. One of the things he loved most about Becky was her ability to make him take a step back, look at himself and, more often than not, have a good laugh.

"I suppose you'll enjoy telling the children about this," he said dryly.

"What children?"

"Our children."

Becky stared at him for a moment before looking off toward the mountains. "What are you tryin' to say, Pete?"

"I want you to marry me."

She didn't look at him, didn't say anything for the longest time. Peter wanted to grab her and shake her again, make her say something, anything, as long as it was yes. But

he held on to his patience, even though he could see a refusal forming on her pursed lips as her mind worked out
what would, no doubt, be a list of reasons five miles long.

When she finally turned her head toward him again, his
muscles tightened, as if he were bracing for a physical blow.

"I've thought about that," she admitted, "but after last
night, I didn't think it would work."

"Because of the dress?"

"No." She smiled slightly and yanked out another weed.
"It was more a matter of seeing a whole new side of you.
The doctor side. That's what you were meant to be, ya
know."

"I guess I've finally had enough time and distance to realize that," he conceded. "But I've learned my lesson,
Becky. I won't let my career eat up my personal life again.
In fact, I think a wife and family are what I need to help me
keep my life in balance."

"You're probably right, but I can't be that wife."

"Why not? Don't you love me?"

She pulled her knees up to her chest and clasped her hands
around them, her cheeks turning pink. "You know I do."

"That's all that matters." He reached for her hands, but
she pulled them away and buried them in her lap.

"No, it's not. You're not just any doctor. You're an oncologist. Your work's in a big hospital in a big city. I'd go
nuts in a place like that."

"Becky, that's ridiculous."

"Think about it, will ya?" she insisted. "I don't have any
job skills that would do any good there—"

"How do you know you couldn't be happy in a city if
you've never lived in one? Washington is a fascinating place.
I'd love to show it to you."

"Shoot, Pete," she answered with a laugh, "Laramie was
too big for me. I couldn't wait to get home."

"That was a long time ago, and you didn't have me. If
you don't like it, we could always live outside the city and I
could commute. There are lots of beautiful farms in Mary-

land and Virginia. We'll buy one and you can raise all the horses you want."

"Just like that?"

"Why not? In case you didn't know it, thanks to Grandfather Sinclair, I've got money I don't know what to do with. You can have anything you want."

"Right," she said, completely unimpressed by his wealth as he'd known she would be. That was another thing he loved about Becky Dawson.

"You can buy me mountains and prairies and clean rivers and not seeing another soul for miles and miles?"

"I can buy you a view of the Appalachians. They're not as high or as rugged, but they're beautiful. I can't give you prairies, but I can give you green, rolling hills and trees that change colors in the fall. As for rivers, not all of them are polluted, you know. Unfortunately, I can't get rid of all the people for you."

"Aw, Pete, it's not really the land." She hesitated, twining the weed around and around her fingers until it fell apart. "It's me. I don't have the kind of education you and your friends have. I just wouldn't . . . fit in."

"So, you can finish your education. You can go to Georgetown or American University. There are hundreds of colleges. Take your pick. I'll hire a housekeeper so you can study."

Laughing, Becky threw the pieces of weed at him. "Lord, you don't know when to give up, do ya?"

Smiling wickedly, Peter tipped her backwards, pressing her shoulders onto the ground and looming over her. "Not when it's something as important to me as you are. Now, do I have to kiss you into submission, or what?"

"You can always try," she retorted, sliding her hands up his chest and around the back of his neck.

And, God, did he ever enjoy trying. Her lips were soft and warm and tasted of coffee. Her breasts cushioned his chest. She smelled of sunshine and crushed grass and Ivory soap. And her soft sighs of pleasure caressed his nerve endings as her strong, wonderful hands caressed his back and shoulders.

She loved him. He could feel it in every touch of her lips and tongue, in the softening of her body as it welcomed his weight and strained toward his hands, in the sweet glow of desire for him in her eyes. Something this special, this wonderful between two people could not be denied for long. Surely she would see that.

He would make her see that. But he had to do it gently, a step at a time. If he pushed her too hard, she would balk and dig in her heels. So he would go slowly in trying to convince her, as slowly as he did when he made love to her and wanted to drive her out of her mind with passion. There was plenty of time. Always plenty of time for Becky.

"How am I doing so far?" he asked, kissing down the side of her neck.

She sighed and arched for him, giving him easier access. "Not bad. Not bad at all."

Then she pushed against his chest. He raised up on one elbow and studied her laughing eyes. "That's good, because we have to stop. Unless, of course, you'd care to get started on the children."

She dug her fingers into his pectoral muscles, as if that idea might be tempting. "I don't think we're quite ready for that yet, Pete. Let me up."

He sat up reluctantly, offering a hand to pull her upright beside him. "How about a compromise?"

"I'm listening."

"Why don't you come to Washington with me at the end of the summer? You can meet my friends and see what it's like for yourself before you decide anything."

"I doubt that'll change my mind."

"Will you at least think about it? Please?"

"All right. I'll let you know after Hank's wedding in August." She held her hand out to him. "Deal?"

"Deal."

Chapter Fifteen

Becky floated along through the rest of the day, feeling as if she'd swallowed a giant bubble of sunshine. Pete loved her. He really, honest-to-God loved her. Every time she thought about the way he'd hollered that little tidbit of news at her, she wanted to laugh. And he wanted to marry her, and have children....

Who'd have thought the man would ask her to marry him beside an irrigation ditch? Lord, she loved him for that. Some women wanted candlelight and champagne, but the utter sincerity in Pete's eyes and voice had made his proposal the most romantic thing that had ever happened to her.

And the dear, sweet, silly man, dangling his money and a horse farm and an education, not to mention a housekeeper, as bait like that. As if he wasn't enough to make her love him all by himself. Men were so wonderfully dumb sometimes. It tickled her no end that Pete wasn't any different.

She drove the pickup back to the house, sneaking glances at him, smiling to herself all the way down to her heels. She didn't know if she could marry him or not, though she wanted to say yes more than she'd ever wanted anything in her life. But for now, it was enough that he'd asked.

If only she wouldn't have to leave the Circle D and her family to have him.... But, by golly, she *would* visit Washington with him at the end of the summer. He'd made it sound pretty darn nice, and it would be worth almost any sacrifice to be able to spend the rest of her life with him.

Realizing most women would hardly think what he'd offered her was much of a sacrifice, Becky chuckled and reached for his hand. He smiled at her and laced their fingers together. They stopped at the horse pasture to visit Dandy and Misty, enjoying the colt's antics for a moment.

Then the back door of the house slammed and Tina rushed down the steps, turning her head this way and that, as if she were looking for someone. When she saw Becky and Pete, she ran toward them, her little legs pumping fast, her arms waving frantically.

"Aunt Becky, come quick!" she shouted. "Uncle Sam needs you on the phone. Hurry!"

Becky raced for the house with Pete right behind her. A sick feeling of fear rose from her stomach to her throat, leaving the taste of bile in her mouth. Oh, Lord, what had happened now? She grabbed the receiver from Grandma D, noting a stricken expression in the old lady's eyes.

"What is it, Sam?"

"We've got cows droppin' like flies. I don't know what the hell's wrong with 'em. Call the vet and get him up here fast. Meet him at the ranger station and guide him in to the watering hole by the giant rock. That's where we'll be."

"Will do."

"See if you can get some men from the Bar Z to stay with Grandma and Tina. I don't like the looks of this at all. Oh, and ya better bring some lanterns and jackets and some food. We might be workin' up here after dark."

''We'll be there as soon as we can.''

Luckily, Becky reached the vet on the first try. Grandma D and Tina made sandwiches and packed a cooler. The neighbors arrived while Becky and Pete were still loading the lanterns and coats into the back of the pickup. As an extra precaution, Becky added six rifles and plenty of ammunition.

Doc Shumaker arrived at the ranger station five minutes after Becky and Pete, and followed them into the mountains at breakneck speed.

Becky stared in horror at the cows and calves already on the ground. Good Lord, there must be twenty-five or thirty, and three more staggered and keeled over in the next ten minutes. Doc Shumaker examined the last ones to fall, then talked to Sam and Hank, asking for more information about when the animals had started showing symptoms.

''I think they've been poisoned,'' he said. ''I'll have to autopsy one of them and run some tests, but you'd better keep the rest of them away from the water and the salt and mineral blocks until we know for sure.''

Sam uttered a vicious curse and started barking orders to the other men. The calves whose mothers had died bawled piteously, shattering the quiet of the forest. Becky and Pete unloaded the supplies they had brought and went back to the ranch for more equipment.

When they returned, ten more cows, four calves and two bulls were down. One of the hands found tainted grain scattered at another watering hole, but the cows in that section hadn't discovered it yet. Becky and Pete spent the night brewing coffee, passing out sleeping bags and feeding the orphaned calves who had managed to survive.

The somber faces around the campfire changed throughout the night as the men took turns standing watch over different parts of the herd. No one talked much. After all, what was there to say? They all suffered with each dying animal, but there was nothing anyone could do to help the poor creatures. A rancher hated nothing more than waste, and this was waste on a scale none of them could have imagined.

By morning, a hundred and ten of the Circle D's pure-bred Angus stock, including five of the best bulls, had perished. The Dawsons' hopes of a profitable year had perished with them. Exhausted and sick at heart, Becky, Pete and Hank went back to the ranch, leaving Sam in charge of the cattle.

Grandma D met them at the back door, her face creased with worry. "Is everything all right?" she asked.

Hank gave her a quick hug. "Yeah, Grandma. It was a rotten night, but everybody's safe. For now, anyway."

"Get washed up, then," she said, "and I'll put breakfast on the table."

"I'm not hungry," Becky grumbled, rubbing her eyes with her fingers. "I just want a shower and then we'll head back out and relieve Sam."

"Nonsense. You need a hot meal and I need to know—" Grandma D gulped "—just how bad things are. Janice took Tina over to the Carters to play with Tiffany, but they'll be home in about an hour. I don't want that child to hear about any of this if we can prevent it. Now get going."

Fifteen minutes later, they all gathered around the kitchen table over French toast and scrambled eggs. Hank filled Grandma D in on what had happened during the night. The old lady sighed and shook her head.

"Dear God, those poor critters. What kind of a monster would do a thing like that?"

"I don't know, Grandma," Becky answered, "but we can thank our lucky stars that Sam's such a good manager. We could be in real trouble if the ranch were mortgaged."

"Yeah, we'll be all right for a while," Hank agreed. "But we can't afford many more hits like this one."

The front doorbell rang at that moment. The Dawsons exchanged puzzled looks, since their friends and everyone else who knew them always knocked on the back door. Becky shoved back her chair and went to answer it.

A stocky, gray-haired man wearing a Western-cut, dark blue suit stood on the stoop, a Stetson held in one hand. Becky cursed under her breath when she recognized Marvin Castle and called for Hank before opening the door.

"Good morning, Miss Dawson," Castle said through the screen door. "Beautiful day, isn't it?"

"I hadn't noticed," Becky replied. "Things are a little hectic around here, Mr. Castle. I'd appreciate it if you'd just state your business."

Hank, Grandma D and Pete entered the living room. Grandma D gasped softly when she recognized the man talking to Becky. Pursing her lips, she marched forward and nudged her granddaughter aside. She gave Becky a now-mind-your-manners-young-lady look, then opened the screen door.

"Come on in, Mr. Castle. Would you like a cup of coffee?"

Smiling, Castle stepped inside. "No, thank you, ma'am. I'd like to talk with Sam, if he's got a minute."

"He's not here," Hank said, walking forward until he stood directly in front of the older man. Hank propped his hands on his hips and tilted his jaw at an aggressive angle. "I'll be happy to pass on a message."

Castle frowned, as if confused by Hank's attitude. "Is something wrong?"

"As if you didn't know," Becky muttered, rolling her eyes at the ceiling.

"I beg your pardon," Castle said. "I've been out of the state for six weeks. Our home office has authorized me to increase our offer for your ranch by half a million dollars. That's all I wanted to tell Sam. Have you folks been having trouble? I couldn't help noticing your barn—"

Grandma D shot quelling looks at both of her grandchildren. "Why don't we all sit down?"

"Mr. Castle won't be staying that long, Grandma," Hank replied. "To answer your question, Castle, we've been havin' a helluva lot of trouble around here. Wouldn't you be a little hostile if somebody stole calves, sabotaged your pickup, burned down your barn and poisoned your cattle?''

"You think I had something to do with any of that?'' Castle demanded, his eyebrows raised in astonishment.

"You're the only one who seems to want the Circle D."

Castle straightened to his full height, which still left him looking a long way up at Hank. "Mr. Dawson, the Executive Cattle Company does *not* do business that way. We've made you an extremely generous offer for your property, perhaps too generous in light of what's been happening here."

"Get this through your head, pal," Hank said, repeatedly poking Castle in the chest with his index finger. "The Circle D has been in our family for damn near a century. It's not for sale and it's never gonna *be* for sale, no matter how much money you offer us."

"That's a foolish attitude, Mr. Dawson," Castle replied, stepping back out of Hank's reach while he straightened his suit coat. "The family ranch is on its way out. You'll never be able to compete with corporate agriculture. Why, I can make you people rich."

"We don't need your money to make us rich," Becky told him. "We've got everything we want right now."

"I'm sorry to hear you feel that way." Marvin Castle pushed the screen door open with one hand. "Nevertheless, our new offer stands. I suggest you talk it over among yourselves and get back to me." He stepped outside and started down the front steps.

Hank shouted from the stoop. "I'll get back to you, all right. If anything else happens to my family or our cattle, by God, I'll get back to you personally!"

The other man crammed his hat onto his head and paused beside his pickup. "Don't threaten me, Mr. Dawson. You'll regret it." Then he climbed into his truck and drove away.

"That mealymouthed little son of a bitch," Hank grumbled as he walked back inside. "I'd like to break him in half."

"What the hell got into you two?" Grandma D demanded, her glare jumping from Hank to Becky and back to Hank. "You don't know that Marvin Castle is responsible for anything."

"Grandma, he just upped an already ridiculous offer by half a million dollars," Becky protested.

"Yeah, and ain't it convenient that he made it right after a hundred of our cows croaked? I'd say that's pretty damn suspicious," Hank agreed.

"You still don't have any proof," Grandma D insisted. "Dammit, Hank, you shouldn't have lost your temper."

"May I say something?" Pete asked. When the others nodded, he continued. "If Castle *is* involved, you've just told him that you suspect him. He's going to be more cautious. Since he knows he can't buy you out or scare you off, he's going to be more dangerous, too."

Becky snorted. "What more can he do to us, Pete?"

"He could kill one of you. Maybe all of you."

"Aw, hell, that little runt wouldn't do that," Hank muttered.

"I wouldn't be too sure of that," Pete replied. "I hope you'll all be extremely careful."

"Lord, I do, too," Grandma D said, shaking her head.

Hank frowned thoughtfully at that. "Well, I'm gonna go call Andy Johnson. He was supposed to check into Castle's background. It's about damn time we found out if he's learned anything. If he hasn't, I'm gonna give him a nudge."

During the first week of August, Hank and Sam guarded what was left of the herd. Becky and Pete started cutting the hay and baling it into small square bales. Then the bales had to be stacked and all of the stack yards fenced to keep the cattle and the moose out until the hay was needed during the winter. The hours were long, the work was exhausting and the threat of another disaster made everyone jumpy.

Despite all of that, Becky had never been happier. She whipped through each day, enjoying every moment out in the fields with Pete, talking and laughing while they worked. It was as if knowing he loved her had given her an endless supply of energy to draw upon.

Whenever they could, they sneaked off to the foreman's house to make love. They learned each other's bodies as well as each other's hearts and minds, and the bond between them grew stronger with each encounter. They avoided the topic of marriage, but it was always present between them.

For Becky, that was the only dark spot in an otherwise sunny sky. As the date for Hank and Janice's wedding approached, so did her need to make a decision about going to Washington with Pete. God, she wanted to go with him.

But how in God's name could she leave the Circle D, when someone was out to get her family? Pete wouldn't understand; she knew he wouldn't. He coaxed her almost daily to make everyone become more independent, but it wasn't as easy as he believed it should be.

To her way of thinking, everyone was upset enough. The middle of a crisis was not the time to try to change long-standing relationships. It was the only bone of contention between them, but it was a frustrating one.

Still, she was happy, and she wanted everyone around her to be happy, too. As the days passed, Becky began to notice that Janice didn't look well. Of course, everyone was uptight these days, and with the wedding only ten days away, she had every right to be a little nervous.

Unfortunately, Becky feared something more than bridal nerves was eating at her future sister-in-law. Janice had lost so much weight that her clothes hung on her already slender frame, she rarely talked at the supper table anymore and there were shadows under her eyes that even careful makeup didn't hide completely. Pete would probably get ticked off at her, but Becky just couldn't sit back and watch Jan's misery without offering to help.

At eleven-thirty one morning Becky and Pete ran out of baling twine and had to go back to the house for more. They ate dinner with Grandma D, Janice and Tina. When the meal was over, Becky sent Pete out to load the pickup, then asked Janice if they could talk for a moment in Sam's den.

Janice agreed readily and led the way. She perched on one corner of Sam's desk. "What's up?"

"I wanted to ask you the same thing," Becky replied, sinking into the overstuffed chair in front of the desk.

"What do you mean?" Janice asked.

"You're lookin' a little strung out lately, Jan. I just wondered if there's anything you need to talk about. Are you gettin' nervous about the wedding?"

Janice laughed, but it was a bitter sound rather than a happy one. "You mean if there *is* a wedding."

"Have you and Hank been fighting?"

"No, it's nothing like that. But with everything that's happened lately…" She shrugged. "Hank doesn't even want to talk about the wedding now. If anything else goes wrong, I'm afraid we'll have to postpone it."

"Aw, he's just upset. It won't come to that," Becky assured her.

Janice's eyes misted with tears. "I hope not. I've got a whole list of things I need to do, but I just can't seem to get anything done. I wish I was organized like you."

"I'll be glad to help, Jan."

"Oh, Becky, you're too busy. I'm going into town this afternoon to get my hair cut and visit with Cindy. Since she's my matron of honor, maybe she'll do some of this stuff for me."

Becky rose to her feet, crossed the room and put one hand on Janice's shoulder. "Well, there must be something I can do. Where's your list?"

"Upstairs on my dresser."

"Tell ya what. When Pete and I come in this afternoon, I'll take a look at your list and we'll talk about it after supper. How does that sound?"

Janice covered Becky's hand with her own and gave her a watery smile. "I'd appreciate that. Thanks."

Becky chuckled. "Hey, I've waited a long time to get one of my brothers married off. I don't want you to have the chance to change your mind about marryin' Hank."

Giving Jan's shoulder a final pat, Becky headed out the door. She found Pete waiting impatiently in the driver's seat of the pickup.

"What took you so long?" he asked.

Becky quickly related her conversation with Janice, and to her surprise, Pete agreed with what she had done. She shot him a doubtful look.

"I thought you'd tell me to mind my own business."

"I'm not completely heartless, Becky," he replied. "I've noticed that she's been awfully down lately, too. It must be hard for her to cope with all of this when she's trying to plan her wedding. It should be a happy time for her. And for Hank. I'll come look at the list with you. Maybe there's something I can do to help, too."

"Hey, you're my kinda guy, Sinclair."

"I've been trying to tell you that all along, Dawson. Besides, I'm hoping that if you help Janice plan her wedding, you'll start thinking about planning your own."

"That's pretty devious. I thought we weren't gonna talk about that again until after Hank's wedding."

He grinned and shook his head at her. "That was a simple, casual remark. No need to get upset, dear."

"Oh, yeah?" Becky drawled, arching an eyebrow at him. "Well, watch those casual remarks, honey, or I won't meet you at the foreman's house tonight."

"Cruel woman. Cruel, cruel woman."

"You want to drive the baler or the stacker this time?"

"The stacker. It's more fun."

"All right, but try not to run over any more bales."

"Nag, nag, nag."

Dark clouds began to gather over the tops of the mountains later in the afternoon, but they were too busy working to pay much attention. When Becky finally noticed the drop in temperature and looked up, a row of thunderheads had swept halfway down the valley.

"Damn and blast," she grumbled, signaling Pete to stop so she could point them out to him. "C'mon, we've gotta get this field finished before that rain hits, or we'll have to wait until it dries out."

Working flat out, they made it, but just barely. They secured the machinery for the night, then ran for the pickup, laughing and trying to dodge the fat raindrops pelting down on them. Sam's pickup pulled into the driveway at the same time Becky and Pete reached the house.

Sam and Hank climbed out, looking tired and dirty. Becky greeted them both with a hug.

"What are you guys doing here?" she asked.

"Couldn't stand one more night on that damn mountain," Sam admitted with a grin. "I'm ready for a hot shower, a hot meal and a warm bed."

"Me, too," Hank said, tugging off his boots in the mudroom. "If somebody wants to mess with our cows in a thunderstorm, let 'em try. Oh, Lord, Sam, it smells like Grandma made a pot of stew. Where's Jan? I haven't seen or kissed that woman in days."

"She went into town this afternoon." Becky leaned close to him and took an exaggerated whiff of his shirt. "Whooee! You'd better get that shower before ya try to kiss anybody."

Hank took a swat at her rear end, but Becky dodged away and ran into the kitchen, laughing when she heard him mutter, "Damn, smart-mouthed brat."

"Did I hear the boys come in?" Grandma D asked, looking up from the rhubarb pie she was lifting out of the oven.

"Yeah, they're in for the night. Looks like we'll all be here for supper for a change," Becky answered.

"Let's go look at Jan's list and let them shower first, Becky," Peter suggested, taking her by the arm.

Becky allowed him to hustle her into the living room and up the stairs before digging in her heels. "What's the rush, Sinclair?"

He backed her up against the wall in the hallway next to Jan's bedroom door. "It seems like I haven't kissed my woman in days, either," he said in a husky voice.

"Poor baby. We'd better take care of that."

She slid her hands up the front of his shirt and linked them behind his neck. His lips were warm and hungry, and she reveled in the way he wrapped his strong arms around her waist, crushing her to him. He smelled of sun and rain, hay and sweat, all the ways a man should smell.

Fortunately, or unfortunately, depending on how one chose to look at it, the door beside them opened with a squeak before they could get carried away. Two little eyes peeked out through the crack, and a soft giggle made Pete raise his head. He heaved a martyred sigh, then inclined his head toward Janice's room.

"We've got company," he whispered.

"So I noticed," Becky whispered back.

Her eyes dancing with laughter, she motioned for him to step out of the way and sneaked up to the door. Light footsteps pattered away inside. Becky grabbed the doorknob, pushed it hard and charged into the room.

"Is there a ghost in here?" she demanded.

Another giggle came from the far side of the bed, which, like the chair and most of the floor, was covered with wadded-up clothes. Uh-oh. Janice was usually the tidiest person in the house. Now her cosmetics and the contents of her jewelry box were spread out over the dressing table in a jumbled mess. Somebody had had a wonderful time playing dress-up in here. Becky didn't need three guesses to figure out who. Janice was not going to be thrilled with the kid.

Pete followed close on Becky's heels. She turned to him, holding one finger to her lips and pointing to the near side of the bed. He nodded and crouched down, ready to catch the little culprit if she got away from Becky.

The instant Becky lunged for the other side, a scrabbling noise erupted as Tina dived under the box springs. Becky latched on to an ankle, however, and pulled the little girl out.

"Oh, my," Becky murmured, then bit her lower lip to hold in a startled laugh.

Tina wore three strands of beads around her neck and had enough lipstick, eye shadow and blush smeared across her face to qualify for either a clown or a junior hooker-in-training. A pair of ratty sneakers and jeans frayed at the cuffs stuck out from under the hem of Janice's favorite pink blouse. Both wrists jangled with bracelets.

"Don't I look pretty, Aunt Becky?" the little stinker asked, batting her eyelashes fast enough to create a breeze.

Pete snorted, then covered his mouth with one hand. Becky sent him a reproving look and turned back to her niece.

"Well, you sure do look different," Becky replied, striving for a firm tone. "Did Janice give you permission to play in her room?"

The little girl started to nod, but changed her mind at the last second and shook her head instead. Becky's stern expression might have had something to do with her decision. Tina lowered her gaze and fiddled with a bracelet.

Becky placed two fingers under the child's chin and forced her to meet her eyes. "Would you like it if Janice went into your room and messed it all up like this?"

"No," Tina answered, her bottom lip poking out.

"Aw, honey, you've gotta try harder to get along with her for your own sake as well as your daddy's. She's gonna be your new mama pretty soon."

"I don't want her to be my mama," Tina complained. "She never plays with me or nothin', an' she's always tellin' me to be quiet. I like you better, Aunt Becky. Why don't *you* marry daddy instead o' her?"

"You know I can't do that, Tina. Sisters and brothers don't marry each other. But I'll always be your aunt and I'll always love you."

"It's not the same. I don't want things to change."

Tina's chin quivered and her eyes welled up with tears. Becky pulled the child into her arms and stroked her soft, shiny hair.

"I know, sweetie. But life changes sometimes, whether we want it to or not, and we all have to learn how to adjust and move on. Your daddy needs a wife and he loves Jan. He'd be awfully sad without her. You don't want that, do you?"

"I dunno." The little girl pulled out of Becky's embrace, wiped her nose with the back of one hand and looked around the room. "She's gonna be awful mad at me."

"You're going to have to apologize to her, but I don't think she'll be too mad if we get this mess cleaned up before she comes back from town. Whaddaya say?"

"I'll help," Tina answered eagerly, already unbuttoning the blouse.

Becky accepted the blouse, then turned the kid around and nudged her toward the bathroom. "Darn right, you will. But first, you need to wash all that evidence off your face."

Tina scampered out of the room without a backward glance. Pete picked up hangers while Becky sorted and straightened, and they both chuckled as soon as the child was out of earshot.

"Honestly, do you believe that kid?" Becky asked. "What in the world will she think of next?"

"I wouldn't dare guess. How'd you get to be so good with kids, anyway?"

"I don't know. I just treat her like a regular person." Becky reached across the bed for a silky navy blue blouse, shook it out, then paused when she noticed one of the small, silver buttons was missing. "Uh-oh. I wonder if Tina did this or... wait a minute."

Pete came over to see what she was holding. "What is it? You want me to look for the button?"

"No," Becky said thoughtfully, "I know where it is. See the little anchors? I found one just like it up at the cabin. It's strange...."

"So, she lost a button. What's strange about that?"

"I don't think Jan's ever been to the cabin. At least not with Hank. He doesn't like to fish, so he rarely goes up there." She hesitated, frowning and unconsciously wadding the blouse up in her hands. "And there's something else."

"What? C'mon, Dawson, you're driving me crazy."

"I thought the button I found might belong to one of the women who cleaned the cabin for us. I saved it because it's not an easy one to match. But when I showed it to Jan and asked her if she knew who might have lost it, she said she'd never seen any like it before."

"She probably just didn't remember seeing them before."

Becky raised a skeptical eyebrow at that. "You or me, maybe. But Jan, the clotheshorse? I've seen her shop for hours and reject a blouse or a dress because the buttons didn't suit her. Something's not adding up here, Pete."

"You don't think Jan is involved with—"

"Dammit, I don't know." Becky wrapped her arms around her waist, as if warding off a sudden chill. "I hope to hell she's not. I can't imagine why she would be. But somebody's been giving information to whoever's been doing all these things...."

Pete put his arm around her shoulders and gave her a comforting hug. "It's probably nothing, honey, but I think we'd better go find Sam."

Chapter Sixteen

Carrying Janice's blouse, Becky stopped at her own room to retrieve the button she'd found at the cabin, then followed Pete downstairs. Her conviction that Janice was involved in the trouble at the ranch grew stronger with every step, as other memories flitted through her mind—Janice talking on the phone in her room, at the dinner table urging them to sell the Circle D, her continuing resentment over the loss of her parents' ranch and the meager price they had received for it.

Becky hadn't been concerned about any of those incidents at the time they had occurred. But looking back on them now, those incidents formed an undeniably suspicious pattern. She hoped like hell that she was wrong, but an awful feeling deep in her gut wouldn't let her believe it.

They found Grandma D in the kitchen, turning down the heat under the stew. She smiled when she saw them enter the room, but her eyes held more than a trace of anxiety.

"What's the matter, Grandma?" Becky asked.

"Sam got a call from Andy Johnson while he was in the shower. I told him Sam would have to call him back, but Andy said to get Sam right away. They're still talkin'. You know, Andy's not one for wastin' time on the phone."

"Is Sam in the den?"

"Yeah."

"Well, hold supper for a while if you can, Grandma. Peter and I have to talk to Sam, too."

"Janice isn't home yet, anyway. The thunder and lightning's let up, but would you look at that rain come down out there?" The old lady wrung her hands. "I'm scared, Becky. I just can't shake this notion that somethin' awful's about to happen."

Becky hugged her grandmother. "Worryin' won't help anything, Grandma."

"Yeah, well, knowin' that and livin' it are two different things."

Taking Pete's hand, Becky led the way to the den and quietly opened the door. Sam looked up and waved them inside, the receiver still clamped to his ear.

"Yeah, Andy, I understand. We'll do anything we can to help. Let me know if you hear anything else."

He hung up the phone, shook his head and wiped one hand down over his face. "We've got big trouble on our hands. Get Hank and Grandma D in here. And, Pete? Would you mind lookin' after Tina? Becky can tell you all about it later, but I don't think Tina should hear this."

"No problem. I'll tell Grandma D," Pete said, and left the room.

Her insides frozen with fear, Becky went to find Hank. Since their father had died, Sam had been their rock, the strong, quiet leader who willingly shouldered the responsibility for the ranch. He rarely showed any doubt or worry, no matter how bad things were, and he was more inclined to understatement than anyone else she knew. If he said they had big trouble, they had *big* trouble.

When they were all gathered in the den and settled in chairs, Sam got right down to business, his expression grim.

"Andy couldn't find out anything about Marvin Castle, but he did find out the ECC is a subsidiary of another company based in Las Vegas. He asked a friend of his at the FBI to check into it, and the guy just told Andy that this bunch has some definite ties to organized crime."

"You've gotta be kiddin'," Hank said.

"I wish to hell I was," Sam muttered. "One of their sidelines is drug running. Andy thinks they're using the ECC as a place to store the stuff before they ship it north. The Drug Enforcement Agency's already lookin' into it."

"They've got five thousand acres," Becky protested. "That oughtta be plenty of space to do whatever they want. Why would they want the Circle D?"

"I don't think it's the ranch they're after, as much as they don't want any close neighbors," Sam explained. "Maybe they're afraid we might see something suspicious and report it. I don't know. Whatever their reason is, these guys don't play games. What worries me is that we still don't have any idea how they've known when and where to hit us."

"Oh, dear God," Becky murmured, her gaze shooting to Hank. "I think I do."

Hank scowled at her. "What are you lookin' at me like that for?"

"I think..." Becky gulped, then forced herself to say the words that could break her brother's heart, "I think it's Jan."

"Have you gone loco?" Hank shouted, coming to his feet. "She wouldn't do a thing like that!"

"Hold on there a minute, Hank," Sam demanded.

Haltingly, Becky told them about the button, the blouse and the other incidents that were troubling her.

"That's pretty damn flimsy evidence, Becky," Hank said, pacing over to the window when she'd finished.

"I know. But did you ever take her to the cabin?"

"No. But she knows where it is and the key's right there on the pegboard in the kitchen with the rest of 'em. Maybe she just went up there for some peace and quiet. God knows she hasn't had much of that around here."

"But why would she lie to me about that button, Hank?" Becky insisted. "That's what doesn't make any sense. Why wouldn't she just say she'd been up there?"

"It would be a handy, private place to meet somebody from the ECC," Grandma D said quietly. "And you can see a lot of the ranch from up there."

"Jan just pulled in," Hank announced, straightening away from the window. "So why don't we ask her instead of talkin' about her behind her back?"

"Fine. Bring her in," Sam replied.

"Hank," Becky said, grabbing his hand as he walked past her. "I'm sorry."

He jerked out of her grasp and stomped out the door.

Becky's eyes misted with tears. "Oh, hell," she whispered. "What have I done?"

"You've done the right thing, that's what," Sam told her. "I think you've made a damn good case. If Janice *is* involved with one of those guys, she's in more danger than the rest of us, because she can identify him."

Grandma D came over and sat on the arm of Becky's chair. "Sam's right. Don't go blamin' yourself for speakin' up."

Then Janice preceded Hank into the room. If her hair had been cut that afternoon, Becky couldn't see it.

"Sit down, honey," Hank said, indicating the chair Grandma D had vacated.

"What's going on?" Janice asked, smiling hesitantly.

Sam briefly repeated what the sheriff had told him about the ECC. She paled visibly at the news that the ECC had connections to organized crime. She turned absolutely chalk white when Sam extended his palm holding the button Becky had found at the cabin.

"Do you know anything about this button, Jan?"

Janice shook her head vigorously. "No. I already told Becky. I've never seen it before." Her eyes darted back and forth, never quite meeting anyone else's.

Sam laid the navy blouse across the top of his desk. "Then why does it match the ones on this blouse Becky and Pete found in your room?"

"Wh-what were you doing in my room?" Janice demanded, looking to Hank. "Can't I have any privacy here at all?"

Hank simply stared at her, his eyes filled with sadness and resignation. "What were you doin' at the cabin? Meetin' Marvin Castle?"

"What makes you think that?" she asked, her spine stiffening.

"Because I don't think you'd lie to me otherwise." He cupped the side of her face with his hand, forcing her to look at him. "We're all in danger, and we need your help. Now tell me the truth, Jan. Have you been helping Castle?"

Twin rows of tears leaking down her cheeks, she nodded, then closed her eyes. Hank inhaled a harsh breath, as if he'd been slugged in the gut. A moment later, he knelt in front of her and grabbed her shoulders.

"Why, baby? How in hell could you do that to us?"

"I . . . I only did it to help my folks. I l-lied about them, too. Dad's a lousy salesman. They're just not m-making it. They can't even afford to come to the wedding, and I couldn't buy a w-wedding dress because I had to send them my wages."

"You should have told me. I'd have been happy to buy you a dress or anything else you needed," Hank said softly.

Her chin came up and her tears dried. "No! I didn't want any more of your damn charity," she said.

"Charity! Good God, woman, you were going to be my wife!" He let go of her shoulders and stood, his chest heaving as he glared down at her.

She rose to face him. "That's right. Charity. You took me in when my folks lost their ranch, gave me a job and even decided to marry me, Hank. But you don't really love me. You never did. Didja think I didn't know that?"

"You're wrong, Jan."

"Hah! You needed a mother for Tina and I was convenient and not too ugly. I suppose you like me well enough, but you don't look at me the way Pete looks at Becky. You don't talk to me or tell me what you're feeling about things. So when I got a chance to earn some real money, I took it and helped my parents. I only did it a few times. Castle promised me nobody would get hurt."

"That's no excuse," Hank snarled. "Becky damn well *did* get hurt. And your folks would be ashamed to accept money you earned by betraying their friends."

"You don't know the first thing about my folks," Janice retorted, bitter venom dripping from every word. "You high and mighty Dawsons with all your money and the latest equipment! You don't know what it's like to watch your ranch go under. We were poor all the time and I hated it. Every blessed minute of it."

"I can't believe this is you talking, Jan," Hank muttered.

Her cheeks flushed and her eyes burned with a feverish excitement. "Well, it is! And I think you're all fools to hang on to this dumb ranch. What have you got to look forward to but work and more work? Freezing winters and lousy cattle prices? Why didn't you take the money Castle offered you and run? He's right, you know. The big corporations are gonna take over agriculture before long and all the little guys like us will be forced out."

Hank turned away as if he couldn't bear to look at her any longer. "Get Andy Johnson on the phone, Sam. Have him come get her."

"Nooo," Janice wailed. She clutched desperately at Hank's arm. "You can't call the sheriff on me, Hank. Even if you don't love me, I've loved you since I was a little girl.

We can still work it out. Just sell Castle the Circle D and everything will be okay."

He shook her off and walked to the door, then looked back over his shoulder at her. "You don't know a damn thing about love, Jan. I'm gonna saddle up Barney and go for a nice long ride. When I get back, you'd better be gone, and I don't ever want to see you again."

Janice stared at the closing door like a lost, bewildered child. When the latch clicked shut, she sank to her knees, weeping. Sam reached for the phone. Grandma D went to the stricken young woman. Becky ran after Hank, her throat clogged with unshed tears of her own.

Pete called to her as she raced through the kitchen and out into the pouring rain, but she couldn't stop and tell him what had happened. She caught up with her brother at the new tack shed, and found him calmly gathering up a bridle, a saddle blanket and a saddle. She was glad to see he'd taken the time to put on his hat and a rain slicker.

"Hank, don't leave," she begged.

He swung his saddle onto his shoulder and brushed right by her as if she weren't there, his expression colder and harder than the snow-capped, granite peaks of the mountains. Becky followed him to the horse pasture.

"Dammit, Hank, it's not safe for you to go off by yourself," she shouted. "The weather's rotten, and who knows what those bastards might do next?"

Ignoring her, he whistled for Barney. The buckskin gelding obediently trotted over to him. In desperation, Becky snatched the bridle from Hank's hand and shooed the horse away. Hank glared at her for a long moment, grabbed the bridle and whistled for the horse again.

Becky socked him on the jaw as hard as she could. He staggered and drew back his arm, his hand clenched into a powerful fist.

"Go ahead and hit me if it'll make you feel better," she raged at him. "I know you're hurtin' and you're not thinkin' straight, but by God, you're my brother and I love you too much to let you leave like this. We need you, Hank."

The veins in his forehead stood out in sharp relief. His fist trembled in midair then gradually dropped to his side, his broad shoulders sagging in defeat. Becky ran to him, wrapped her arms around him and rested her head on his chest. A moment later, he hesitantly returned her embrace. They rocked back and forth, sharing what comfort they could.

"I didn't want to hurt you, Hank," she said.

"It wasn't your fault, Beck." He sighed and rested his chin on top of her head. "It's better I found out before the wedding than afterward."

"I feel awful about it anyway. I still can't believe some of the things she said."

"I can't, either. I think she needs professional help. Will you ask Sam to arrange it for her?"

"I'll do it myself."

Hank pulled away. He rubbed his jaw as he looked at her, then managed a lopsided smile. "That was a pretty damn solid punch you threw. You're lucky I didn't pound the hell out of ya."

She shrugged, as if it had never occurred to her to be afraid of him. "Did I hurt you bad?"

"Nah. Just enough to knock some sense into me. I'm all right now, sis, but I still need some time alone."

"Nobody'll bother you at the foreman's house."

He shook his head and swallowed. "I don't want to be here when Andy comes for Jan. I don't think I can...you know."

"Yeah, I know. Will you at least take some food, a rifle and a bedroll?"

"All right. I'll spend the night at the old line shack Grandpa built and be back in time for breakfast."

"Okay. I'll go pack your saddlebags for you."

Becky ran back to the house. Pete had settled Tina in front of the television in the living room with a bowl of stew and a glass of milk. Becky filled him in while she made sandwiches for Hank. Then Sam walked into the kitchen.

"Where's Hank?" he asked.

"Out saddling Barney."

"Is he okay?"

Becky shrugged. "I don't know. I think so. He's gonna spend the night at Grandpa's line shack, but I don't think he should go. Will you talk to him, Sam?"

Sam thought about it for a moment, then shook his head. "I'd feel the same way."

"But, Sam—"

"Dammit, Becky, Hank can take care of himself," Sam snapped. "Now, let him be, will ya?"

Becky shut her mouth and added an apple and a brownie to Hank's supper. She doubted he'd eat any of it, but it seemed this was all she could do for him at the moment.

Sam came around the counter and patted her shoulder. "I'm sorry, sis. I'm worried about him, too. I'd better get back in there and see if I can help Grandma with Jan."

"It's all right, Sam. Go ahead."

Tears welled up in her eyes; there were too many to hold back, though she certainly tried. She lowered her head and hastily wiped them away, but a moment later a pair of strong arms wrapped around her. She turned into Pete's embrace, taking comfort from his warmth, the steady beat of his heart beneath her cheek and the familiar scent of his body.

"Cry if you need to, sweetheart," Pete said softly. "You don't have to be strong all the time."

"I c-can't. I have to take Hank's supper to him. Oh, Pete, he's so hurt. Dammit, I should have noticed there was something wrong with Jan. Maybe I could have stopped her."

Pete held her away from him, a frown wrinkling his forehead. "That's ridiculous. Hank and Grandma D spent more time with her than you did, and they didn't notice anything. Your feeling guilty won't change what happened."

Becky moved away from Pete and wrapped her arms around her waist. "Hank's my *brother*. When he hurts, I hurt with him. You just don't understand."

"I *do* understand. But you can't fix this for him, Becky. He's a grown man and he's going to have to handle it in his own way. Stop trying to rescue him."

"You're right," she said stiffly, picking up the saddlebags. "I'd better get this out to him."

She stepped out the back door. Hank had ridden Barney up from the pasture and was waiting impatiently for her. She handed him the saddlebags, and stood silently stroking the horse's neck while Hank tied them in place.

"Thanks. I'll see you in the mornin'," he said gruffly before reining Barney around and kicking him into a trot.

Though he couldn't see her, Becky nodded and raised one hand in a half-hearted wave. "Be careful," she whispered.

Hank held Barney to a trot until they were well away from the house. Then he let the buckskin have his head, and before long the gelding moved into a smooth, rocking lope. The rain dripped off the brim of Hank's hat, but he paid no attention to it. The only thing he was aware of was the question that repeated itself over and over in his mind.

Why?

Why had Jan betrayed him and the rest of his family? Why hadn't she trusted him enough to tell him about her parents? Why hadn't she believed in his love for her?

Dammit, he *had* loved her. As much as he'd ever loved any woman. Certainly more than he'd loved Tina's mother, Christine. He'd known right from the start that Christine was a party girl. She'd been attracted to him because of his prowess on the rodeo circuit, and they'd had a helluva lot of fun together.

When Christine told him she was pregnant with his baby, Hank had offered to marry her because to his way of thinking, a man accepted responsibility for his actions. He hadn't expected a great marriage, but he'd been willing to give it a shot. He'd even given up rodeo to provide a stable home for his wife and kid. Still, he hadn't been all that surprised when Christine had left him and their tiny daughter.

But, dammit, Jan was supposed to be different. She was used to living on a ranch. Hell, she'd grown up right next door. She might be a little young for him, but they'd known and respected each other for years and they both liked the same things. At least he'd thought they had.

He'd enjoyed being with her, looked forward to seeing her at the end of the day, and though it hadn't been easy, he hadn't even pushed her to sleep with him before the wedding because that was what she'd wanted. If that wasn't love, it was close enough to it for Hank Dawson.

What more had Jan wanted from him? Love poems, for God's sake? He snorted in disgust at that idea.

The ground sloped upward into a series of sage-covered hills. The line shack was only two or three miles away now. Twilight had come early because of the cloud cover. Hank reined Barney back to a walk, and settled deeper into the saddle as the gelding picked his way down the other side of the first hill, struggling for purchase on the muddy path. Suddenly Barney's head reared up and his ears rotated toward the north.

"What is it, Barn?" Hank asked, glancing around. "You hear some—"

He never got a chance to finish the question. A sharp crack sounded from some scrubby trees twenty yards away. Hank ducked instinctively. Barney lunged forward, caught his front left hoof on a rock and stumbled. Another shot rang out. The gelding jerked and started to fall.

Trying to keep his head low, Hank kicked his right foot out of the stirrup, but he wasn't fast enough. Barney crashed onto his side, trapping Hank's left leg beneath him. Hank felt the sensation of bones snapping, a feeling he'd become all too familiar with during his rodeo days, then grunted with pain as the rest of his body hit the ground.

His vision blurred. It hurt like hell to breathe, but he struggled to sit up, reaching for the rifle in the scabbard. He managed to snag it, his fingertips brushing sticky, wet blood on Barney's twitching hide.

The gelding thrashed his hooves, grinding the bones in Hank's trapped leg against each other, pushing the man deeper into the mud. Hank gritted his teeth in agony. He dropped the gun and stroked the animal's neck in a vain attempt to quiet him, and found another patch of blood high on the horse's shoulder.

Unable to withstand the pain, Hank flopped onto his back again. He heard a rustling in the trees where the shots had originated. He grabbed his rifle and cocked it, hoping the son of a bitch who had fired at him would try to come finish him off. But then he heard an engine start up—probably a motorcycle from the sound of it—and a moment later it faded into the distance.

Barney twisted his head, as if trying to see Hank. The gelding's breathing was tortured now, and he grunted with pain every few seconds. A lump formed in Hank's throat as his fingers tightened around the gun. Barney was a damn good horse who had served him well for the past five years.

Nobody would come looking for them until morning. Barney would bleed to death long before then. Hank felt woozy enough himself; he wasn't all that sure he was going to make it, either. There was nothing he could do to keep the gelding alive, but he could save him from any more suffering.

"I'm sorry, old buddy," he said, choking the words out, lovingly smoothing Barney's mane.

Then he clenched his teeth, put the rifle barrel to the back of the horse's head and pulled the trigger. By the time the echoes of the blast died away, Hank felt his grasp on consciousness slipping. When he closed his eyes, a vision of his sister's worried face wavered before him like a reflection on a rippling pond.

"You picked one helluva time to be right, Beck," he murmured, then surrendered to the rain and the darkness.

Chapter Seventeen

Becky greeted Andy Johnson at the back door, answered Tina's questions as best she could about what was going on when the sheriff took Janice back to town with him, and put the little girl to bed. She found Janice's address book listing her parent's phone number, called them, then went through the motions of having supper with Sam, Grandma D and Pete, and cleaned up the kitchen. She worked until she couldn't see straight.

Pete finally forced her to go to bed and sat with her while she dozed off, but nothing could stifle the awful feeling deep in her soul that something terrible was going to happen to Hank. She dreamed about him repeatedly throughout the night, and got up at four o'clock because she couldn't stand to lie there any longer.

The rain had stopped sometime during the night. She paced at the kitchen windows, guzzling coffee and straining for a sign of her brother as the first rays of dawn came over the mountaintops. Then she fixed a hearty breakfast of waffles, eggs and sausage for everyone, but couldn't choke down a bite herself. When he still hadn't returned by seven-thirty, she felt she had to do something or she'd go completely crazy.

Fortunately, Grandma D agreed with her, and Sam and Pete were more willing to listen than they had been the night before. They decided to trailer the horses as far as they could to save time and have a CB as close as possible.

While the men went out to saddle and load the horses, Becky packed a pair of saddlebags with a couple of blankets and every first-aid supply she could lay her hands on. After hugging her grandmother and niece goodbye, she ran out to the horse pasture.

She found Pete shoving his medical bag into another pair of saddlebags, and Sam sliding a rifle into his scabbard. Without speaking, the three of them climbed into the pickup and drove off to the west. Becky silently prayed that they would meet Hank on the trail and feel like a bunch of over-protective idiots. They had no such luck.

When the terrain became too rough for the truck and trailer, they unloaded the horses and mounted up. Becky silently cursed the soggy ground forcing them to move slowly. The animals heard Hank before Becky, Sam or Pete did. They snorted and tossed their heads, ears twitching, their pace increasing without any urging from the riders.

At last Becky heard it—Hank's voice, weak and thready, coming from over the ridge. She couldn't understand what he was saying, but at least he was alive. Sioux carried her to the top of the hill, and there Hank was on the other side, down at the bottom, lying in a puddle of murky water.

Becky gasped at the sight of him, flat on his back, his head rolling back and forth while he babbled, his left leg buried under an obviously dead horse. She heard Sam mutter, "Sweet Jesus." Then they dismounted and slid down the muddy slope, hell-bent-for-leather to get to Hank.

Sam reached him first with Becky close behind. Pete dug out his medical bag and joined them a moment later. Hank looked up at his brother and sister and gave them a woozy smile.

"'Bout damn time you guys showed up," he said, his words slurring.

"Shh, we're here now," Becky said, smoothing his hair back off his forehead with a trembling hand. His skin felt cold. So damn cold.

Pete gently pushed her aside and started examining Hank.

"What happened?" Sam asked.

"Bastard shot at me. Twice," Hank answered, grimacing when Pete probed at his ribs. "Hit poor Barney." His eyes filled with tears and his voice broke. "Hadta put 'im down."

"You didn't have any choice," Sam told him. "You rest now, Hank, and we'll get you outta here."

Pete stood and moved away, motioning for Sam and Becky to join him.

"How bad is he?" Becky asked quietly.

Pete shook his head. "I don't know yet. He's in shock, but his pulse isn't too bad and he's lucid. Those are both good signs. He's got at least two broken ribs, but I won't be able to tell how bad his leg is until we can free it."

"All right," Sam said. "Pete, you stay with Hank. Becky and I'll rope Barney's feet and use the other horses to drag him off. Then I'll ride back to the pickup and raise Grandma on the CB. She can call for a helicopter."

"It's a good plan," Pete agreed. "We may do more damage to his leg by pulling the horse off, but I don't want to wait to do anything else in case he's bleeding somewhere I can't see. The sooner we get him to a hospital, the better."

It took twenty minutes to free Hank's leg. He fainted in the middle of the process. After assuring himself that his brother was still alive, Sam rode off toward the pickup. Becky helped Pete drag Hank out of the water and cut away his jeans and boot.

When she finally saw his mangled limb, she stumbled off into the sagebrush and lost every drop of the coffee she'd been drinking since dawn. Then she went back to her brother. Pete's calm, skillful attention to Hank's injuries awed and comforted her. At last, they had done all they could to make him comfortable, and sat close together on a large rock.

"God, I'm glad you're here," she said, laying her head on Pete's shoulder. "Thank you."

He smiled at her. "You're welcome."

She indicated Hank's leg with one hand. "Do you think he'll . . . lose it? You know, from Barney layin' on it?"

Pete sighed. "I can't promise you anything, Becky. I think the mud may have saved him from having his circulation cut off completely. He's lucky none of the bones came through the skin. That'll cut down his risk of infection. Let's hope for the best."

"I wish he'd come around."

Pete wrapped his arm around her. "It'll be better if he doesn't until after we get him loaded onto the helicopter. It's going to hurt him a lot if he gets jostled."

Sam returned a moment later. Pete updated him on Hank's condition, and then the three of them sat in silent agony, sweating out the time it would take for help to arrive. Finally, a tiny speck appeared in the sky above the horizon and gradually the whomping sound of the helicopter's rotor blades grew louder and louder.

Becky jumped to her feet and waved her arms to attract the pilot's attention, then ran to make sure the horses didn't bolt when the chopper landed. Sam and Pete stayed with Hank, ready to assist the medical personnel in loading him onto the craft.

After waiting so long, Becky was stunned by how quickly the task was accomplished. It was as if Hank had been there one minute and had vanished the next. She didn't have any time to think about it, however. When the helicopter lifted off, Sam and Pete ran for the horses.

"Let's go," Sam ordered. "We've gotta get to Jackson."

Four weeks later Peter sat at the Dawsons' kitchen table, watching Becky whip up yet another treat—a chocolate milk shake this time—to tempt her brother's finicky appetite. Peter gritted his teeth and held on to his patience, but he doubted he could continue to do so much longer. He'd barely had a moment alone with Becky since Hank's injury, and it didn't look as if there would be a change in the situation any time soon.

Unfortunately, his time at the Circle D had already run out. He should have been back in Washington to resume his duties on September first. Today was the fifteenth. Eric Goldman, the hospital administrator, had phoned twice in the past week demanding a definite date for Peter's return.

While Hank had been in danger of losing his life, and later his leg, Becky had turned to Peter for comfort and support. He'd given it gladly, finding the experience of being needed by someone other than a patient a heady one. He'd felt close to her and the rest of the family, in a new, almost frighteningly wonderful way.

However, Hank had been home for two weeks now. He would need two or three more surgeries and extensive physical therapy, but his prognosis for a complete recovery was excellent. But you'd never guess that from observing Becky.

She hovered over her brother as if he might die at any moment. Of course, being human, Hank lapped up all the attention she lavished on him, and kept her running from dawn until long after dusk. As far as Becky was concerned, no request was unreasonable, and no one else could possibly care for the man as well as she could. God forbid Hank should have to wait five seconds for something.

Worse yet, in Peter's opinion, the rest of the family appeared to agree, even expect her to carry on this way indefinitely. No one seemed to notice that Becky had grown thin again. Or that she drank gallons of coffee every day in order to keep moving. Or that the circles under her eyes were starting to look like bruises. No one but him.

Peter rubbed his eyes when Becky hurried out of the kitchen, glass in hand. She was headed for the den, which had been converted into a bedroom to save Hank from climbing the stairs. Peter supposed he ought to be glad the new arrangement saved Becky innumerable steps, as well.

Yes, it was back to business as usual at the Dawson ranch, all right. With a vengeance. Besides catering to Hank's whims, Becky was also cleaning the house, doing the laundry, taking care of Tina and helping Grandma D with the cooking. She'd probably still be milking Gertie if Peter hadn't lied and insisted that he'd always wanted to learn how to milk a cow.

It was absolutely infuriating, and he was beginning to believe he was wasting his time and endangering his employment for no good reason. He didn't want to provoke Becky; she had more than enough to cope with. He didn't blame her for loving her brother, either.

But dammit, he thought, drumming his fingers on the table, what about her relationship with *him?* Did she even remember she *had* a relationship with him? Or had he simply become a hired hand who worked with Sam now, instead of her, and happened to live in the house?

Peter felt small and petty for feeling jealous of a seriously injured man, but he couldn't help it. When was the last time Becky had sat beside him and given him ten minutes of undivided attention? It seemed like forever.

And it had to stop. Now.

Peter shoved back his chair and stalked into the den. Becky sat on the side of Hank's bed, eagerly waiting for his verdict on the milk shake. Hank took his time about giving it to her, Peter noted darkly. The injured man held the first sip in his mouth and drew his eyebrows together in a thoughtful pose. He swallowed, wiped his mouth with the back of his hand and finally gave her a smile.

"It's great, sis, but do you think you could add just a little more chocolate syrup?" he asked.

"No, she couldn't." Before Becky could draw a breath, Peter stormed into the room.

She reached for the milk shake automatically. "It's no trouble, Pete. It won't take but a minute."

"It won't even take that long," Peter assured her, snatching the glass from her hand and slamming it down on the bedside table, "because you're not going to do it." Acting on instinct and an adrenaline rush fueled by anger, he grabbed Becky's hand, hauled her to her feet and slung her over his shoulder in a fireman's carry.

She screeched with indignation. She pounded on his back and flailed her legs. Peter was extremely glad he'd built up his muscles with hard physical labor all summer: Becky was a strong woman, even when she was exhausted. He whacked her bottom once, hoping it would discourage her from thrashing, and headed for the doorway.

Turning back to an astonished Hank, he said, "You've had a personal slave long enough, Dawson. Drink that milk shake the way she made it or starve."

Sam and Grandma D came running to see what all the noise was about. Peter marched right by them, and was gratified when neither tried to stop him.

"I'm taking her to the foreman's house for the night," he said without slowing his pace. "We'll see you in the morning."

Then he hauled Becky outside and dumped her into the passenger seat of Hank's pickup. By the time he raced around to the driver's seat, she had righted herself and already started cussing a blue streak at him. Ignoring her tirade, he started the engine and drove away from the house.

"What the hell do you think you're doing, Sinclair?" she bellowed when he'd parked in front of the cottage and dragged her inside. "I've got a million things to—"

"Shut up, Becky."

Peter propped his hands on his hips and leaned back against the door, studying her calmly while she stared at him in surprise, her mouth opening and closing several times. He gestured toward the sofa. "Sit down. We need to talk."

She sighed and rubbed the back of her neck. "Can't it wait?"

"For what? Until Hank can walk again? Or until you turn him into an invalid?"

Her head jerked as if he'd struck her. Well, good, he thought grimly, ignoring a twinge of guilt. At least he finally had her undivided attention.

"That was a rotten thing to say," she said, her chin coming up. "I'm doing the best I can to take care of him."

Peter crossed the room, took her arm and gently pushed her onto the sofa. When he sat beside her, she scooted into the corner out of his reach.

"I'm not criticizing your nursing skills—" he began, ignoring her muttered, "Ya coulda fooled me."

"—in fact," he continued, "you're doing too good of a job of taking care of him."

"Oh, now, *that* makes a helluva lot of sense."

"Will you knock off the sarcasm and listen to me?"

She rolled her eyes at the ceiling, then nodded when he glared at her.

"Thank you. What I'm trying to say is that you're not doing Hank any favors. He's facing months of recovery. He needs to learn to do things for himself."

"For God's sake, Pete, he's been through hell," Becky protested. "Everybody needs a little TLC after they've been through something like this."

"Granted, but you've given him enough TLC to last a lifetime," Peter argued. "You can't let him become too comfortable in that bed or he may not have the will to fight and get himself out of it."

"Hank wouldn't do that. Give him a little time. He just got out of the hospital."

"He's been out long enough to run you ragged, Becky. He plays on your sympathy constantly. He should be getting up and around more by now."

"It hurts him to move around."

"Of course it does. And so will his other surgeries. And so will his physical therapy. He's going to have to get used to it, and you're going to have to let him."

"Dammit, Pete, I can't do that."

"Then you'd better hire someone who can, or Hank will end up so dependent, you'll have to take care of him for the rest of his life. Is that what you want?"

"Oh, come *on.*"

If looks could kill, Peter thought, he would be on his way to the nearest mortuary, but he met her fierce scowl steadily and crossed his right leg over his left.

"I'm serious, Becky. Hank needs a professional nurse and you need some help."

"Gimme a break. We're doing just fine."

Peter sighed with exasperation. "I've been trying to talk to you for days, but you never have a second to spare. How long do you think you can keep up this pace?"

"As long as it takes."

"I'm afraid I, or maybe we, don't have that long."

"What do you mean by that?"

"I have to get back to my own life while I still have one," he said quietly.

She shook her head in confusion. "You're leaving?"

"I'll lose my job if I don't. I'm already two weeks overdue. I promised my boss I'd tell him tomorrow when I was coming back."

"Oh, hell."

She lay her head back against the sofa cushion and closed her eyes as if she simply didn't have enough energy to cope with this latest complication. Peter's heart wrenched at the sight, but he had to hold on to his resolution. For her sake as well as his own.

"I want you to come with me," he said after a long moment.

She turned her head and looked at him, her eyes so sad, he could hardly bear it. "You know I can't do that, Pete."

"Yes, you can." He slid across the cushions and took her hands in his. "You can hire a nurse to take care of Hank and a housekeeper to come in and help Grandma D. I'll be happy to pay for them if your family can't afford it."

"It's not the money. Don't you see? My family really needs me now. Especially Hank. He's still worried about Jan, and—"

"Jan isn't your responsibility. She's cooperating with the authorities, and since your family won't press charges against her I'd say she's gotten off pretty easily."

"But she still has to testify against Castle and the guy he hired to shoot Hank. Andy says the DEA agents think he's a professional hit man. The bullets they found in his gun when they raided ECC matched the ones they found in Barney. And they found all that cocaine. How would you like to identify people like that in court?"

"She's going into the Witness Protection Program, Becky," Peter argued. "They won't even let you see her."

"But—"

"Jan is *not* the issue here. *We* are." Peter slid off the sofa and knelt on the floor in front of Becky. He framed her face between his hands and spoke in the most earnest tone he possessed. "I love you, Becky, and I need you, too."

"I know. And I love you, too, Pete, but..." She paused and gulped before continuing. "This just isn't a good time for me to leave."

The plea for understanding in her green eyes sliced into his heart like a scalpel, but he had to know where he fit on her list of priorities. He dropped his hands to his sides.

"Is there ever going to be a good time for you to leave your family?" he demanded. "Or are you going to martyr yourself again and destroy our chance for happiness?"

"I'm not trying to be a martyr," she answered, her voice twenty degrees cooler. "We were lucky the grand jury was meeting so they could indict Castle and the hit man, but we don't have a trial date yet. And then we'll be filing a civil suit against the ECC for damages. Maybe in another month—"

"In another month Hank will be ready for his next surgery, and it could be a year before they bring those guys to trial, Becky. Come with me now, and you can come back when the action starts."

"Look, can't you give me six months? Just to get things under control here?"

"You mean when your life is all neat and tidy, and everyone else is happy, then you'll have time for me?" Peter rose to his feet, then walked to the window.

"That's not fair!" she shouted.

Peter turned to face her. "You're right. It isn't fair. To you or to me. I'm thirty-eight years old. You're thirty-four. We both want a home and kids, and neither of us is getting any younger. It's weird, but this whole situation is starting to make me feel sympathy for my ex-wife."

"What's that supposed to mean?"

"She always complained that I didn't pay any attention to her. Now I know how she felt."

"It can't be *that* bad. Good Lord, you sound like a whiny little kid."

"Maybe I *feel* like a whiny little kid, okay? Blame my parents if you want to. They always had too many other demands on their time to bother with raising me. I can't handle the same kind of treatment from my wife, Becky."

"I can understand that," she said softly, her shoulders slumping in defeat. "And I guess we might as well end the whole damn thing right now."

Peter crossed the room in three strides and clamped his hands onto her arms. "No, dammit! That's not what I want at all. How can you give up like this without a fight?"

"We've had the damn fight. I can't take much more, Pete."

"But aren't we worth fighting for? Sweetheart, we've been so happy together here."

"Yeah, that's right. We've been happy together *here*. But being here has been kind of like an adventure for you, not real life. I've known from the beginning that we were just too different to make it work."

"That's not true," he said, giving her a gentle shake.

"Yes, it is. I'd never fit in with your crowd, and you know it. I'm not the kind of woman you need. Just go back to Washington and forget about me for your own sake."

He inhaled a deep breath and rammed his hands into his jeans pockets for fear he would shake her hard enough to give her whiplash.

"Tell me you're afraid. Tell me you don't love me enough," he said in a deadly quiet tone that should have scared her witless. "But don't tell me you're doing this for my sake, Becky. It's not your job to decide what I need. And don't make decisions for me."

She stiffened and turned away. "I'm not doing that."

"Aren't you? You do it so often, you don't even realize it anymore. You're so much smarter than everyone else, you just have to step in and rescue people from themselves. That must be quite a power trip."

"Oh, shut up. If I'm such a damned awful person, then shut up and leave me the hell alone."

The hurt in her voice and in her eyes made him soften his tone. "I don't think you're an awful person at all. You just don't know when to stop giving."

"Oh, *please.*"

"No, listen to me. You never had a chance to be on your own long enough to form your own identity, and you've allowed your family to become that for you. I think you're scared to find out they can get along without you. Maybe you're scared you can't make it without them. You're scared to be free, aren't you?"

"And now the mighty Dr. Sinclair is a shrink," she retorted, bitterness dripping from every syllable. "Thank you for your analysis."

"Hey, even an amateur shrink can see things with the right perspective. Remember, you don't have to do it all alone. I'll be with you every step of the way. But *you've* got to take that first step. Take it, Becky. Rescue yourself for once and come with me."

She turned back to face him, her shoulders straight, her chin raised, her eyes dry, and Peter knew he had lost.

"Believe whatever you want, Pete. I don't need to be rescued from my own family. Go back to your job and your friends and don't contact me again."

"You really mean that."

"Yes, I do."

"All right. We'll go to the house and I'll pack."

"You go on ahead. I'd just as soon walk. I need to check on Misty and Dandy, anyway."

He stood there for a moment, memorizing her face, loving her for her stubborn pride and strength, even though they had ultimately cost him her love. He wanted to hold her one last time. Kiss her one last time. Make love to her one last time. She wouldn't let him do any of that, of course. It wouldn't change anything if she did. Except to make leaving her that much harder.

So he turned, walked out to the truck and drove away, feeling as if his internal organs had been shredded with a hot fork. When he parked at the back door of the house, Peter made a final decision regarding Becky Dawson's future. He knew he wouldn't be allowed to share in it now, but perhaps this one time somebody needed to rescue her.

Becky held herself rigidly in place until she heard the pickup's engine fire up and gradually die away. Then she collapsed onto the sofa and felt the sudden, oppressive silence and the loneliness close in on her. The tears she'd come so close to shedding during her argument with Pete were locked inside her now—a painful lump beneath her ribs.

God, she wanted to hate him for what he'd said. Of course, she couldn't. She knew he hadn't said those things to hurt her. They'd hurt like hell anyway, but that hadn't been his intention. One of the hardest parts of being Becky Dawson was that she could always see and understand the other guy's side in an argument.

Unfortunately she couldn't change that about herself, and she couldn't seem to change anything else, either. Maybe she was unreasonably concerned about her family, but that was who she was. At least that was the person she'd always thought she was.

Why couldn't Pete understand that she couldn't leave Hank now? And where did he think they were going to find a nurse and a housekeeper to hire way out here? In Pinedale? Not likely. After all this time he'd never figured out that Wyoming and Washington were like two different planets.

She started to get up and go tell him that, then realized it was just another example of how different she and Pete were. They didn't see things the same way, and they never would. He wasn't only talking about her leaving her family for a little trip. He was talking about a lifetime.

Why, the big dope had actually forced her to choose between loving him and loving her family. How could she love a man who was that selfish?

"I don't," she muttered. "I won't."

Now, if she could only make herself believe that, she just might survive this god-awful pain until morning.

Chapter Eighteen

Becky stood at the kitchen sink after supper, looking out the window while she washed the pots and pans that wouldn't fit into the dishwasher. Bear Dog, Sam's Australian shepherd, slunk into the backyard, stalking Grandma D's pet rooster, Clyde. Clyde continued pecking at the ground, supremely indifferent to the pup's presence. At the last possible second, he would squawk and fly into the lower branches of the apple tree, frustrating Bear Dog again.

This game had been going on all summer, and Pete thought it was hilarious. Becky turned to call him, then sighed and slumped against the sink when she remembered he wasn't there. Damn the man.

She'd thought that after a month the urge to share things with him would fade. She'd hoped the worst of the pain of missing him would be over. She'd prayed he would at least phone or write to see how Hank was getting along, and maybe they could talk....

But none of that had happened. She was just as miserable as she'd been the day he left—all right, more miserable, if she was honest about it. To her knowledge, nobody in the family had heard from Pete, and she supposed that after all this time that wasn't going to change.

Some other things *had* changed at the Circle D, however. Hank had suddenly become determined to do everything he could for himself. When she asked if he needed anything, or offered to bring him a snack, he always shook his head and said, "No thanks, sis." He even yelled at her on occasion, and demanded, "Quit tryin' to baby me, will ya?"

Tina had started spending more time away from her aunt, insisting she wanted Uncle Sam to read to her at bedtime, and she wanted Grandma D to tuck her in. Becky missed those cozy moments with the little scamp, but she wasn't about to force herself on the kid. Besides, Sam and Grandma D appeared to be enjoying the new arrangement.

Becky couldn't be absolutely certain, but she sensed that something was going on behind her back between Sam, Grandma D and Hank. If she walked into a room where the three of them had gathered, there was always a pause in the conversation, as if they were all quickly shifting gears and changing the subject. She figured they were worried about how she was taking Pete's leaving.

Shoot, she wasn't fine and she wasn't okay, but she *was* surviving. She got up in the morning and did her work, and if she wasn't as cheerful about it as she used to be, tough toenails. The truth was, she had too much time for thinking and regrets, and she wished like hell that she could have found a way to go with Pete.

The ranch didn't excite and challenge her the way it once had. The jobs she had taken such pride in doing and doing well seemed repetitive, even boring, when Pete wasn't along to talk and laugh with her. Life just didn't have any zing in it anymore and she wanted that zing back, dammit. She couldn't help feeling resentful and angry about it, though she tried not to let those feelings show.

Well, tomorrow she and Sam were driving Hank to Jackson for his next operation. She'd get a break from her routine, even if it wasn't a very pleasant one. She wrung out the dishrag and hung it on the rack, then started the dishwasher and headed up to her room. She might as well pack a few things in case they needed to stay overnight.

"Becky, will you come in here, please?" Hank called from the den when she reached the bottom of the stairs.

Shrugging, she went to find out what he wanted. Though he was fully dressed, Hank lay on the bed, his head propped up on a mound of pillows. Sam and Grandma D occupied a pair of wooden chairs on the left side of the room. Sam indicated a third one set at the foot of the bed.

"Have a seat, sis. We want to talk to you."

"All right," she said, warily eyeing their somber expressions as she crossed the room and slid onto the chair. Good Lord, the three of them looked as if they were about to witness an execution. "What's going on?"

Sam's gaze darted to Grandma D. She nodded at him, obviously lending encouragement and support. Then he said, "You won't be goin' to Jackson with us tomorrow."

"Why not?"

"You'll be busy movin' into your new house," Hank told her with a strained smile.

"My new house? What are you talkin' about?"

"It's plain as day you're not happy here, Rebecca Anne," Grandma D said. "We've leased you a little place so you can start raisin' your Appaloosas."

Becky jumped to her feet in protest. "Wait just a damn minute, here. Have you all lost your minds? And who said I wasn't happy?"

"We may be crazy, but we're not blind, Beck," Hank said. "You've hardly smiled or laughed since Pete left."

"Well, excuuuuuse me. I didn't know smiling and laughing were part of my job description. I'll try to do better in the future."

"Now, Becky, don't get your bowels in an uproar. We're only doin' this 'cause we care about you," Sam put in. "It's time for you to have your own life for a change."

Becky pointed her index finger at Sam. "Pete put you up to this. Didn't he? Where the hell does he get off?"

"It doesn't matter who gave us the idea," Grandma D replied tartly. "It's the right thing for you to do, and by God, you're gonna do it."

"And I suppose you're gonna take care of Hank and Tina and everything else around here I've been bustin' my butt over? Huh, Grandma? You can handle all of that?"

"I'll be bringin' a nurse back from Jackson to take care of Hank when he comes home from the hospital," Sam informed her, obviously struggling for a patient tone. "And Mary over at the Bar Z is gonna come in every day and help Grandma."

Becky plunked herself down on the chair again, feeling like a punctured balloon. "I see." She shrugged and let out a bitter chuckle. "Well, I guess it wasn't so hard to replace me after all."

"Quit feelin' sorry for yourself," Hank ordered her. "Most people your age left home years ago. It's high time you grew up and learned how to stand on your own."

"It doesn't have to be forever," Grandma D said gently, "but we want you to try it for six months. If you don't like it, we'll love havin' you back home again. And of course you can come visit whenever you want."

Perilously close to tears, Becky nodded, stood and left the room without another word. She pounded up the stairs to her bedroom, slamming the door behind her. The tears gushed down her cheeks then. She went to the window and leaned against the casing, telling herself she was grateful for what her family had done.

Because now she could prove Pete had been wrong about her—she wasn't afraid her family could get along without her and she wasn't afraid of freedom, either. Now she could finally really hate the man and enjoy it. Oh, wouldn't she just *love* to get her hands on him—like around his throat.

It hadn't been enough that he'd taken her heart and her joy in life with him when he left. Oh, no. Now he had to take away the only people she cared about, the only people who cared about what happened to her.

"Well, I hope you're satisfied now, Sinclair," she muttered, wiping her eyes with the backs of her hands. "I hope you're just happy as hell."

"Sit down, Peter," Eric Goldman said, indicating the chair across from his desk.

Stifling an impatient sigh, Peter looked at his watch, then subsided on the leather cushion. "I don't have much time, Eric. What do you need?"

Eric fiddled with his pen, a thoughtful frown on his wrinkled face. "I need you to tell me what's wrong."

"What do you mean? Everything's fine."

"That's not what I've been hearing, Peter."

"Come on, Eric, cut to the chase. What's this all about?"

"It's about three good nurses we couldn't afford to lose resigning in the last month."

"I don't have any patience with incompetence."

"You don't seem to have any patience with anything lately. Frankly, Peter, I'm worried about you." When Peter opened his mouth to interrupt, Eric stayed him by holding up one palm. "Please. Let me finish."

"All right."

"I thought time off last summer would help you put your work into its proper perspective. Unfortunately, you've been back for five months now and your workaholism is worse than it was before you left. As your hospital administrator, I'm delighted to have so much of your time and energy. But as your friend, I simply can't allow this to go on. You're risking another breakdown, Peter."

"I'm fine, Eric." Peter ran one hand through his hair. "I'll take the weekend off. All right?"

"I'm afraid that's not enough."

"What do you want? My resignation?"

"Of course not. Perhaps some therapy—"

"Therapy!" Peter stood, smacked both hands on the desk and loomed over his boss. "Forget it. I don't need it and I don't have time."

Eric adopted the same posture, meeting Peter's glare with an equally fierce one of his own. "Then talk to me, Peter. Tell me what happened to you in Wyoming. Douglas told me you'd met a very special woman out there. Does she have anything to do with your present mood?"

Just the mention of that very special woman brought a vision of Becky's face to Peter's mind, and with it a stab of longing so sharp, the air rushed out of his lungs. He sat before his knees gave out and covered his face with his hands.

Eric left his desk, locked the door and closed the mini-blinds on his office windows. Then he opened the bottom drawer of a file cabinet and pulled out a bottle of Scotch and two glasses.

"I bought this especially for this discussion," he said, waving the bottle. "You're officially off duty for the rest of the weekend and so am I." He poured them each a drink and pushed one of the glasses across the desk toward Peter. "Now, then. Tell me about her."

Peter downed the three fingers of Scotch in one fiery gulp. When he finished gasping, he settled back in his chair, propped his feet on Eric's desk and started talking. Once started, he couldn't stop, and by the time he'd told Eric everything, the bottle was half-empty. Surprisingly enough, he felt better than he had since leaving Becky.

God, the nights. The long, lonely miserable nights without her, dreaming about her, missing her so much he wanted to scream. His damned, empty apartment. His phone that only rang when a patient needed him. His heart stopping every time he saw a tall, auburn-haired woman on the street.

"What are you going to do?" Eric asked after a long moment of silence.

Peter shrugged. "What *can* I do? If her family did what I suggested, she probably hates my guts."

"Perhaps she's missed you as much as you've missed her."

"If she hasn't worked herself to death," Peter agreed, covering his mouth with one fist to stifle a belch.

"Why don't you go find out?"

"It would . . . hurt too much if—"

Eric laughed softly, then held up his hands in a peacemaking gesture. "This isn't like you, Peter. I can't believe you're giving up so easily."

"You think leaving her was easy?"

Eric raised his eyebrows at that outburst, then continued in a calm, reasonable manner. "You know, you demanded an awful lot of her. You really picked a miserable time to ask a woman like that to leave her home and family. Wasn't there any room at all for a compromise?"

"Like what? I offered to live in Maryland or Virginia and commute, but this is where my work is, Eric. Surely you can see that."

"There must be some place you could work that would be closer to her home. Denver? Seattle? Salt Lake City? Don't people in Wyoming ever get sick or hurt? You're licensed for general practice and you've kept up. You've done a good job here, but we all know your heart's not in it."

"If she didn't have to be so far from home . . ." Peter murmured, his thoughts suddenly starting to race.

A smile, the first sincere smile he'd felt in months, slowly spread across his face. Rising, he leaned across the desk and shook Eric's hand.

"Thanks, Eric. Start looking for a new oncologist immediately. I'm going home."

Eric shook his head, then jumped to his feet. "Wait a minute. It's been a long time since you've seen her. What if she's . . . found someone else?"

"No problem," Peter replied confidently. "If she's found someone else, I'll just have to kill him."

Sputtering, Eric followed Peter out into the hall, but he couldn't keep up with the taller man's eager strides. "I'm calling you a cab, Peter," he called. "You're in no condition to drive."

Peter waved in acknowledgment and hurried past the nurses' station, poking the elevator's down button with a flourish. Before three astonished nurses' eyes, dignified, often irascible Dr. Sinclair stepped into the elevator when it arrived, turned and jumped into the air, clicked his heels together and bellowed, "Yeeehah!" as the doors rolled shut.

Becky sipped from a scalding cup of coffee and glanced at the calendar. Valentine's Day. Terrific.

Irritated that some idiotic, stubborn part of her wished she would get a gushy, sentimental card from Pete, she banged the mug onto the counter and marched out her back door, grabbing a hammer on the way. A bitter wind from the north stung her cheeks and the air smelled as if more snow would fall before morning.

She'd put her three pregnant mares in the barn tonight. For now, however, they could stay in the pasture and enjoy the sunshine. They came up to the fence to greet Becky, nipping playfully at her parka while she used the hammer and broke the ice in their water tank. Then Misty raised her head and pricked her ears toward the road.

Becky turned and saw a shiny blue Bronco pull into her driveway. She wasn't expecting anyone and she didn't recognize the vehicle, but she wouldn't mind having a visitor as long as it wasn't a salesman. Waving goodbye to the animals, she headed back to the house.

A tall man wearing a white Stetson and a dark brown, sheepskin-lined coat stepped out onto the gravel as she rounded the barn. There was something familiar about the way he held his head. For a second, her heart refused to beat and her blood practically curdled in her veins.

Chuckling wryly at her wishful thinking, Becky lowered her head against the wind and kept walking. *It's not Pete, you idiot. It's over. Done. Kaput. So stop thinking about him.*

But when she looked up at the man again, the impression was stronger. He stepped away from the Bronco, one hand raised in a hesitant greeting, and suddenly she knew. Dear, God, it *was* Pete!

Her feet slowed automatically. Her mouth went dry. The fur lining of her gloves clung to the sweat springing out on her palms.

"Hello, Becky."

She halted at the sound of his voice, the voice that had haunted her dreams for months until she'd stopped hating it because that was the only way she would ever be able to hear it again.

He took off his hat and held it in front of him. The sunshine glistened on his thick, glossy hair. His cheeks and ears were red with cold. His smile was tentative, but his gaze raced over her, his eyes taking in every detail of her appearance the way hers were devouring him.

"I'd like to talk to you. Have you got a little time?" he asked.

She couldn't talk, couldn't think, couldn't breathe. Instead she nodded, then led the way into her house. Moving carefully, as if it was extremely important that her coat and hat be hung just so, she removed her cold-weather gear on the back porch, motioning for him to go ahead of her into the kitchen. When she joined him, he was looking around the room, smiling in approval.

"Want some coffee?" she asked, relieved that her voice sounded reasonably normal if a bit gruff.

"I'd love some." He draped his coat over the back of a chair and laid his hat on the table. "You've got a nice place, Becky."

She shrugged and reached into the cupboard to get him a mug. "I guess I've got you to thank for that."

"I imagine you were pretty angry at me for talking to your family," he said, taking a seat at the round oak table she had refinished during the long winter evenings.

"I was at first." She set a steaming mug in front of him before sitting on the other side of the table.

"Are you still angry?"

"No," she admitted. After all, what was the point in denying the truth? Damn, but she was glad to see him, even if she felt as uncomfortable as a sinner at a revival meeting.

"Why not?"

"The first couple of months by myself were pretty awful. I guess it took me that long to figure out what to do with myself. I mean, the horses keep me busy and all, but it's not like it was at home. Lately, though, I've learned to enjoy being on my own. Have you seen Grandma D and Sam?"

He nodded. "That's how I found you. They said to tell you Hank will be coming home again at the end of the week. I was sorry to hear he'd had a setback."

"He handled it pretty well. I don't care what happens. He'll walk again come hell or high water."

"I'm sure he will."

They both sipped from their cups and looked at each other. Becky couldn't read the expression in his eyes and hoped he couldn't tell what she was thinking, either. Finally she couldn't stand the suspense another second and blurted out the question she'd wanted to ask all along.

"What are you doing here, Pete?"

He leaned forward, resting his forearms on the table. Then he cleared his throat. "I, uh, wanted to know how you were, of course. And I wanted to apologize for the things I said to you the last time we were together."

"No apology needed." She gave him a crooked grin and heard her voice drop to a husky whisper. "You were right, you know. Everybody's benefited by my moving out."

"I know it must have hurt you. A lot." He reached out and covered her hand, sighing quietly when she didn't pull it away. "I'm sorry for that."

"I'm getting over it."

"Did you get over me?"

His eyes met and held hers prisoner. His gaze suddenly burned with intensity, as if her answer meant more to him than anything else on earth. Lord, she'd forgotten just how blunt he could be.

"That depends," she answered, feigning nonchalance.

"On what?"

"On whether you got over me."

A low, rough chuckle came out of his throat. "Good move, Dawson. Make me stick my neck out first."

"Well, Sinclair," she drawled, "what can I say? I've already admitted you were right. Seems t'me it must be your turn to squirm a little."

"All right." He moved the mugs out of the way and took both of her hands between his. "The truth is, I haven't gotten over you at all. I've missed you so much...."

"You're doin' just fine, honey," she said, her eyes misting with happy tears. "How much did you miss me?"

How he got to the other side of the table so fast, she would never know; she didn't give a rip, either. The only thing that mattered was that she was finally in his arms again, laughing and crying, kissing and hugging, telling him how much she had missed him.

"I can't believe I'm really here," he whispered, running his hands over her back and hips, nipping down the side of her neck with his lips. "God, Becky, I love you."

"I love you, too, Pete. I wanted to call you so many times, but I didn't think you'd want me anymore."

"Not want you?" He pulled her hard against his groin, dispelling any further doubts on that issue. "I was such a grouch, three nurses resigned rather than work with me. All I could think about was you and how much you must hate me."

She started nudging him toward the bedroom, unbuttoning his shirt as he walked backward, whispering fevered confessions of her own. They were both naked to the waist by the time they stood next to her bed. The whispers became naughty giggles, the giggles became moans of delight and then gusty shouts of pleasure.

Here was freedom and passion and sharing, all the zing any two bodies could ever hope to endure. Here was love and tenderness and completion, a union of hearts and minds and bodies that never should have been parted in the first place. Was it possible to die of happiness?

He collapsed into her arms, his chest heaving, his heart hammering in rhythm with hers. She stroked his hair and his neck, still unable to believe that he was really here and that he loved her this much. She whimpered when he rolled to his side, then snuggled willingly into the warmth of his open arms.

"Marry me, Becky."

"Okay."

"Just like that?" he asked, cocking an eyebrow at her.

"You wanted an argument? Well, tough, Sinclair. You're not gonna get one from me."

"Does that mean you're going to be an obedient wife?"

She raised up on one elbow and smiled down at him. "I wouldn't bet my stethoscope on it, Doc. When do I start packin'?"

"Packing for what?"

"The move to Washington," she said patiently, wondering if all that heated sex had scorched his brain cells. "You know, our nation's capital? The one with all the monuments and politicians?"

"What about your family?"

"We'll have a phone bill that'll make your eyes roll back in your head, even if you are rich. And I'll want to come back for the trial and visit at least once a year. I'll miss 'em like hell, but not as much as I've missed you. Besides, once we start our own family, I don't reckon I'll have much time to miss Wyoming."

His throat worked down a gulp and he gave her a wobbly smile. Then he reached up and stroked her cheek in a gesture of such tenderness it brought tears to her eyes.

"That won't be necessary, sweetheart," he said.

"Well, why not? I really don't mind, Pete."

"I can see that. And you'll never know how much it touches me for you to make that offer. But I've decided to try general practice for a while."

Pursing her lips, she eyed his smug grin suspiciously. "What have you done now, Sinclair?"

"I've bought into Dr. Miller's practice. We'll have enough work to keep us both fairly busy, and we can share the on-call duty, so either of us can get away for a vacation when we want to. I'll have plenty of time to be with my family."

"But you're used to so much more," she said hesitantly. "Are you sure a small-town practice like this will be enough of a challenge for you?"

"Becky," he said, his voice taking on a warning note.

"What?"

"You're not going to say something noble, are you? Like 'don't do this for my own sake'?"

"Who, me?" she asked, trying her darnedest to keep the guilt out of her eyes. "Of course not. You're a grown man. Perfectly capable of taking care of yourself and making your own decisions about what's best for you."

"Thank you," he said dryly.

"There's one little thing I'd like to know."

"What's that?"

"Do you still jog and take vitamins?"

"Yes, but what's that got to do with anything?"

"Keep on doin' it for my sake, will ya? I want a man with a lot of stamina."

He rolled her onto her back and moved on top of her, his hands braced on either side of her head. She ran her fingers through the hair on his chest, loving his arrogant, macho smile.

"You're just what I've always wanted, Becky Dawson," he said, bending to kiss her lips.

"Oh, yeah? What's that?"

"A woman who knows what she wants."

"Dang right. I'll want you with me forever. And you *can* bet your stethoscope on that, Doc."

* * * * *

COMING NEXT MONTH

#745 SILENT SAM'S SALVATION—Myrna Temte *Cowboy Country*
Reluctant rancher Sam Dawson hadn't envisioned a housekeeper like Dani
Smith. Fast-talking, stylish, two kids in tow—Dani swept up so well, she
uncovered his secret . . . proving herself Silent Sam's salvation.

#746 DREAMBOAT OF THE WESTERN WORLD—Tracy Sinclair
Struggling single mother Melissa Fairfield wasn't acting. But when movie
star Granger McMasters gazed upon the graceful, capable woman tending
his garden, he saw the makings of a lifelong love scene. . . .

#747 BEYOND THE NIGHT—Christine Flynn
Mitchell Kincaid was drawn to the thrill of dangerous pastimes. He
thought nothing of taking risks, until Jamie Withers made him face the
biggest risk of all—falling in love. . . .

#748 WHEN SOMEBODY LOVES YOU—Trisha Alexander
Only one thing kept Laura Sebastian and Neil Cantrelle apart: Laura's
engagement—to Neil's brother. Brokenhearted, she struggled not to break
her vow, waiting . . . hoping . . . for mending, magical love to prevail.

#749 OUTCAST WOMAN—Lucy Gordon
Mystical beauty Kirsty Trennon was a woman scorned and alone, until
runaway prisoner Mike Stallard appeared. Both outcasts, they shared
earthly passion; could they clear their names and find heavenly love?

#750 ONE PERFECT ROSE—Emilie Richards
Wealthy executive Jase Millington wanted to give homeless Becca Hanks
everything she needed. But to win the strong, independent Becca's love,
Jase needed to take a lesson in receiving. . . .

AVAILABLE THIS MONTH:

"GET AWAY FROM IT ALL" SWEEPSTAKES

HERE'S HOW THE SWEEPSTAKES WORKS

NO PURCHASE NECESSARY

To enter each drawing, complete the appropriate Official Entry Form or a 3" by 5" index card by hand-printing your name, address and phone number and the trip destination that the entry is being submitted for (i.e., Caneel Bay, Canyon Ranch or London and the English Countryside) and mailing it to: Get Away From It All Sweepstakes, P.O. Box 1397, Buffalo, New York 14269-1397.

No responsibility is assumed for lost, late or misdirected mail. Entries must be sent separately with first class postage affixed, and be received by: 4/15/92 for the Caneel Bay Vacation Drawing, 5/15/92 for the Canyon Ranch Vacation Drawing and 6/15/92 for the London and the English Countryside Vacation Drawing. Sweepstakes is open to residents of the U.S. (except Puerto Rico) and Canada, 21 years of age or older as of 5/31/92.

For complete rules send a self-addressed, stamped (WA residents need not affix return postage) envelope to: Get Away From It All Sweepstakes, P.O. Box 4892, Blair, NE 68009.

© 1992 HARLEQUIN ENTERPRISES LTD.   SWP-RLS

"GET AWAY FROM IT ALL" SWEEPSTAKES

HERE'S HOW THE SWEEPSTAKES WORKS

NO PURCHASE NECESSARY

To enter each drawing, complete the appropriate Official Entry Form or a 3" by 5" index card by hand-printing your name, address and phone number and the trip destination that the entry is being submitted for (i.e., Caneel Bay, Canyon Ranch or London and the English Countryside) and mailing it to: Get Away From It All Sweepstakes, P.O. Box 1397, Buffalo, New York 14269-1397.

No responsibility is assumed for lost, late or misdirected mail. Entries must be sent separately with first class postage affixed, and be received by: 4/15/92 for the Caneel Bay Vacation Drawing, 5/15/92 for the Canyon Ranch Vacation Drawing and 6/15/92 for the London and the English Countryside Vacation Drawing. Sweepstakes is open to residents of the U.S. (except Puerto Rico) and Canada, 21 years of age or older as of 5/31/92.

For complete rules send a self-addressed, stamped (WA residents need not affix return postage) envelope to: Get Away From It All Sweepstakes, P.O. Box 4892, Blair, NE 68009.

© 1992 HARLEQUIN ENTERPRISES LTD.   SWP-RLS

"GET AWAY FROM IT ALL"

Brand-new Subscribers-Only Sweepstakes

OFFICIAL ENTRY FORM

This entry must be received by: May 15, 1992
This month's winner will be notified by: May 31, 1992
Trip must be taken between: June 30, 1992—June 30, 1993

YES, I want to win the Canyon Ranch vacation for two. I understand the prize includes round-trip airfare and the two additional prizes revealed in the BONUS PRIZES insert.

Name _____

Address _____

City _____

State/Prov._____ Zip/Postal Code_____

Daytime phone number _____
(Area Code)

Return entries with invoice in envelope provided. Each book in this shipment has two entry coupons — and the more coupons you enter, the better your chances of winning!
© 1992 HARLEQUIN ENTERPRISES LTD.   2M-CPN

"GET AWAY FROM IT ALL"

Brand-new Subscribers-Only Sweepstakes

OFFICIAL ENTRY FORM

This entry must be received by: May 15, 1992
This month's winner will be notified by: May 31, 1992
Trip must be taken between: June 30, 1992—June 30, 1993

YES, I want to win the Canyon Ranch vacation for two. I understand the prize includes round-trip airfare and the two additional prizes revealed in the BONUS PRIZES insert.

Name _____

Address _____

City _____

State/Prov._____ Zip/Postal Code_____

Daytime phone number _____
(Area Code)

Return entries with invoice in envelope provided. Each book in this shipment has two entry coupons — and the more coupons you enter, the better your chances of winning!
© 1992 HARLEQUIN ENTERPRISES LTD.   2M-CPN